KU-762-875

JO-ANN GOODWIN grew up in Sheffield and Doncaster a... English at Hull University. She followed this with an M.Phil. in Dickens at York. Now a full-time journalist, she has previously worked for the Labour Party. Jo-Ann is married and lives in North London. She is currently working on her second novel. *Danny Boy* was longlisted for the Orange Prize.

Further acclaim for
DANNY BOY

'A fast-paced but thoughtful and moving spin on the spiralling-out-of-control theme. Think a spiritual *Trainspotting*' *The Face*

'Danny gradually reveals himself to be a bruised romantic. He possesses a cynical charm, grudgingly confiding to the reader emotional depths he hides from his mates . . . What emerges is a clash that is comedic, brutal and poignant' *Express on Sunday*

'Excellent . . . A mesmerizing read' *The Big Issue*

'Jo-Ann Goodwin has tempered her own savagely down-at-heel tale with a gleaming thread of redemption, and in her nineteen-year-old anti-hero Danny McIntyre, an unbreakable spirit. She has also a lyrical way with language that elevates the novel way above its street setting . . . Goodwin's first novel drags you deep into a vibrant realm from which there is no escape. And you don't need to approve of drug culture to appreciate it' *Daily Mail*

'Goodwin writes consistently scintillating prose. The pages are peppered with sly references to Freud, Milton, the Bible, Irvine Welsh and Quentin Tarantino' *The Times*

'A gutsy foray into the grime of a drug user's underworld. This surreal slice of life is redeemed by a sense of hope and some upbeat humour' *Mirror*

'The inventiveness of Danny's vernacular – a mix of northern dialect, drug argot and, of all things, Spanish – and the evocation of sudden, convincing moments of pathos mark *Danny Boy* out' *Times Literary Supplement*

'You will seriously enjoy this book' *Pulp.com*

'Beneath the harsh reality there is something much deeper going on: a host of rich symbolism and religious iconography which gives the book a mythical resonance . . . Goodwin has come up with a formula for the perfect book' *The Big Issue in the North*

'Goodwin differs from [Irvine] Welsh in that she has created, in Danny and his friends, individuals that the reader can care about and cheer on as the sad, sick world throws its worst at them . . . *Danny Boy* is an unflinching and honest début by a natural storyteller' *Tribune*

'Streetwise . . . and very readable' *Daily Telegraph*

'A new generation of British writers has been playing with the forms of violence and brutality – pain as comedy and savagery as high art. In *Danny Boy*, Jo-Ann Goodwin goes one better, she adds a lethal dose of compassion to the mix, a much-needed undercurrent of grace to temper the pain. Danny McIntyre is a street-smart, thieving, heart-breaking bastard. And he's beautiful. And he has a heart'
STELLA DUFFY

'Danny . . . is a wonderful creation, with a nicely misanthropic and bitterly funny stream of consciousness . . . Does for Doncaster what Irvine Welsh did for Edinburgh . . . A terrific début' HELEN ZAHAVI

danny boy

JO-ANN GOODWIN

BANTAM BOOKS

LONDON · NEW YORK · TORONTO · SYDNEY · AUCKLAND

DANNY BOY
A BANTAM BOOK: 0553 812610

Originally published in Great Britain by Bantam Press,
a division of Transworld Publishers

PRINTING HISTORY
Bantam Press edition published 2000
Bantam Books edition published 2001

1 3 5 7 9 10 8 6 4 2

Copyright © Jo-Ann Goodwin 2000

All of the characters in this book are fictitious, and any resemblance to
actual persons, alive or dead, is purely coincidental.

The right of Jo-Ann Goodwin to be identified as the author of this work has
been asserted in accordance with sections 77 and 78 of the Copyright,
Designs and Patents Act 1988

Lyrics from 'The Skye Boat Song' by Harold Boulton reproduced by
kind permission of Cramer Music Ltd.

Lyrics from 'The Boy From Tamlaghduff' by Christy Moore
reproduced courtesy of Bal Music Ltd.

Lyrics from 'No Man's Land' by Eric Bogle reproduced courtesy
of PLD Music Ltd.

Lyrics from 'A Windmill in Amsterdam' by Ted Dicks and Myles Rudge ©
1964 and 1973 Westminster Music Ltd, London SW10 0SZ. International
copyright secured. All rights reserved. Used by permission.

Condition of Sale
This book is sold subject to the condition that it shall not,
by way of trade or otherwise, be lent, re-sold, hired out or otherwise
circulated in any form of binding or cover other than that in which
it is published and without a similar condition including this
condition being imposed on the subsequent purchaser.

Set in 11/13pt Sabon by
Phoenix Typesetting, Ilkley, West Yorkshire

Bantam Books are published by Transworld Publishers,
61–63 Uxbridge Road, London W5 5SA,
a division of The Random House Group Ltd,
in Australia by Random House Australia (Pty) Ltd,
20 Alfred Street, Milsons Point, Sydney, NSW 2061, Australia,
in New Zealand by Random House New Zealand Ltd,
18 Poland Road, Glenfield, Auckland 10, New Zealand
and in South Africa by Random House (Pty) Ltd,
Endulini, 5a Jubilee Road, Parktown 2193, South Africa.

Reproduced, printed and bound in Great Britain by
Clays Ltd, St Ives plc.

To Gilmar Cruz Silva

acknowledgements

Thanks to Father Gerard Harney, Stewart Hennessey, Ginny Till, Ted Verity, Tad Williams and my agent, Stephanie Cabot, or help and advice.

I am especially grateful to Cachorro Louco, Helen Windrath and Steve Carr for their insight and encouragement.

And to Deborah Thorpe; todos de todos, amiga.

chapter one

IT'S FUCKING FREEZING. THE RAIN IS HALFWAY THROUGH my jacket, and every so often I have a sort of mini spasm, a jerk of the backbone, like some half-arsed break-dancer. I know junkies whine – permanent residents in self-pity city. But I'll tell you, it's not an easy life.

Given the choice I wouldn't have moved today. I'd have stayed in bed with Regina, got a bit of breakfast out of her and started out leisurely. Maybe gone down the market for a couple, maybe just gone home to chill out. But I don't have no fuckin choice, do I? Thirty-six hours since the last jag and I feel like shite. My kidneys are aching. I don't know why, but they are. And the cold; oh, the cold. I had a bath at Reg's. I thought I was going to have a cardiac when the water hit me, but once fully submerged I was OK. But then the fuckin hot water ran out, didn't it? I suppose I'd known, theoretically, that if I got in I would, at some time, have to get out. But dear God, save us, the shivering, shaking, snivelling misery of it all. Desperate to get dry and get me clothes on, but too fuckin feeble to hack it. Oh, I tell you, it's a killer.

Anyway, that's what I went through at Regina's place.

Normally I wouldn't have bothered, but I felt so fuckin ackie. For a start I stank of her, not something to cart round for the rest of the day. I mean, Reg is OK, as far as it goes, which is strictly not the daylight hours. Secondly I stank anyway. The thing about starting to withdraw is you sweat – buckets of it. I hate it. This morning, my side of Reg's pale pink sheets were a sight to behold. Sodden, with a sinister-looking brown ring spreading round the edge of the wet stuff. She knew better than to say anything. Anyway, I had to get up. You can't sleep in a fuckin puddle, and it was freezing. Every time I turned over it was like falling into cold water. Even so, it took me a fair while to get going. The thought of what was coming was a major disincentive. Optimistically, it's going to be at least one o'clock before I plane out. Possible fuck-ups taken into consideration, it could be tomorrow, which doesn't bear thinking about.

The plan is simple enough. I've got the cash, which must be counted as a major plus, and I know who's got the gear: Tinnsey did a chemist last week and is still playing Wall-Street games with the DDA box. It's a bull market, and Danny MacIntyre has just put in a mega-bid for world-wide diconal stocks. Buy! Buy! Buy! But, but, but, Tinnsey's a twat. He may have shifted the box to safer territory; he may have contracted out the whole retail operation; he could have got lifted; he could have OD'd in the overexcitement. Who knows? There's only one option, and that's to get on the bus and find out. The crucifying thing is, if I don't score I've added another hour plus to the tally of misery.

Oh fuck, where is this fuckin, bastarding bus, and why am I stood with this bunch of cripples and losers? What is it about buses? Do they have a social-rejects-only policy? 'Sorry, you're too normal, you can't get on this bus.' I mean, fuck me, I'm in a state, right enough, but compared to the rest of the crips in the queue I'm Michael Jordan. I fuckin hate this. 'Waiting for the Man'. Nearly thirty years since Lou wrote that and personally I'm sick of fuckin waiting. What's happened to progress and the market? All this shite about pushers at the school gates, I wish to fuck it was true. Fat fuckin chance. Instead you're chasing all over town and – witness today's nightmare – shithole pit villages beyond, begging and grovelling. Dealers are so crap; I could do that job with one hand tied behind me back. Maybe I could get the dinos together and set up . . . Oh, at fucking last. Never has a lover greeted his lass with more sincerity and affection than I give to thee, single decker, Donny Dodger, number 29 bus for Rossington. Get out the way, crips. If I have to kill every last one of you, I'm getting on this fuckin bus.

Of course Tinnsey would have to live in Rosso, wouldn't he? I mean, there's no fuckin shortage of competition, but Rosso could truly lay claim to being the arsehole of South Yorkshire. Twenty-five minutes of pure purgatory – and we're talking each way here – and finally we arrive in the badlands. My bones feel like glass, I just can't cope with it. There are monsters out there who'll rip your head off for not being one of the tribe, and weird women with funny stiff hair. But you can't look too long, it's dangerous.

They built the place on a grid system, and Tinnsey's is on Seventh Street. So it's going to take me another ten minutes to walk it from here. Oh, let him be in. Oh, please God, let him be in. I can't bear it, I honestly can't. Then there's his house. I can't remember the fuckin number. You can usually tell a junkie's house from the general shite and filth about. Garden full of weeds and dog turds, no curtains, filthy toddler in the window, door with a spyhole at the top that's been kicked in once too often. But here you wouldn't know, you honestly wouldn't.

The whole place is full of mutants. They all dress the same: bleached-out denim, bleached-out hair, backed up by the dead-eye stare. It's the land that time forgot and no fucking joke. They pile on the bus on Friday night and head for Donny and the heart of metropolitan glamour. After that it's pretty straightforward. First head for the market pubs and get as pissed as cunts. Whilst you're staggering round the market with your mates you're obviously on the lookout for anyone who's not from Rosso. If you're lucky enough to find some poor bastard from Edlo or Askern you naturally smack his teeth straight down his throat. Next move is to stagger to the nearest club, hoping to find something shaggable. At 3 a.m. you totter off for some speedy scran, which you stuff down your face in preparation for chucking up in the taxi back home. The entire fuckin village will probably end up on the *X Files* or something, cos this lot are beyond the laws of nature. You wouldn't want to accuse them of keeping a welcome in the hillside neither. They'll fuckin kill me if they find out I'm from town, and I don't know if I can fake the accent. Oh Christ, here we go.

'Alrate, marrer, thou nos Tinnsey?'

'That twat's off 'is box, foteen, marrer.'

Pissed it, absolutely pissed it, ya shit-thick Rosso bastard. See you in town an I'll have your balls for breakfast. Please let him be in. Answer the door, you cunt, you can't be that stoned already.

'Alrate, Danny, how's it goin?'

'Pretty plaza. Bit of business, Tinnsey. Can I come in?'

'It'll have to be quiet; June's been up all night an the kids are giving her jip.'

June, as scrawny wet and dismal as a wanking

pensioner. Three kids, all under five, all disgusting. Just get in there and give me the gear, Tinnsey. I know as I follow him in it won't be that simple. The smell of nappies and dog nearly knocks me backwards, and there's stringy June and the three brats, half-naked and covered in welts and spots. It's no surprise Tinnsey's a smack-head, I mean, you couldn't face this lot on reality, not a chance.

Getting gear off Tinnsey is like being at the court of Louis XIV. I observe the formalities, ask about the kids (who gives a fuck), his mam (ditto), the success of the chemist job (more interesting) and his general health (crap). This takes twenty minutes of bleedin agony. The sweat inside my clothes is meeting the rain on the outside. Finally I judge the time to be right.

'Any gear about then, Tinnsey. We're talking proper paper; I've got the dinos.' He keeps his eyes averted, attention bent on crafting his roll-up.

'Not really, marrer. I've shifted it away, like.'

I feel my heart lurch, but keep the affable expression stuck on my face. I'll pay the power-tripping bastard for this one day. I get out my wallet and count 500 quid in tens and twenties.

'Come on, Tinnsey, stop arsing about.' For a long moment he just sits there, looking shifty, and then, finally, he makes up his mind. I've joined the charmed circle; he's going to let me buy.

'What you after, mate? I've got smack, morph, powder and amps, pinkies, phy tabs, phy amps, peach palf and a bit of coke. That's the grade-one gear, plus there's a lot of rammy stuff about – DF118s, naps and the like – but you'll not be wanting, to my mind that's strictly jayjay stuff.'

'How much for the dikes and the smack? White smack, pharmy, right?' He nodded. 'I'm looking to buy a bit.'

Tinnsey's prices weren't that bad, not that I cared much.

13

I'd cleaned out Regina's handbag *en route*, besides which I had dinos from a couple of enterprises earlier in the week. The wash of relief from knowing he had the gear was enough to take out every other consideration. Twenty-five dikes and six grams of white should do it.

My works was flashing the minute I grabbed the gear out of his hands. Four dikes first jag, that's right enough. With dikes it can be a thin line between planing and OD'ing, but four should see me cruising. June made some whiney remark about not wanting me to hit up in front of the kids, but both Tinnsey and I told her to shut the fuck up. It took me a while to get a vein; it always does when you're strung out, when you really want it. The kids made it worse; the eldest kept asking if he could hold my quet. I kept telling him to fuck off, but it had no effect. In the end I got in such a state I backhanded him, which on reflection I should have done in the first place, cos it finally got rid of the little bastard. And then . . . and then I got it – the dark red rushing into the barrel to lie with the pink. Dike Utd, the colours of the world's best team. I put it in slowly – you got to treat dikes with respect – and then flushed it. I couldn't stop once I'd started; I was on my fourth flush when it hit and the world turned over.

June made tea while I packed my stuff. I was chatting to Tinnsey, just rabbitting really, about various mates and downtown stuff and whether the Queen should come to the St Leger. He's all right really. Could do better than fucking June. I mean, he's got the gear. He could get almost anybody, yet he's stuck with that clapped-out old tart. Anyway, she made some tea, as I've already said, which I drank before I left, with many a formal thanks and lots of 'Any time, marrer. Pleasure to do business.' Greasing up to Tinnsey is good policy; he's a total cunt, but he gets a lot of gear, and in a way he's grateful to anyone who comes out to Rosso and gives him a bit of human contact, and takes his mind off his fuck-awful wife and the howling brats. Leave her, mate, why don't you just do it? Town's full of sixteen-year-olds desperate for their first hit.

Anyway, Tinnsey's fuck-ups aren't my problem. I saunter through Rosso in the early sunshine, and there's a garden that's escaped the mutants, full of little gold and purple flowers. I pull up a few for Reg, or maybe for Janey. For somebody anyway. There's nobody else at the bus stop, and I hope it's a while, I want to have a smoke (gear always makes you smoke more – tastes better you see) and think about things.

By the time the trusty Donny Dodger has carried me back to home turf, I can sense I'm losing it slightly. I'm precise about these things because it's important. Two and a half hours at Tinnsey's, forty minutes' journey and the dikes are wearing off. I'm not turkeying, but I'm sliding perilously close to normality. That golden beneficence and euphoria is leaving. I can't go to one of the oh so many junkie houses about, because whoever I land on will demand a hit as ground rent, and I haven't been through the Rosso horror show just to give it away. Janey, sadly, also falls into this category, being a bit partial herself, which is a pity, cos I quite fancy seeing her. Going home runs the distinct possibility of bumping into the creature from the black lagoon, and if anything can ruin your drugs it's her. So it looks like Reg's lucky day. She'll be made up.

I was going to give her the flowers, but I lost them some-where. I was still feeling good enough to buy her a half of vodka, though. I like vodka with orange juice when I'm planing; it's clean and healthy. Reg reminds me of a puppy, you know. Sort of pathetically grateful and excited to see you, wriggling and squirming, not quite daring to

15

get too close, but heart-flipped with desire. We all know what to do with puppies: they're cute and cuddly and you stroke and snuggle with them, then you kick them in the gob to get rid, because they just won't go away if you ask nicely, and eventually they learn. After a while, all you have to do is look the wrong way and they go all quiet and terrified, just waiting for the slap. That's how it is with Reg. I don't enjoy it much; she's too supine, too wretched and beatable. If you're going to get something out of beating up women, then it's only any good if they fight back a bit. You want to feel the surrender, the muscles straining, the snarling mouth and hating eyes. Something worth breaking. If they don't fight, then they're not worth much more than a casual backhander; there's no sex and no science in it.

Anyway, I digress. As I say, Reg was chuffed as little apples, just couldn't believe her luck. Danny Boy two nights in a row, and one of them a Friday. The angels were singing for her. She started trying to cook for me, but I stopped all that and told her I was after a jag and then I'd think about it. She's very good when you're hitting up. It's a neglected branch of the service industry, but Reg could operate nicely as a shooting-gallery hostess. And she's learnt it all by hard work and careful observation, cos, astoundingly enough, she's not interested in taking gear. I've offered once or twice. You know, you get these fits of ridiculous stoned generosity, but she's never been tempted. She's quite classy like that. One of the reasons I've put up with her for so long.

Anyways, as I was saying, she's got a professional flair. She got me a quiet, a spoon, hot water and a mat to put me works on. Quietly and efficiently, which I appreciated. She then held my quiet and rubbed up my vein. There's one just down near my wrist which is a real contender if you

16

can get it up. It goes without saying, of course, that both my mainliners are fucked. Anyway, Reg did a nice competent job. A few light slaps, a bit of a rub, quet tightened properly and there it was. I hit it second time, which is not at all bad. Reg, in beautiful clinical form, loosened the quet and, once the flushes were through, put her finger on the vein to hold it while I withdrew. A brief massage to stop the bleeding and bruising, and then she was away, cleaning out the works and tidying the debris. Sometimes I think I'd like to get her a nurse's uniform. Not for some sexual thrill, you understand, but in recognition of a job well done. It's when she's helping me like this that I like her best. Smooth, efficient, engrossed in her work, you can forget how crap and usable she is, and just sit back and admire.

I spent the entire evening holed up at Reg's. I was frankly too stoned to be let loose in public, and quite happy to sit back and watch the telly while Reg ran about catering to my needs. Isn't telly crap on a Friday, by the way? I suppose it's because only sad cases and pensioners are watching, and who cares about them? By this time, you see, I was gauching, and that's a private pleasure. I mean, there's few things worse than sitting in a pub watching some lucky stoned bastard slowly slipping face-first into his pint. Equally, people have no manners, no understanding or proper etiquette. If you're gauching, you've moved out, absconded to a better world, and the last thing you want is some concerned tosser saying, 'Ere, pal, you're falling asleep.' Yes, you cretin, I know; that's the whole purpose of the very expensive drugs I just bought, and if you prod my shoulder one more time to 'bring me round', I'll smack your teeth right down your throat. You'll understand, obviously you just can't be doin with the hassle. So anyway, I stopped in and watched

17

Bob an Noel an Bruce as they cavorted about. At about one in the morning I told Reg to get us some scran. She was a real good girl all night, quiet and attentive, and she did sausage, beans and lasagne – made a nice job of it too – but in the end I couldn't get it down, the dikes had closed up my throat and I couldn't swallow, but I said 'ta' to her anyway.

We went to bed about 3 a.m. She'd changed the sheets to white, which I liked. Sometimes I feel tender about her, you know, and I did tonight. She's got long hair, pale brown and halfway down her back; it makes you want to stroke her. At twenty, she's a year older than me, and gettin close to being past it, but she's tiny and, with the long hair, like one of those Victorian dolls that fetch a packet. She's even got the big, round, china blue eyes. When we fucked I told her about Janey. She kept silent, totally still, but the eyes became more and more intense and shiny, until they spilt down her face in this glittering line. It was magic. Pure, pure magic. I slept like the dead that night, soft and warm and comfortable, stroking her hair as it fell on my pillow.

Of course nothing lasts. Life is a vale of tears, as they say, and when Saturday comes I have to get off my arse and move to sort out the dinos. Anyway, two days of Reg is enough for anyone.

Town was rolling, the market full of old biddies and bints, shoving their shopping in your face and elbowing through to get at the tomato sausage. I just dandied about for a while, showing off me new strides and generally feeling fine. I was looking for Dekka, to do a spot of business – the dinos were well and truly calling.

In the end Dekka found me, spotted me over the road and weaved his way through the shopping and stilettos to get to my side, like a good lieutenant should.

'Danny, kay passer, marrer?'

'Cruisin, hombre, just cruisin. What gives?'

'Nowt much. Round town last night with a few of the lads. We went up the Roxette. We missed you, marrer. Where were you?'

'Down at Reg's, keeping her happy. Listen up, Dekka, we've got a job on.'

I ought to explain about Dekka. Me and him go way back. At primary school together we formed a seven-year-olds' alliance, and we've stuck with it ever since. If you think my mam's bad – and believe me, she is – Dekka's family can give her a twenty-yard start in the hundred metres worst-parent-of-the-decade dash. His mam's an alchy – well, isn't everyone's? But the worst sort, you know? I mean, my mam's a screaming, shouting, dancing drinker. I'm allus coming home to find her chucking the china at some no-hoper she's picked up down the Pelican. I can't pretend it's fun, dealing with the debris, human and inanimate, but at least it's lively. Shows a bit of zest, a teeny suspicion that things ought to be a wee bit better. But Mrs Dixon, oh dear God, give me strength. You've never heard whining like it, I promise you. As constant as the stars is Dekka's mam's self-pity. Nor time nor tide make an atom of difference. You can shout, reason, sympathize or physically abuse, she barely breaks stride. Thirteen years she's been at it, to my knowledge.

Then there's Dekka senior, his da, another complete disaster area. Mr Dixon makes his living taxiing on the black and dognapping. He's got this deal with some local lab you see. So he's driving his beat-up Datsun round Donny, and sees some unsuspecting canine dandying about, and before you can say 'beauty not cruelty', the Bonios are out and the dog's in the back seat on the way to the sharp end of the appliance of science. He does cats as well, but they're harder to catch.

When we were about nine or ten, he caught a labrador puppy, just like the one on telly. Anyway, I don't know what went wrong, but he didn't go straight to the lab, he took it home for a few days. Dekka fell in love and asked if he could have it for his birthday. Mr Dixon, all heart, says, 'Of course, son, the dog's yours.' Two weeks later – you know the end to this story, don't you – Dekka comes home to find that Striker – fuckin stupid name – has gone. His da has got back on bargaining terms with the lab, and the furtherance of humanity's cause has, naturally enough, come before Dekka's birthday pressie. The uproar was unbelievable. Oh the wailing and gnashing of teeth; it pierced the very heavens. Mr Dixon asserted his authority and solved the matter by knocking seven shades of shite out of Dekka and locking him in his room for two days. I have to say it worked, because he's never mentioned the dog since, and now he's older he's even been known to give his da a hand with the business.

Anyway, I digress. Suffice to say that me and Dekka have been amigos durandes for many a long year and that, despite his many and manifest shortcomings, you couldn't find a more useful oppo. A sort of sub-commandante to my jefey, if you get the way the water's flowing. So, we've done loads of jobs together, and there's one coming up tonight. I'm a bit cleaned-out after the Tinnsey trip, and there's an urgent need to rapidly replenish the dinos. I have noted, being smarter than your average pudding, a house down the posh end, which has an extremely portable set of elecs: vid, telly (small but perfectly formed), computer and wee mico, for irradiated speedy scran. In addition, there's probably a bit of sparkle kicking about. All we need to do is put the master plan into operation, because the owners of this enviable loot always piss off out on a Saturday night. People are so predictable, you know. Nah class, nah style, too right. The fuckin bourgeoisie deserve all they've got comin.

'Anyway, Dekka, amigo mio, what you think?'

'Sound as a pound, Danny. Do we go mob 'anded or is it a dos job?'

'Dos, I think. We need the wheels, but thee and me should sort it. Waiting round the Chequered Board I thought, marrer? Sisi?'

'Sisi, Danny. Esso es.'

Dekka and I arrange to meet at eight thirty and we go our separate ways. Ordinarily I'd spend Saturday afternoon in the pubs with me mates, but I don't drink before a job, which is why I'm still dandering round the streets of Donny whilst half the toerags of my acquaintance are hoping for a trustee's job in Armley. Besides which, I have to go back to the asylum and change. Dekka's a pro and won't drink, either; he's on the hunt for some gear to take after we've done the job. I know, I know, you think I'm a cunt for not giving or at the very least selling him some, don't you? Well, you know fuck all. You're still thinking about little Dekka and his fluffy golden puppy, aren't you? Well little Dekka is nineteen now, he's five eleven and weighs thirteen stone. Last year his girlfriend got an abortion, not on demand, although there's some would say she asked for it. No. You see, if I told Dekka about my gear, I'd be forced to give him some, cos we're amigos, an all that shite. Then he'd lose respect for me, for being soft enough to give him gear I'd paid for, then I'd have to do something really vicious to him to win his regard back. So really I'm doing us both a favour by keeping me gob shut. Look, it's difficult to explain. Just take my word for it.

21

So it's deep breath and hit the road for home. I'm just walking out the market and steering down for the Axside bus when a hand grabs my jacket. Luckily I'm in a good enough mood not to throw a punch. I can't bear people touchin me uninvited, and they will do it. Anyway, it was Janey, half-cut and raging about Friday night.

'Danny MacIntyre, you lying, conniving tosspot. Where the fuck were you? I stayed in, twat-face. Stayed in till 'alf ten waiting for you, you wanker, and you never showed.'

At this point she began screaming about what a bastard I was. Now you know why I didn't turn up, and I did try and explain – things to do, people to see – but she was having none of it, still screaming, and she hadn't let go of my jacket. Only eighteen and already a complete pain in the arse.

'If you don't shut up now, you stupid bitch, I'll smack your ugly teeth straight out. I didn't come round cos I've got better things to do with me time than fucking you. Now get your hands off my fucking jacket. It's new.'

This quietened her down somewhat, and I was able to soften up slightly. Told her if she played her cards right I'd see her later on that night, maybe in the Queen of the Sea, which shut her up and got rid. But my mind's made up: she's not worth the hassle. I might ask Dekka tonight if he fancies taking over. Even if he doesn't it's definitely adios to Jane. Jesus, I mean, I have status in this town. I can't have some silly tart mouthing off at me in public, like I was just anybody. Nah, fuck right off is the order of the day, sisi?

So, it's off to home sweet home. I took the back way – more scenic – and walked down the canal past St George's, which is the biggest parish church in the whole of England. No-one ever goes to it, cos it's totally stranded behind the ring road. But then it's C. of E., so I don't suppose it matters. Anyway, I trotted on at a fair clip, past the dole office and the bingo and the back end of the Frenchgate. It's marvellous what exercise can do for you. By the time I reached the Northern Bus Station I was perky as you like, and doing the odd dance step as I dandered down for the Axside bus.

Unfortunately, as some poet or other pointed out, happiness doesn't last, and good moods don't hang around. No sooner had I hopped on the bus than a voice piped up behind me, 'Danny? Danny chav, all right then?' Sodding Teapot, who else? Every time I turn round, there's Teapot. I mean, me an my shadow ain't in it. Of course, there's acres of empty seats but, natch enuf, he plonked himself next to me and droned on about his court case for the entire journey, which was mercifully short. I mean, who cares about his miserable twocking? Certainly not me. I also suspect that he's a grass, which places him beyond the moral pale, down there with the sickos and the psychos. To be honest, I didn't even want to be seen with him – you know, guilt by association. I got off the bus two stops early just to get away. I've heard it rumoured that Gibbsey's got a squad out for him, and he certainly seemed jumpy enough. I sat as far away from him as the double seat would allow. If they catch up with him it'll be a serious case of physical rearrangement, and that's one gig I'm not buying a ticket to.

When I finally trailed up to number 66, after a brisk yomp down St Stephen's and a nifty cut across the jennel into St Cath's, the signs weren't good. The lights were blazing and I could hear the Rod Stewart from fifty yards. If approached with real skill and caution – you know, like tribesmen in the forests of Borneo, who melt on silent feet into the morning mists – there was a hope I could make it to sanctuary without disturbing the beast, but my chances weren't good. Inhabiting Pandemonium has done nothing to lessen the senses. Her hearing's like the lynx; eagle-eyed and nostrils flaring, she scents me from afar and cryeth, 'Ha Ha!' And it's such a fucker, you know.

I took a deep breath, dropped down to my knees and, half running, half crawling, made it down the side passage. My key was primed and to hand. The lock turned with silky smooth silence and I paused immobile and unbreathing. I'd drawn the door to, of course, or else she'd clock the extra light, but closing it was another game entirely. The click – you can't avoid it – it stops my heart. I waited for Rod, body rising and falling with the beat, and 'Hot Legs' did it. I was paralysed for a minute, but she missed it. I cross the kitchen on soft feet, and now I'm risking visibility. Three strides across the hallway to the stairs and twenty-one steps up to the first landing. Once there I turn the corner and it's all about sound and smell. This is the worst part of the journey. The temptation is to get out of sight as quickly as possible, but speed means sound. You have to hold your nerve, move like a dancer, all grace and silence, and pray that God is with you and the old bat's amidst some Rodney-induced euphoria, her eyes firmly fixed on 1974, and not you. I did it well. A cat-like glide and then I started the climb in smooth arcs, like a hovercraft. I travelled on air and finally made it. I had to stop and steady myself before the second ascent, gob-smacked by my own success.

'Daz, is that you, baby? Come to Mummy. Come and dance with me.'

Oh fuck. Oh sweet, suffering Jesus. Oh no. Don't ask me how. It's like a sixth sense. She says her blood beats in rhythm to mine, and sometimes, loath as I am, I can almost believe it. In the front room the curtains are drawn and the joss sticks are out; Rodney wants to know if I think he's sexy. Frankly, mate, you haven't a prayer; just go and get your bus pass now. She's wearing stretch denims, tighter than her skin – well at her age it's not difficult. On top there's this blood-coloured silky halterneck affair, and a dark purple velvet jacket. Beads, and black feathers in her ears, bracelets, and lots of lipstick. I'm going to get covered in it. She always says she was beautiful, and you know, from the photos you can see it. Eyes black as death, with hair to match, and a look which held you. She should have been OK, but no, my mam fucked up on a grand scale. There's no-one between the ages of twenty and forty-five in Donny who hasn't had her, including quite a few of me mates. For what it's worth, they say she's not at all bad, especially with her mouth – when it's full that is.

'Come here, darling. You look lovely. You've got my hair, of course; such a good colour. I always loved dark men. Dance with me, now, darling.'

I'd like to gloss over the next hour, like to say never mind, didn't happen, dreamt it. But if I've got to live the horror show I don't see why you should escape without a full viewing. To be grateful for small mercies, she's chucked the tartan terror. In his place we've got the Mambo Kings, which in a weak moment I'd been stupid enough to buy her for Christmas. Well, our sins find us out. You see, me mam started me dancing when I could barely walk. The entire deal, Viennese waltz, foxtrot, tango, disco, mambo, samba. When I was barely able to stand she was battering me for not matching up to the video of John Travolta. Anyway, I can do it – eventually you learn – and I've inherited enough of me mam's mad genes to half like it. Not like this, but who said we were choosing? There's something iffy about smooching with your mother. The Mambo Kings sing songs of love, yeah,

25

but not for you and me mam. I've tried to tell her, but you can't really tell much to my mam. So there we were, mamboing round the front room to the likes of 'Guantanamera' and 'Quiereme Mucho' (oh I do, I do). As the songs go by, me mam gets more gropey, her arms entwine round the back of my neck, her body leans into me and our hips move in concert. Now I'm so post-Freudian I've missed the second backlash. I know how it goes – you can keep the psychoanalysis for me lawyer – what I can tell you is that I don't want to screw me mam, no matter how good a blow job she gives. I hate this, fucking hate it, but deny her nothing; just a boy who can't say no.

Several decades later I escape. No pretence of stealth – I leg it up to the bathroom and slam the bolt. Predictably enough she follows, but not quick enough. Leaning against the door I can feel the reverberations as she hammers, screams, threatens and pleads. After ten minutes or so she gives up and goes back down. I've got about an hour before she gets her second wind, so it's into the pit, off with the kit and back to the shower. I stand under the hot water for ages. Such a feeling; like washing your soul. I dress carefully for tonight. They've got to be loose, easy to move in yet compact. I feel tight, frustrated; I've got to get out of the house before she starts again. I make it down the stairs in five easy bounds, a 'ta ra, Mam' and I'm out and running. I hope to Christ she brings someone back tonight. I can't do another one of those, not for a while.

I meet Dekka in the Chequered Board bang on time. He's sat nursing the ritual bottle of Becks. I bought me own and joined him.

'OK, amigo, tranquilo?'

Dekka nodded, tight and sure. I like this about him: he

isn't a flapper. His approach to work is proper and serious. We had an hour to kill, and we spent it going over the details. I could feel the ice beginning to enter my blood and my mind narrowing down to nano-focus: I could see the house, them locking up (don't waste your time, my angels), laughing as they got in the car, the gravel shifting under the wheels. It was time, now it was surely time.

With one mind we rose, moving quiet and sure, the predator's step, heavy and silent. It was only a mile and a half and we flew there, Dekka talking her through the bends and smooth as milk down the main drag. We were peaking, throbbing with tension and anticipated release. Suburbia was silent and we respected the mood, jemmying off the back window in balletic slow-mo. Leg up and I wriggle in, dancing hips standing me in good stead. Dark and so silent inside, but I'm no fuckin amateur and I go straight for the turnables, always same place. Tick 'em off: vid, telly, mico, CD, kettle (I know, I know, but it was a posh one, and I get carried away on the job), all straight out to Dekka, who's ferrying bootwise. The computer weighed a fuckin ton, but it looked like a top-end job and worth the struggle. He'd got loads of games too, so I popped into the kitchen for a plaggy bag and handed them through. I had the good manners to leave his disks alone, even pulled out the one he was working on. You can't say I'm not thoughtful, and they're worth nowt anyway. Then I'm away, onto my second set. Upstairs in the bedroom, marvelling that so many flower motifs can be crammed into twelve square feet, and totally disgusted by the net drapes on the four poster. What world are these fucking people living in? I ask you, you can just see the silly bitch, can't you, sat there in her bleedin Victorian nightie, being all coy and romantic, and her wanker of a boyfriend thinking, Oh well, at least I get a shag at the end of it. What a tosser. Women don't like it, you know. They think they do, but they don't. If she starts traipsing about in pink silk and lace, rip it straight off before she's had time to light the first aromatic candle. In the long run she'll be grateful.

Anyway, back to the job. It didn't take long to locate the sparkles – in a fucking box on the dressing table, aren't they? How very cunning. Well, following a quick reccy I shove the lot in my pocket and start to go. I've been in a good fifteen and it's starting to get risky. I was halfway down the stairs before I stopped, overcome by this weird compulsion, and I went back, blade in hand. I did a job on the drapes, on the sheets and duvet. Don't know why; they just offended me. I wanted to give them another chance, to let them do better. Anyway, end of story. And as me and Dekka drove down past the race course we were singing, 'Glory glory, Leeds United. Glory glory, Leeds United.'

chapter two

IT WAS THE FOLLOWING TUESDAY IT HAPPENED. I KNOW it was Tuesday because it was market day, and I was sat in the Fort with me marrers. Dekka was there, so was Chico Latino, Scaz, Teapot (who'd managed to sit next to me – marvellous), Kev, Janey, Mad Dog and Angie. Janey was still pathetically attempting to grovel her way back in with me. I was leaning back, lordly style, accepting the drinks and the manifest crawling and keeping tranquilo. She had no chance, but it was fun watching her try. Why is it the more they want you the more you despise them? It was good to be out, money in me pocket, smack running in my blood, sitting with me marrers and the day to kill – no wonder the sun was shining. To add to the entertainment, Angie was definitely after me, and showing. Now, if you've pegged Reg and Janey as four-star basket cases, I have to tell you they're shiny-faced amateurs in the fucked-up stakes compared to a hardened pro like Angie. At the relatively tender age of twenty-five she can lay claim to real prestige loony status. Her career has been pretty impressive. She started early, falling pregnant to her older brother when she was just eleven. Made the local papers

29

and even copped thirty seconds on *Look North* – SHOCKING CASE OF DONCASTER SCHOOLGIRL. The social services, in a rare outbreak of sanity, took the kid off her. The next major escapade came two years later when she torched the family home. Unfortunately Ma, Da and bro all escaped, and the only victim was Peter the budgie. Angie was thereafter nicknamed 'Kentucky' as in fried chicken, and if you want to see her lose her rag just ask for a family bucket with extra beans and coleslaw and watch her go.

Since then it's been the usual stuff: bit of smack, bit of whoring, perfecting the shoplifting technique, but still showing flashes of real nutter potential – one of her 'clients' had to take an emergency trip to DRI after she almost bit his dick off. Some say she was simply carried away on the job, others that he'd tried the Kentucky joke at a particularly stupid moment. Such highlights are fairly sporadic. Most of the time she's as sussed as they come and a born survivor. Her interest in me was not for my bonny blue eyes, most likely she'd heard I was in mega-dinos and thought it would be nice if I spent some of it on her. Fat fucking chance. What with Care in the Community it's not hard to fuck a loony nowadays, if that's where your interests lie; and they let you do it for free. Angie's stock is falling; they're flooding the market. Anyway, call me old-fashioned, but I prefer my women to have at least a passing acquaintance with sanity, which I'm afraid rather rules out Angie. Truth to tell there was another, less lofty reason for my disinterest. I mean, as someone like the New Seekers once sang, we all love to be loved, but, Angie baby, with you, I *know* it's just the dinos, just another bit of trade, and I don't like it.

Well, what of the rest of the gang who witnessed – and as with most witnesses, hadn't got a clue what was going on – the moment of my epiphany? Well, Teapot you already know. He was the centre of attention that afternoon, as we amused ourselves by suggesting what Gibbsey and the boys would do to him as revenge for grassing, watching the blood drain from his face and following his eyes shooting perpetually towards the door. He knows it's coming, but don't ask me for sympathy. He's a pain in the arse, and he fuckin volunteered for it, didn't he?

You see grassin is one of those things you just don't do. Personally, I don't know if Teapot sang to the polis or not, but Gibbsey thinks he did, an that's all that matters. Everyone knows the score: break the rules and you'll get a good slapping. Discipline has to be maintained – fair enough really. Interestingly, there's two distinct philosophical schools in Donny regarding necessary batterings. When it comes to a beating, Dekka and I can hand it out with the best of them, especially Dekka, who has weight on his side. But, and this is important, we never lose it. If you've got to do someone, you do them, but it's work, not leisure. You keep control. The Gibbsey camp says bollocks, go for it 110 per cent, they say, and find your fun where you can. Anyway, if the lesson is delivered with enthusiasm, it will be better received and better remembered. They may have a point, but the kickback is that you end up on a murder charge when you merely intended to point out that owing £25 for over two weeks is not a good idea. Sometimes the game's not worth the candle. Gibbsey recently went round to see someone who owed him drug money. He took the lads with him, and the unfortunate victim was bundled into the car and taken to casa Gibbsey. Afterwards they left him by the railway line, and when the police found him they thought he'd been hit by a train. No, officer, it wasn't a 125 on the East Coast Line, doing a ton on its way to the Cross. No, it was four hours spent in the company of Gibbsey and the boys.

Anyway, there you go. Aside from Teapot there's Mad Dog, a barking-mad heavy, built like a brick shithouse, with brains to match; Kev, a dismal junkie with a bad complexion; and Scaz, his even spottier younger brother. That just leaves the big 'itters: myself, of course, and Dekka, amigo mio. Apart from us there was only one serious contender present.

I've left the real competition till last; the only one that counts. His mouth as full and shapely as the loveliest girl, skin golden as the sunshine. Chico Latino, beautiful as a fallen angel, walked straight off the front cover of *Vogue* into Doncaster marketplace. Chico's parents came from some fly-blown death hole in South America; at some point in the Eighties they finally saw sense and clambered aboard a plane bound for the First World. Some cruel twist of fate then dumped them and little Chico in darkest Doncaster, and they run a caff just off the market. Chico's turned into a class act, sauntering round in his shades, dealing the drugs and screwing the girls – you wouldn't believe it, they practically line up and beg for the privilege, they do. He's sitting across from me, holding a cigarette and smiling. Teapot is almost in tears by now, but Chico's not one to give up. His voice is silky-soft, the accent thick as butter.

'Sisi, eet's a problem, to lose your balls, eet's a bad thing. You think they use a blade, or sceesors maybe? When they find the boy by the train lines, ees thighs, they were covered in blood, and they break ees legs with a spade, I theenk. Is a spade, Ma Dog?'

Mad Dog nods assent, smiling, and Teapot looks as though he's going to be sick. Such fun we were having, I can tell you. The sun was streaming in, fighting its way past the barrier of filth on the windows and striking a pathway through the thick, dark air. You could see tiny bright things dancing in the light. Outside the window the barbarous multitude are thronging by, intent on their dismal lives. Why do we put up with so little? Are we – me, Chico, Dekka and the lads – are we the only ones with any ambition in this town? I sometimes wonder, I really do.

I get a nasty twinge sometimes, you know. I look at the shagged-out crew of thirty-somethings sitting in their corner of the Fort, or watch me mates' older brothers. From where I'm standing it don't look good, I'm telling you. Where are the mob you see on telly? Those women who still look sexy when they're practically forty? All those people who seem to live in a perpetual gleam of assurance. Well, they're not here, I'll tell you that for certain and sure. Maybe I should go, while there's still time. Only trouble is, where to?

The bang, when it came, shattered even my legendary cool, and Teapot looked as though he'd just suffered a major coronary – a sign of things to come. The punters sitting behind the door stared at the pool of glass and beer that had been their pints, but wisely refrained from moving. Waltzing across the carpet with that rhythmical, shoulder-swinging, you-are-fuckin-dead-mate tread were Gibbsey and the boys.

He went without a murmur. Finished his Guinness – good for you? I wonder – and just stood up and nodded. 'Right. See youse later, lads,' he said. This proved not to be true, but Teapot had never been overly gifted with prescience.

There were six of them that took him. A tad excessive, I thought, even at the time. Teapot wasn't much to shout about physically; his skills had always been more of the ducking-diving kind, which I suppose lends a kind of poetic symmetry to the eventual outcome. No-one said a word, of course, when he went. You don't interfere in matters of this kind. We didn't even acknowledge his goodbye; that would suggest partisanship, some smidgin of support. Sympathy even. Nah, we looked straight through him as he walked out with the bodies of Gibbsey's mob closing round him. Silly twat shouldn't have grassed. Beggin for it really, as I said.

Once the doors closed and normal service resumed we got more drinks in. Chico, typically flash, on the San Miguel. St Michael – like unto God. Captain-general of the angelic hosts, supreme commander of the nine orders, vanquisher of Satan, commandante in chief of God's army. That's Chico for you, fairly sure of his place in the scheme of things. Deprived of Teapot we had to find other amusement, and Kev entertained us with a story of a girl from the deaf college that his brother had brought home one night last week. Of course the possibilities for fun in such a situation are endless, and Kev and his bro had not been slow on the uptake.

I was slightly off on one when it happened. You know, half paying attention but not really joining in. I was thinking about other things, toying with various ways of spending my cash – clothes, I thought, a holiday maybe, a car, whatever – and I was looking at the girls, like you do, but not really seriously. Maybe I was dreaming. Anyway, I looked up. I looked up past Chico's beautiful face, past the accumulated grime of decades, past the red velour drapes, held in place by lacquered brass fittings and costing, the landlord reliably informs me, a packet. I looked up and through the window. The shoppers were still at it; their enthusiasm for Ron Law's cut-price cucumbers undiminished. Then I saw her, and whilst she remained I saw nothing else.

She was surrounded by stars, and the starlight made her shine, silver and blue. And she was the most beautiful thing, the moon at her feet and stars in her hair. White light. And I wanted to, oh I wanted to. To what? To hold her very close and dance, and to hear her voice. I wanted to keep her with me always. Always. She was looking straight at me, her eyes as deep as the oceans, the starlight shining on me, too, taking us a million miles away. And it was like the best and brightest of heaven. When she turned away I shouted, but I couldn't move, couldn't follow cos I was trapped, hemmed in by my tosspot mates and fellow drinkers. She was almost round the corner when I grabbed Chico, hauling him to his feet.

'Look! Can you see her? Just turning, just going. Who is she? Where can I find her?'

'Eh, hombre, tranquilo.' Chico looked at the creases in his T-shirt and then back out the window. 'I see nada, amigo. Nada de nada. What chica you talk about?'

I shoved Chico out my way, and was past him before he'd finished talking. I knocked someone's pint as I went; I could hear the smash of glass and the shouting, but I didn't even turn my head. I had to get out there. Had to find her.

I was out the back door and round the corner like a rocket. I was movin so fast I nearly took a header onto the dual carriageway, and had to grab the safety railing to stop myself going straight over. That's when I thought I'd lost her. I was looking round, searching through the crowds, but she'd gone. No sign, and the longer I looked, the more normality began to reassert itself. I mean, no-one wants to be a daft cunt, do they? Stands to reason. And you don't get much dafter than running out of a pub full of your mates in hot pursuit of some mystery bint you've never seen before. I was making an utter twat of myself, and it was time to pack it in.

Across the other side of the dual carriageway the bus for Firstlanes pulled in. I turned to look, still getting my breath back, and I saw her. She was getting on the bus, waiting patiently for some doddery old bloke in front of her. Standing at the edge of the bus shelter, the last one in the queue, shining like silver, waiting there in the grime and drizzle and shite.

'Oh look, love,' said a woman's voice behind me. 'Isn't that Eleanor?'

I turned round. It was a couple of old biddies. One was pointing across the road. Pointing at the bus stop. I took hold of her arm.

'Is that her name?' I said. 'Who you pointing at? Is it that lass over there? Do you know her?'

The two of them just stood there, gawping at me. I shook the one I had hold of, the one who'd spoken. 'Who's Eleanor?' I said. 'Come on, you daft bitch, tell me. Is it her?' I shoved the old cow towards the railings and pointed, but it was too fuckin late. The bus was moving off, picking up speed as it rolled away. I let go of the woman and clenched my fists. I had to make them tell me.

'I'll call the police.' It was the friend talking now. The two of them were backing away, inching down the street. 'You come near again, and I'll do it. Get away. Go on, get away from us. Leave her alone or I'll have the police on you.'

'Just tell me,' I said. 'Was it her? Eleanor? Is that her name?'

They were a good distance away now. The one I'd had hold of was white in the face and silent, the friend had an arm around her. Just as they turned away she shouted at me, 'You're on drugs. You should be locked up. They should lock you up and throw away the key.'

36

I watched them as they disappeared into the market, then I turned and walked back to the Fort.

Chico thought it was the funniest thing he'd seen in years.

'Hey, amigo, she run too fast for you to catch her?' he shouted as I slid back into my seat. There was lots more of the same. I kept a tight, non-committal smile on my face, but I was close to decking the cunt. One day Chico and I would have to sort out who was boss. In the meantime we got in a bit of practice for the eventual decider. For the moment Chico thought he was on a winner. On and on it went. Oh, there was no stopping him.

'You reach too igh, amigo. Thees girl too fine for you. She no fuck standing up down the back alley. She no for you. Listen to me, muchacho. Stay where you beelon, with your leetle amiga, Reggie. This way you no get urt.'

'My round,' said Dekka. As he got up to go to the bar he almost kicked Chico's chair from under him. Dekka leant forward, arm on Chico's shoulder. 'Sorry, marrer,' he said, flat as the marshes, and smiled at me. I smiled back. That was Chico's problem, two of us, you see. Against me he'd have an even chance, but me and Dekka, we'd kick him to death, and, not being a stupid boy, he knows this very well.

It was gone six when I left the Fort, and I was more than half-cut, but the gear was keeping me straight enough to operate. I told the boys I was going to Reg's, to get rid, and then I slipped across town to the bus station.

It was only after I got off the bus that I began to wonder what I was at. What was I going to do? Knock on the door of every fuckin house in Firstlanes? For a while I just dandered around a bit, sat on the wall by the pub, walked round a bit more. I thought about going into the corner shop and askin for her. But what if I found her? What if

37

the bloke behind the counter said, 'Oh yeah, mate, Eleanor. Lives at thirty-three Coronation Close.' What then? What the fuck do you say? 'I saw you through the grimy windows of the Fort this after and I think I'm in love'? Nah. I don't think so. Eventually I had enough. Fuck it, I thought. What am I doing? Me, Danny Mac? And I turned for home. Just another bint. Have to put the wasted bus fare down to experience.

The bus, when it came, was almost empty. Just a couple of pieces of wreckage leaning against the windows and one brave soul in newly ironed denim out on a bender. It was on the bus that I first saw him. You couldn't really miss him, come to that. Chico, for all his pouting and eye flashing, is one of us; easier on the eye, maybe, but still essentially made of the same material. This one could have descended from the gods in a chariot of light. Sitting on the number 77 he – and I use the term loosely – was a tad incongruous. Golden as the sunlight, it sat on the corner of the back seat, humming to itself, tossing back blond hair that was definitely on the puffy side. Very tall, the limbs were too long for the space, and arms and legs were folded up. I wondered how such a creature had survived in Donny without a battering. They, our municipal leaders, once tried to put swans on the lake up at Adwick, but the initiative fell a bit flat when three of the birds were found crucified with crossbow bolts to the trees in the park. I knew one of the lads involved and he'd said it was harder than it looks; they're heavy things, and the noise had been appalling. This particular swan on the back seat of the number 77 looked ripe for crucifixion and, feeling as I did, I was more than half willing to start the job.

He looked up and half smiled; his mouth was very pink. 'Come ere, marrer. We need to talk,' he said.

I was so shocked I did it, I mean, weird or what? I sat

well away from him, in the middle of that long back seat, but he flowed out of his folded corner and leant towards me, looking straight into my eyes. His aftershave was so strong I almost OD'd on it. He was trying to pick me up and my whole body tensed to deliver the blow.

'Hombre, it's no good dandering up and down the road. Where's that going to get you? You want her bad, sisi? Te quiere, entiendo. Yo say, todos. Mira, muchacho, mira. I'll sort you. Stick with me and you'll be sound.'

His hand was on my thigh, but I didn't move, cos I couldn't. I couldn't break eye contact; couldn't move a muscle.

'She's shifted, carino, and you've got to get after her. I'll help you. Although it won't be for free. Comprende, muchacho mio, comprende? Wait on. There's mas.

'Mira, it's going to get very heavy, and you've got to get out. I'm talking about los tres – you'll sabey soon. Follow her. South it is, south. From grey to green, devils for company. Should suit, eh, muchacho?

'Don't worry, marrer, I'll be back. It'd help if you looked for us. Then you'd be in with half a chance. Valey? Luego.'

After this he vanished. Walked down the gangway and jumped off at Hyde Park flats. Turned the corner and disappeared. And that was it. It was as if he'd never existed, except the scent still lingered in the air and my leg still felt warm from the pressure of his hand. The bus swayed back into town beneath the orange lights, and I pondered the madman. Well, what I really pondered was me. You see, I wanted him back. Now why was that? What's the attraction in some pretty nancy who talks in riddles? Search me. By the time we free-wheeled into Donny I'd made up my mind to forget.

*   *   *

39

It was the kids that found him. He hadn't been there very long, only an hour or so. They were down at the canal, under the North Bridge; three of them, two air guns between them. They go down to shoot sparrows, starlings and pigeons. By the bridge there are fields bordering the canal, wide patches of pale brown scrub and, just occasionally, you get a benighted rabbit to have a blast at. It's a lark when you're too young to get in the pubs or make serious news with drugs or shagging. The papers didn't name them, just gave their ages – two brothers, aged eight and ten, and the third one, who was ten as well. They'd been happily popping away and, as is the way of these things, not hitting much. The birds had caught the lie of the land early on and fucked off home, so our young companyeros were reduced to creating targets, and the bits of flotsam and jetsam floating on the canal's oily surface served well. Moving, but not very quickly, they made ideal practice.

They told us this in school. Local claim to fame. We don't have many, but this is a good one. In 1536 the Pilgrimage of Grace halted on North Bridge, Doncaster. They marched under the banner of the Five Wounds of Christ, and they'd already captured York and Hull. Their leader, Robert Aske, was persuaded by a fellow Catholic, the Duke of Norfolk no less, to stand down his troops and go south for parley with Henry VIII. His escort took him straight to Henry's torture chambers, and he never saw the northern hills again. In 1537 he was hung, drawn and quartered on Tyburn Hill. The lesson of this is only leave home on your own terms and never trust a southerner. As the traffic roars past Hyde Park Corner, spare a thought for Robert Aske, brave and honest and totally stupid. As for Henry Tudor: 'He should be as Ahab, and the dogs would lick his blood,' Friar Peto prophesied in 1532, and he was right, wasn't he? They brought Henry's corpse to lie in state at Greenwich. He was six foot three, and weighed half a ton. The lead casket that was coping with this gargantuan mound of rotting flesh gave up the ghost and cracked open. It was Easter Sunday, so it can't have been that warm, but he'd been dead a good few days by this time. Liquid began to seep from the body and pool on the stone floor beneath, and one of the workmen's dogs was seen to creep beneath the coffin. It was hungry probably, this being well before the advent of salmon-and-chicken-flavoured Mr Dog for the 'friend you really love'. Anyway, hungry or not, it was none too fussy. It crept under the coffin table and started lapping up the mixture of blood, pus and God knows what that lay congealing there. They're disgusting, dogs; they eat their own vomit, you know. But you have to hand it to Friar Peto, he wasn't far off the mark. He fled to Rome and became a cardinal.

When it floated down the canal the kids were made up. There were considerably more than five wounds by the time they'd finished thudding the pellets in, although it ought to be acknowledged that there were more than five wounds before the kids even started. It seemed to twitch a bit as the shots hit home, then one of the kids took aim and started screaming. Turned by the current, a face had appeared – wet and mangled, but nonetheless definitely human. And the pellet holes seemed to be leaking blood.

They'd bent him back, bow-like, and tied his elbows to his knees. They'd snapped his spine whilst doing it, but who's counting? Both his legs had been broken first, possibly by a sledgehammer, the pathologist thought, and he'd been raped, probably by a broom handle the pathologist thought. There were splinters you see. Petrol-soaked rags had been pushed into his mouth and set alight. He'd been finished off with a knife. Before the rags scenario they'd cut his tongue out, and then, the pattern being set, they'd carried on cutting at any extraneous bits that caught their fancy. The pathologist thought he'd probably bled to death. Finally they'd shoved what was left in the boot of Gibbsey's Audi, driven to a reasonably quiet spot and dumped the whole shebang in the canal, including the two bin bags they'd thoughtfully put down to stop the blood getting all over the carpet in the boot. An hour later the sluggish motion of the canal had taken its unhappy cargo a mere quarter of a mile downstream to the North Bridge, where our three playmates were practising their visual and motor co-ordination.

When I strolled into the Fort I knew none of this, of course. Looking round, I saw Chico, Dekka and a few other like-minded souls. I'd had a hit before I came out, showered and changed. I felt better. Forgotten about the benighted bus trip, shining girls and queer men. I'd returned to normality, which was a relief. I fancied a few bevvies and a bit of joshing with the boys, something uncomplicated and easy. But, as Mick once poetically put it, 'You can't always get what you want'.

It must have been around tennish when I made my entrance. I'd resolved to make good use of the scant hour we had left before we were cast out into the cold and comfortless streets to make our own fun. I was on my second pint and playing pool. Me and Dekka were taking on Chico and Kev, best of five. It was two each and all to play for. We were on stripes, and I was trying to work out where the white would end up if I went for the purple, when the Fort suffered its second over-dramatic entrance of the day.

There were six of them this time as well. Three came through the main door, three in at the back.

'All right, everybody stand still while we sort this out. DI Stockwell, Serious Crime Squad. I said, don't move, fuckwit, and I meant it.'

He was around five ten, stocky, and dressed in a navy blue raincoat, with the belt doubled round and fastened at the back. I knew him, of course, as did half the clientele. As coppers go he scored about eight out of ten on the gratuitous-unpleasantness scale. I had a sinking feeling he'd come for me an Dekka about our recent foray into leafy suburbia. He hadn't the slightest chance of proving anything, of course, but being slapped round the head by Stockwell down the station wasn't how I'd planned to spend my evening. He was talking to the landlord and waving his ID about, not that mine host needed to see it; he'd let the entire Donny drugs squad shag his daughter and make a video of it if he thought it would help get his licence renewed. His current body language gave a whole new impetus to the word obsequious. Stockwell, who resides in some *Sweeney*-esque fantasy land, was lapping it up. I caught Dekka's eye and we exchanged smiles that bespoke solid, mutual confidence. The stars could shine at noontime before either of us would grass. The gear was long since shifted many leagues away and they had nothing to go on and nothing to come. Nah, nah, nada.

His moment of glory with the landlord over, Stockwell turned to the room, which was starting to resemble a game of musical statues when they've forgotten to restart the music.

'So, here they are, the fuckin Unholy Trinity. Didn't take much finding, did you, lads? MacIntyre, Dixon, da Silva, you're coming with me.'

We were surprised at the inclusion of Chico, but I have to say, all three of us handled it beautifully. Chico shrugged with casual elegance and picked up his jacket.

'I suppose someone as to geeve your life a leetle glamour, eh, amigo? Someone as to ease the soledad. So we spend the evening with you. It's a peety you 'ave no friends of you own.'

Before going I leant back over the pool table. With unhurried serenity I made my shot, rocketing the purple into the left-hand pocket and spinning the white back to settle perfectly in line for the next shot on the yellow. Sometimes God is smiling. Several people clapped. 'Hasta luego, amigos,' I said, and the three of us waltzed out, cool as the alpine snows.

'I'll wipe the smirks off your faces, you cocky, heartless little twats,' said Stockwell. I sighed; it looked set fair for a long and tedious night.

By the time we reached the station – only a ten-minute drive – I sensed something was going off. They'd sent three cars for us, and there was something in the pigs' demeanour – I don't know: pent-up excitement? Expectation? Dread? – which suggested rather more than a stolen vid was on the cards. I sat quiet and kept tranquilo, conserving my energies for what lay ahead.

Once inside we were taken straight to the interview room. Claustrophobic and permeated with the smell of smoke, unwashed bodies and sweaty panic, Stockwell paid me the compliment of personal attendance.

'Where were you between the hours of one and eight this afternoon?' he asked. Tape machine switched on and caution given. Oh he was practically bursting with the importance of it all.

I stared at him, dead-eyed. 'Why?'

'Just answer the question. What were your whereabouts between one and eight p.m.?'

'No say.'

'MacIntyre, I don't want to hear any of your fuckin

44

stupid slang. Speak plain English, do you understand?'

'Claro, conyo.'

He was beginning to twitch a bit. It's so easy to piss them off, and such fun to do. But there was still a worrying note of excitement beneath the frustration. He was like a poker player who can't quite hide the fact that he's staring at a straight flush.

'I'll try again. Where were you between one o'clock and eight o'clock today? I warn you, we're not playing, MacIntyre. This is serious. You and your animal friends have gone too far on this one. I have witnesses who say that you were in the Fort between three and seven p.m. and that you returned again at ten fifteen.'

I shrugged.

'I also have witnesses who say you were drinking with Stephen Furst.'

It was all becoming clearer. Teapot had been battered, and had completed his grassing career by limping up to the polis and displaying his wounds. Some people would never learn. What a total cunt. I shrugged again.

'Friend of yours, wasn't he? You were with him today, weren't you, in the Fort? I know you were. I've got witnesses who say so.' His face assumed a benign, fatherly cast. It was a bit of a struggle, but he got there. 'Look, we know each other. Are you going to talk to me, Danny, or are we going to stay here all night?'

I hate it when coppers try and get matey; they're inevitably crap at it. Two can play that game. I leant forward, confidentially. 'Well, Ken, or do you prefer Kenny?' He winced but kept quiet. 'I think, on the whole, I'll go for the second option.'

It took him a moment to catch on, then he got up from his moulded plastic chair and walked across to the tape machine. 'DI Stockwell, ending the interview at twenty-three oh seven hours.' He walked over to me and hit me across the face with an open-handed blow that carried all the force of his fourteen stones.

'I've got something to show you, Danny Boy. You just wait there.'

It took him less than a minute and he was back, blue folder under his arm and an odd expression on his clock.

He logged back on to the tape and sat down.

'I want you to tell me everything you can remember about drinking in the Fort this afternoon. What time you got there. Who was with you. What was said. Who left with who. Every single little thing. I know you were there, MacIntyre, so cut the crap. I have witnesses who will happily swear on oath that you were drinking in the Fort with Stephen Furst for most of the afternoon. What I'm interested in is who he left with, and when.'

I kept completely blank throughout this little speech. Total silencio. He obviously had some tired old strategy and I hadn't the faintest intention of joining in. It's the classic station etiquette. First thing you learn, don't talk to the sweaty bastards, don't give them the pleasure of even registering that you've heard them. Save it for the solicitor.

The pause lasted a good minute, then he tried again, repeating the same formula. Silencio. The look on his face became even odder; combined with the frustration was a panting eagerness. He had a big moment coming and you could see the excitement building.

'OK,' he said. 'You're refusing to co-operate, MacIntyre. I'm now going to show you some pictures. I am now passing MacIntyre the photographs of the deceased taken prior to post-mortem.'

This last bit was spoken in a self-consciously clear tone and addressed to the tape. He didn't pass me the folder, though. He got up and walked round to my side of the Formica table and opened it up. The pictures were large, the size of a sheet of plain paper, and they were very clear focus. Stockwell pointed to this thing on the page. I wasn't sure if he'd got the photo upside down or not; it didn't seem to make much sense.

'Recognize him, do you? That's your mate, Teapot.'

I felt the blood rush in my ears and kept perfectly still. 'Hail Mary/Full of grace/The Lord is with thee/Blessed art thou amongst women/And blessed is the fruit of thy womb, Jesus.' I was very aware of how still I was. Could see the arms on the table, which seemed to belong to someone else. They were on either side of the thing in the photograph, like I was holding it. I knew I mustn't move. I looked at the thing again. I'd thought it was upside down because his head was at the bottom of the photo and his legs were somehow folded up beneath him. It was definitely Teapot – even had the Stone Roses T-shirt on. Stone Roses, I ask you. Where his legs disappeared at the knees there was something poking out – turned out to be bone; his femur I suppose, although I don't know what happened to the kneecap. Because of the position his hips were thrust forward and his jeans were half down, all the buttons on his fly undone. But it wasn't indecent, not in that sense, cos there was nothing left, you see. They'd chopped it all off. Just a matted mess with a lot of dark stuff – dried blood? No say, you'd've thought the canal would've washed it off. 'Holy Mary, Mother of God/Pray for us sinners. Mother of God/Pray for us sinners. *Ora pro nobis.*' If I concentrated on remembering the words I could keep hold. Those arms, you see; they still belonged to somebody else. His face was the worst bit. He'd never been pretty, but he looked fuckin awful now. He had no ears, you see, and his nose was a bit of

47

a mess. But his mouth. Oh dear, sweet, suffering Jesus; what had they done? The mad bastards; what had they done? All the skin around it was black and bubbly and sort of cracked. His mouth was open, so you could see inside, and it looked like melting plastic, all sort of gooey and misshapen. I could see something was funny. Well, Stevie Wonder on a dark night could see something was funny. But it took me another take to get there. That black stumpy thing at the back of his throat. They'd cut his tongue out. That'll teach him to grass. 'Pray for us sinners/Now, and at the hour of our death. *Ave Maria/ Gratia plena.*' Doing it in Latin was good, I had to try a lot harder to remember.

He put me through the lot, you see. Seven of them, in all – various angles highlighting various bits. A couple from the back, which was where I finished off the Latin, and close-ups of the head and hips. No wonder Stockwell had been so fuckin thrilled with himself. But they made a mistake, you see: when they showed me the first one, well, I'd nearly lost it – the shock more than anything – but by the time I'd done the full seven stretch I was back. I mean, Gibbsey and the boys had obviously gone a little too far – well, a lot too far – but that's not my problem. The long-term thinking here was clear: first move, say nothing, and vamos from this unholy dump of a police station; second move, get the hell out of sunny Donny and as far away from Gibbsey and crew as physically possible. However, first I had to deal with Stockwell.

He put his folder away and started on me straightways.

'Look, MacIntyre, I know you were in the pub with Furst and I know you saw him go. Who did he leave with?'

'No say, hombre. No say.'

It went on like this for quite some time. We had the

48

entire repertoire: the threats (You could be up on a murder charge. Twenty years. I can keep you in here as long as I fucking want), the blandishments (He was a good friend of yours, Danny. Give us the name and we'll keep you out of it) and the slapping about. He got nothing, nada absolutamente. In the end he lost his rag and started shouting at me. But before he left to try his luck with Chico and Dekka he asked one last question. 'Don't you feel anything when you see those pictures? Are you that far gone?'

I answered him truthfully.

'Dolores. Dolores an temeroso. Muchisimo.'

As intended, he didn't get it.

They finally let us go the next morning. The three of us strolled out into the early spring sunshine and, as is customary, kept total silencio until we were back in the safety of town and neutral territory.

We needed to talk, obviously, and we were all starving, the bastards had kept us scranless for the entire night, so we walked down to Betty's, ordered our tea and fry-ups and sat down.

'So,' I said, 'we all got the million-pound picture show?'

The others nodded.

'Not looking too good, was he?' said Dekka.

'Nah, marrer, I've seen him look brighter.'

'Eets that orrible T-shirt,' said Chico. 'Yellow was not ees colour.'

I sniggered. 'Blood red didn't seem to suit him, either.'

We all laughed. Predictably, I know. How's it go? Something about a nervous compulsive reaction to inner trauma? Shite anyway. I thought it was funny. When the fry-ups came we amused ourselves by identifying bits of Teapot. The bacon was an obvious starter for ten, and, as

49

Dekka pointed out, it helped that nobody had ordered sausage. Much fun was had with the tomato ketchup. In the end Betty told us to shut up, as we were annoying the other customers, who were furrowing their brows over the *Sun* crossword before they staggered off to their lorry cabs, crappy factory jobs or beds – depends which shift you're on y'see. You can either stick in a 6 a.m. breakfast before days, or go for the quick bite before hitting the sack if you're on late. Afters are a bit of a problem, cos Betty isn't open at 10 p.m.

When she cleared the plates we ordered a second mug of tea and started on the serious stuff.

'What we need to know,' said Chico, 'ees eef anybody talked.'

This annoyed me. It was my role to say these things.

'Well, let's start with you, shall we?' I said, smoothly regaining control. 'What did you say, amigo?'

Chico favoured me with his best affronted caballero look.

'Nada. I say nada. I keep tranquilo. I smile and say nada.'

'Dekka?'

'Nada, marrer. Dint even acknowledge me name. Well fucked-off they were.'

'Right. So they got nowt. No-one mention Gibbsey?'

'I tell you, I say nada.' Chico was earnest now. The world's most beautiful eyes were fixed on me. 'I mean eet, Danny. Not one word. I'm not crazy.'

Dekka nodded. 'Same for me, marrer. Like Chico says, we're not fuckin stupid.'

We talked for a while longer before coming to a basic agreement. Gibbsey had fucked it, that at least was pretty claro. Loads of people had seen him take Teapot, and some snivelling git with a death wish was bound to crack eventually. We talked and talked about what we would do, but it was all balls. There was fuck all we could do. Teapot was dead, horribly dead, and Gibbsey and his boys had done it. Those two clear facts meant that our world was about to turn upside down. The polis, obliged by media attention, which was fixated on the supposedly traumatized air-gun-toting kids (little bastards doubtless loving every minute of it), were going to have to get off their fat arses and do something about this one. The whole scene implied vast amounts of shite for us. The polis would doubtless keep dragging us in as known witnesses of the late lamented's last visible moments. Never one to underestimate human frailty, Gibbsey would be nervous of the possibility of us coughing. It wasn't beyond Stockwell to take Gibbsey in and tell him we'd made a statement in the hope of pulling a confession out of him. We already knew what Gibbsey thought about grassers. I could feel my stomach turning over. South it is. South, you sabey? I stood up.

'I'm getting out. Hanging around here is buying a ticket for me own fuckin funeral. I'm off down the smoke.'

Exiting to London is the time-honoured last resort of generations of Donny deadbeats. Basically, the thinking goes that the polis are too lazy, too stupid and too skint to be bothered to find you. Also, out of sight is out of mind. Once you're out of the picture, you're also out of the frame, if you get my drift. A couple of weeks should do it, and once Gibbsey was safely locked up we could return, in security and tranquillity, to the pearl of the north – which is what no-one has ever called Donny.

Dekka, as expected, immediately threw his lot in with me, which was fair enough, as I didn't particularly fancy dandering round the streets of London on me tod. We looked at Chico.

'I 'ave this girl,' he said. 'A leetle crazy, but OK. She live in Lincoln now, I theenk she want me to stay a few days. I theenk that would be nice. Juliette is her name. If you like you can come with me. Stay a night, or maybe two, and then to London?'

I looked at Dekka and nodded. 'Sound,' I said. I looked at my watch. 'Let's give two hours for whatever fucking about we need to do. Meet up at eleven thirty, Southern Bus Station I suppose?'

'Nah, amigo, they know we buy teeckets. Eetch it, sisi?'

Chico was right. 'OK, marrers. Same time. Balby roundabout. Anyone who's late gets fuckin left.'

We split outside Betty's and legged it back to our various abodes. She was in, of course. Never rains but it pours, as they say. The good news was she was still sober, and I made it upstairs unmolested. It didn't take long; I just stuffed a few basics in a wee bag and then I was ready. She was in the kitchen when I came down, so I had to walk past her.

'Just off round to Reg's, Mam.' My voice sounded wrong, a bit wavery, like I was going to cry or something.

'Baby, baby, are you OK? Look at me, baby. What's happened? Tell Mummy, baby. Tell Mummy; she'll make it right.'

She came up to me. She's not as tall as I am, so she put her hand on the back of my neck and drew my head down.

'Stop it, Mam. Get off. It's OK.'

It was too late, she was away. My head was on her shoulder and she was stroking my hair and crooning to me. 'Speed, bonny boat, like a bird on the wing/Onward the sailors cry/Carry the lad that's born to be king/Over the sea to Skye.' Rocking me to the rhythm. I kept my eyes open, seeing nothing, wishing it was different, wishing me mam wasn't crazy, wishing the tears weren't rolling down my cheeks. I don't know how long it was before I shrugged free. 'I've got to go, Mam,' I said, and picked up my bag and headed out.

chapter three

I WAS THE LAST ONE THERE, AND DEKKA AND CHICO WERE concentrating hard on looking smug.

'We nearly gave you up, amigo,' said Chico. 'You ten meenites late.'

'Yeah, yeah,' I said. I looked over the roundabout and past the bridge, towards the streaming, fleeing cars. 'Come on, marrers. Let's go.' We turned, so smooth it could have been choreographed, and dandered down the slip road.

It wasn't too bad, weather-wise, for the time of year, but standing on the gravel by the A1 isn't anyone's idea of a groovy good time. Fifteen minutes in and we were all fuckin freezing. Two hours later me hands and feet had gone numb, and Dekka was bitching at Chico.

'"Let's eetch"' he says. 'You stupid spic bastard. If we'd got the bus we'd be halfway there by now. Who's going to stop for us? Not a fuckin chance. Me toes are ice. One more hour an' I'll need another hit.'

And so on, until I told him to shut it. I mean, it wasn't the most fun I'd had standing up, but listening to Dekka whingeing made it infinitely worse. I told him to get behind me and Chico – him being the least presentable of the trinity – to stick a smile on his clock and keep totally silent. Being essentially a good NCO, and totally outgunned in the brains and mouth department, he did as he was told. Then, just to cap a perfect day, it began to rain; well, sleet really. It was clearly time to take up the white man's burden and sort this out before we all died of hypothermia, no help needed from Donny drug squad or Gibbsey.

'OK, guapo,' I said to Chico. 'I'm going to try and make Dekka invisible, cos no-one in their right mind would give im a lift. You're going to front the operation. Give us your jacket and jumper.'

'Are you crazee? I going to fuck die.'

'Listen to me, amigo. No-one wants to pick us up, claro?' Chico nodded. 'Ta bom. We need to change their minds. Number one, we keep the Incredible Hulk hidden at the back and I try and look friendly, but badly done to. Number two, you put on your best beautiful-but-damaged. You give me your clothes and stand out there looking pitiful and frozen. Go for the eye contact, and the more like a whipped puppy you look the better for all of us. Now, get your gear off.'

Chico is many things, but stupid isn't one of them. He got the plot and stripped off accordingly. I stuffed his clothes into my back pack, shouted at the sulking Dekka to get behind me and Chico trotted out front.

It speaks volumes for the breakdown of our social fabric that the cunts were able to keep driving past. His white T-shirt got soaked in seconds. The silky black hair dripped into his eyes, globules of sleet sticking to it like Woolworths pearls. His lips were blue, and the normally honey-coloured skin turned a nasty mottled tone. Several people slowed down, but saw there were three of us and thought better of it. Fifteen minutes passed. Dekka hadn't been joshing, either. I could feel the shivers starting. I was going to need another hit soon.

'Danny, Danitito, Danizinho, amigo mio, this has got to stop. I'm fuck dying. Look at my face, my hands. I'm seek, I shake. Eets nice idea, but eet no work. Geeve me my clothes.'

I looked critically at Chico. Yes, he looked awful, but then again, Dekka didn't look much better and he had all his clothes on. It was five to two. The sleet, if anything, was heavier and the traffic was still roaring past.

'Listen, marrers. What say we give it five more minutes, and if nothing's doing by two o'clock, let's fuck off to the Fairway for a pint and a hit, and think again?'

I'm a natural leader of men, and this flawless plan was immediately acceded to by the weary troops. Chico trotted back out front, Dekka stood behind me and tried to look human, I fixed the snug, dry, selfish, car-driving bastards with a classic expression of urban deprivation which would have had the editor of the *Guardian* wetting his knickers. It was during a gap in the traffic that I let my eyes wander. What's that silly fucker doing out, was my first thought. My second thought was, Blessed Holy Mary, Mother of God, get us out of here. The silly fucker in question was Ticka. Sixteen stones of muscle and bone, entirely unhindered by intellect or soul, and Mr Gary Gibbson's right-hand man. Teapot's more unpleasant final moments would have come, most likely, courtesy of Ticka. He was stood on the top of the embankment, at the back of the pensioners' bungalows. Maybe his gran lived there, maybe he was on the rob, maybe he was looking for a new girlfriend. Fuck knows. I wasn't sure if he'd clocked us or not.

'Dekka, marrer, look, arriba, tranquilo. Arriba, marrer, on the left.'

'Oh shit,' was Dekka's response. 'Has he seen us?'

My answer was lost in a tidal wave of water and a squeal of tyres. A huge artic, bearing the legend 'ICELAND, FREEZER FOODS', juddered to a halt, and Chico was shouting, 'Come on. Vamos, amigos! Vamos!'

Dekka and I ran after him, and Ticka's looming profile was blocked from view by the white-wheeled monster. Chico was already halfway in, and I climbed after him, four steps to the cab, which was way above my head, then all three of us were making puddles on the bench seat and nearly swooning in the unaccustomed heat.

The bloke who'd stopped was wiry, with muscular arms, and he had a tattoo on his forearm – very delicately drawn, all in blue; a crescent moon, crowned with seven swords. I'd never seen one like it before. He caught my look and smiled.

'Used to be in the Merchant Navy. Far East. You wouldn't get work like that in England.' He took his eyes off the road for a moment and looked at us. 'You look like a pack of bleeding drowned rats. Mek im take his jacket off to get a bit of sympathy, did you?'

There didn't seem to be any point in trying to continue the blag, so the three of us nodded mutely.

'Aye, well, it's a bugger trying to get a lift with three of you. Anyhow, where you headed?'

'Lincoln,' we chorused.

'Aye, well, that's fair enough. I'm straight through to the smoke. But I can drop you at the turn-off; it's only a couple of miles from there.'

As we bowled down the A1, the spray rising in grey sheets and the giant windscreen wipers sweeping to and fro, I felt myself drift. The heater was blasting out – you could almost see the steam rising from us – and I was further insulated by being squashed between Chico and Dekka. Thigh to thigh, shoulder to shoulder.

What with the warmth and the sway and bounce of the bench seat, I felt myself slipping. Leaning against Chico, I could feel sleep stroking with soft hands and my eyelids sliding. Through the great washes of water, I could see the road ahead. The Old North Road it was, built by the Romans; straight as an arrow.

I was jerked awake as the lorry bumped and slowed. We'd turned off the main drag of the A1 and were pulling into a petrol station, flanked by a Happy Eater. The driver was talking to Chico.

'Oh, you're back with us, are you?' He looked at me and grinned. 'Out for the count, you were.'

'Bit knackered,' I said.

'Happens to us all. Anyway, I was just saying. I've got to fill her up, and I'm going to snatch a bite. If you lads fancy a cup of tea and a sarnie, I'll stand the bill.'

'Thanks very much, mate,' I said. He was right enough, you had to admit it.

We helped him with the diesel pumps, and then he tooled the white monster round the back of the grinning Happy Eater and directed us towards a small brick affair at the back of the car park. 'Where those in the know go for some decent snap,' he told us.

The caff was packed with lorry drivers, all drinking tea and shovelling vast amounts of scran down their throats. Your man ordered a pile of megamush, whilst us three stuck to a mug of tea – welcome enough, after the wet, cold purgatory of the past few hours. The respite also gave us a chance to have a quick hit in the bogs. I finished me tea quite quickly, and left the others at the table while I went off in search of some fags. I don't know why, but I felt restless, anxious to be moving, to get some distance between us and Donny.

I bought twenty Benny, then went for a slash. There was another bloke in the bogs, but I didn't really clock im. I was just zipping up when I heard this voice in my ear.

'Straight as an arrow, for it turneth neither right nor left, but remains straight, and our souls should take heed and follow the path, which is straight, like an arrow in flight.'

The man was tubby and middle-aged, with a completely ridiculous fuckin haircut. Bald on top, with a funny little fringe round the sides. The clothes were as mad as the hair. He was wearing what seemed to be a white T-shirt kind of thing hanging outside white trousers. Over this natty little ensemble he had a very long, very loose black coat. It had big wide sleeves and a hood at the back, and was made out of a sort of woven material. On the left side, about where a breast pocket should be, was this embroidered silver star. Obviously a total nutter.

'The hounds of God seldom lose their quarry,' he said, 'though I must confess, the task has been light and the hunt affords poor sport.'

He had a really irritating way of looking at me, with this smug half-smile on his face. What the fuck was he doing, bargin into the bogs and talking bollocks? I dried my hands and turned to face him.

'And who the fuck are you?' I asked.

'I am Dr Aquinas, lately travelled from Pisa. Wide is the gate and broad is the way that leadeth to destruction, and many there be that go in thereat. Strait is the gate and narrow is the way which leadeth unto life, and few there be that find it. And you, who might you be?'

'Danny MacIntyre, lately travelled from Donny. Good enough for you?'

'Most probably not, but that in itself is no oddity.' He gave another of those mega-irritating smirks.

He paused, looking at me, as if considering. Then raised his eyebrows and gave a sort of half-shrug. He beckoned to me and, half intrigued, half unwilling, I moved closer.

'I am the bearer of instructions. There is a storm at your heels. If you wish to outrun the tempest you must take heed.'

'What the fuck are you on at, fat twat?' I said. I didn't like this bloke. I didn't like his funny fringe of hair, I didn't like his tone, and his clothes were totally weird as well. He gave me a patronizing little smile.

'Obviously the greater amount of your talents and virtues remain concealed. For my immediate understanding offers little more than empty bluster and bravado, such as could be found in a dozen young men, on a dozen streets, in a dozen towns, in a dozen lands.'

So opined this tubby middle-aged git, wearing his floppy black coat with silver embroidery. 'OK,' I said. 'You've made your point. You don't like me. Well, I don't like you, either. So why don't you just fuck off?'

He smiled and said something in a language I didn't understand, then he was back into English. 'Listen, for I will speak but once. Eleanora has sent me.'

At the mention of the name I started, but he held up a hand to shut me up and continued, 'Take therefore no thought for the morrow, for the morrow shall take thought for the things of itself. The road is plain before you; do not turn aside.' He smiled and made an ironic little bow of the head. 'I leave the rest for you, my friend. For now I must make my valedictions and depart. We shall meet again. Remember, straight as an arrow.'

He turned away, then paused and looked back at me.

'You don't recognize me, yet you know me.' He nodded, as if to himself, and smiled. 'Yes, we are acquainted. Eventually you will remember me.' And with that he headed out.

I half opened my mouth to tell him to explain the bull-shit, but thought better of it. As he went through the bog doors I caught a glimpse of another figure, apparently waiting for him. It looked like a kid, and there was something odd about him. He was sitting in a wheelchair or something. I couldn't really see. When the door closed, I stood for a while, just looking in the mirror. Either I was hallucinating, or the bloke was a nutter. I settled on the latter, ran my hand through my ultra-cool pelooque, splashed my face with cold water and left.

When I came out of the bogs the others were in the lorry park, climbing back into the white monster. In the far corner of the parking lot I could just make out two shapes. One looked like a tubby, middle-aged man, the other, holding his hand, was sitting in a kind of wheeled contraption, a bit like a go-kart. I shook my head and climbed into the cab.

It wasn't long before the heating blasting out in the lorry cab sent me off again. It wasn't a deep sleep, more a semi-unconsciousness. I couldn't be bothered to make the effort to speak, or even listen. I just opted out. I kept hearing his voice. 'Straight as an arrow, straight as an arrow, straight as an arrow.' The words ran into each other, blurring into nonsense. My eyes glazed sightlessly. I was lost, abandoned somewhere in a world of grey water.

It was some time before I could discern the flickers of the passing white lines. The rain was even heavier, washing the windscreen in great rivers that were swept aside by the muscularity of the wipers. Dekka was fast asleep, snuffling and twitching on my left side. On my right Chico was chatting to our rescuing knight on a white charger.

'Yeah,' the driver was saying. 'Funny, really, just can't forget her. She was a lovely girl. Graceful like. You don't often see that nowadays: graceful women. Women's lib and all that, I suppose. But this one, like poetry just to watch her serving breakfast. Gave her a pound tip, I did. Told her it was worth double just to watch her walk. Beautiful smile, she had. Went to Spain with the missus last year – Tossa del Mar. Very nice. Anywhere near where you're from, mate?'

Chico began explaining that Medellin was in fact no nearer to Spain than Cape Town was to England. I sat quiet. Then the driver smiled across at me.

'She was another one as admired the tattoo. Said it brought back memories. Funny really.'

'What was she like?' I asked. 'This girl?'

'Well, like I said to your mate, she made an impression. Lovely. No other word for it. Graceful, like I said, and sweet. Lovely smile. Really lovely.'

'Did she say her name?'

'Never asked her, mate. None of my business. She's not there now. Stopped at the same place on me way up yesterday, just to get another look at her really. But no dice. I must have been smitten, because I even asked the gaffer. He said she was only helping him out whilst one of his regulars had gone sick. Thought she'd left for some-where down south. I wasn't after her, you know.'

'Dun't sound like it,' I said.

The driver shook his head, eyes on the road.

'No, you don't understand. I just wanted to watch her. She was poetry, that girl. Lovely, really lovely.'

'Yeah,' I agreed. 'So you said.'

Chico rolled his eyes at me and I smirked back. Dekka

started to snore. The rain washed sheets across the flat expanse of glass and the road, the Old North Road, stretched in front. If you kept on going, then you'd get to the end of the world.

It didn't take long to get to Lincoln. I was dreading the journey ending as the rain continued unrelenting. He was a really decent bloke, though, cos instead of dumping us at the turn-off, he took pity and tooled the artic a couple of miles off his route down to the outskirts of town.

'OK, lads, this is as far as it goes. Hop out, and best of luck.'

We all chorused our thanks and clambered out. The white monster turned on its eighteen wheels and lunged southwards once again, sheets of spray and smoke rising in its wake. As the last gleam faded, Chico reached into his jacket and began quickly filleting. There was only about twenty in cash, but two cards. The rest we pushed down the drain at the road side.

'You see the picture of his wife?' said Dekka.

I nodded. 'Total dog.'

'Woof woof,' said Dekka. 'Woof woof.'

By the time we got into the town centre it was already dark. Chico said this girl would be home about sixish, so we adjourned to a pub hidden in one of the dark, narrow streets that radiate down the hill away from the towering bulk of the cathedral. We jacked up in the bogs – not that hygienic, but I've seen worse – went back to the bar and Chico got the drinks in with his new-found wealth.

The pub was as dark and pokey as the streets around it, and the locals – a dismal crew whose snaggle teeth and knock knees bore witness to generations of fishing in the same genetic pond – had obviously never seen anything so exciting in their lives. They didn't quite have the nerve to stare outright, but when they thought we weren't looking they darted a continuous stream of fascinated little glances, boss eyes struggling to focus under the thatch of hair. Why do these mad-professor types insist on trailing off to Africa for their anthropological digs? It must be the climate and the cheap labour. Cos the missing link ain't missing; we all know where it is – alive and well and living in the English countryside. I mean, just listen to the pig-shit barmy accents and you can tell they're not like the rest of us. They looked at me, Dekka and Chico like we'd just landed from another planet, which in a way I suppose we had. Planet humanity, which clearly had only just swum into their ken – it's life, Jim, but not as we know it. Stalin had the right idea with the kulaks – forced labour camps, only thing to do with them. They'd be glad of someone to tell 'em what to do, they really would. Grateful for a bit of organization and discipline. Give their benighted existence some point and purpose. Anyway, why am I wasting my time? Forget it, ignore them. Leave them to sink unlamented into the flat mud of the Lincolnshire fields. It's raining down in Lincolnshire, but then again, it always bleeding is. Charlie knew the score all right.

As you've maybe gathered, my mood wasn't of the best. I was damp, cold, hungry, pissed off and bored. Chico looked at his watch for the millionth time and made yet another trip to the payphone on the bar. Quarter past seven and still no sign of the silly tart. When I was young and impressionable, and had heard one too many Irish rebel songs, I'd given serious thought to offering my services to the IRA. Sometimes in the summer I used to go and stay with me Aunty Bernadette and Uncle Jim. Mam would put me on the train to Liverpool and then I'd get the ferry. At the other side, me aunty and cousins would be waiting. I loved it. I used to sit with me cousins and

Uncle Jim and shout at the telly when the Brit politicians came on. Uncle Jim taught me all the words to 'Men Behind the Wire' and 'My Little Armalite'. The idea of having a personal Armalite greatly appealed and, in my opinion, any outfit that can blow up Lord Mountbatten deserves respect.

I went to see Celtic a couple of times, and they had this great song on the terraces: 'Old Lord Louis had a boat/ e i e i o/And on this boat there was a bomb/e i e i o/With a boom boom here/And a bang bang there,' and so on. Not sophisticated maybe, but very catchy. Anyway, I fancied myself in the 'Ra. I daydreamed about my coffin, adorned with tricolour and black beret, being carried into Rosehill cemetery, followed by Mam, head to toe in black, and sober. Martin McGuinness due to give the funeral oration, and the mandatory IRA colour party ready to fire the final salute. They'd sell my picture at Celtic souvenir shops and make up songs about me. This was before the ceasefire, natch. I mean, it would all be a bit pointless if there wasn't a war on.

My hero was Francis Hughes, the second hunger-striker to die, aged twenty-seven. Killer of thirty-odd Brit soldiers and RUC men, inventor of the booby-trap bomb, six foot tall and handsome as they come. He was on the run for years, living rough around the border, wearing army fatigues with 'Ireland' and a wee flag embroidered very small on the pocket. He was finally captured on the Glenshane Pass by the SAS. He killed one and severely wounded the other, but they shot him in the thigh. They got dogs and followed his trail of blood. He was so tough that he refused to have anaesthetic when they operated on his smashed leg. He was scared he might babble under the influence and give something away. When they buried him, there was the biggest thunderstorm Ireland's ever seen, and they said they were burying a body and raising a legend. 'As I walked down the Glenshane Pass/I heard a young girl mourn/The boy from Tamlaghduff, she said/Is ten years dead and gone/Oh how my heart is torn apart/At this young man to lose/Oh I'll never see the likes again/Of my brave Francis Hughes.'

Why am I telling you this bollocks? Yeah, because my hero spent months, years, on the run. Most wanted man in Ireland. Reading about it in my bedroom in deepest, darkest Donny, it all seemed dead romantic, but the grim reality was, as grim reality always is, rather different. Here was I, dashing Danny Mac, having been on the run for precisely eight hours and twenty minutes, and I was already tossed off. I still had some gear. I was sitting in a pub, with half a Becks, with two mates and a clean T-shirt in me bag, and I was losing it because some dopey bint was late turning up. What would Francis have done in my situation? Probably shot up the pub and shouted, 'Ireland unfree will never be at peace,' but I didn't have a gun and I wasn't Irish – well, not strictly speaking anyway. Bobby Sands was a poet. 'Oh the radio said/There's another man dead/And he died with a gun in his hand./But they didn't say why/Danny Mac had to die/Cos he died to free his land.' He didn't write that, by the way.

'Danny. Oi, muchacho, I talk to you.' I looked up and saw Chico staring at me across the table.

'Sorry, marrer. Miles away. Kay passer?'

'At last, I speak with her. She has taxi, so she come here for collect us. I tell her to come quick. I tell her I spend too long in this shithole already.'

'And amen to that,' I said.

Dekka's face broke into a rare smile, wrinkling the freckles on his nose. 'Aye, amigos,' he said. 'I'm desperate for some scran.'

66

The fair Juliette arrived shortly thereafter, a sight to be seen. When she turned her back I raised my eyebrows at Chico, and he shrugged, half-embarrassed.

'Kin'ell,' said Dekka, never famed for subtlety. 'Weird or what?'

She was tiny, not even five foot. She had black leggings on her matchstick legs and little black monkey boots with Day-Glo pink laces. On top was a baggy grey jumper about five sizes too big, her hands entirely hidden by the length of the sleeves. She was whiter than the chalk on the dartboard scores and looked about as substantial. There were lots of spots and an angry-looking sore on the corner of her mouth. Her hair, dyed bright orange, was cut short and close to her head. She had piercings all over the fucking place: ears, nose, eyebrow and tongue. There were probably more to discover under the jumper, if anybody had the courage to look. If poor Chico had to sleep with her as ground rent then we definitely owed him one. I mentally reminded myself to warn him against a blow job. That cold sore could be herpes.

'Tewwibly sowwy, gwoovers. But who cares about stoopid time anyway? I was skipping wound town, looking at the pwetty, pwetty fings. So I wasn't home when you twy to wing wing.'

I'll spare you more, because more there was. She kept on like this all the way back to the fucking flat, which turned out to be in one of Lincoln's leafy suburbs. From the outside it looked brill, one of those sloped-roof 1930s jobbies. All pointy gables and black-and-white mock-Tudor beams. Inside was another story.

There was loads of space. Great big front room, kitchen, two double bedrooms and a massive bathroom. Someone had carpeted it – every fucking inch, wall to wall. Soft dark-grey carpet went everywhere, even the bathroom. Really luxurious, Costa packet. There wasn't much furniture: a white, squashy, Hollywood-style monster three-piece in the front room, settled around a long, low, smoked-glass table. There was a state-of-the-art hi-fi and a wilting cheese plant, and that was about it. Turned out Dad had bought it for her. She'd kept jagging off school and running away from home and, finally, los parentez got the message and thought that if they bought her somewhere, then at least they'd be able to keep an eye on their darling daughter. She'd been there seven or eight months. I'd imagine it was spotless when Juliette's dainty little feet first stepped over the threshold. Now it was utterly and completely fucking filthy.

Juliette didn't live alone, you see. She lived with Rusty and Dandy. Rusty was an Alsatian of doubtful lineage, Dandy was a lurcher with a skin disease, which gave the dog a strange, patchy appearance. Everything in the house was coated with their detritus: hair, slobber, chewed-up toys and the overwhelming smell of dog piss. Nice. Not that our little elfin princess hadn't made her own contribution to the overall squalor. Dirty clothes, dirty ashtrays, dirty glasses and cups were everywhere. The small mercy being that there weren't any dirty plates, cos Juliette didn't eat.

'Here, gwoovers, you two cheeky boys can west your curly heads here.' She giggled. 'And you, Mr Latin Lover, can share my woom. You lucky, lucky fing.'

Chico shot me a look that spoke volumes. You poor, poor bastard I thought. I imagined the bony, chalk-white, dirty little body beneath that sweater, and shuddered. Even with her clothes on she smelt of sweat and dog and, worse, of that rancid odour you get from winos and sad old bastards in the street. The smell that says I haven't washed for a fucking decade. For months and years I've

68

let my bodily secretions dry on me, until every pore is permeated with the stink. I hate dirty girls, hate the thought of what lies between their legs; the slimy horror of it all. Reg may be crap, but she's clean. Spotless in fact. Wouldn't go near her otherwise.

Juliette's fridge contained half a pint of curdled milk and a half-eaten tin of Chappie. The three musketeers set out for the corner shop, where we purchased Fray Bentos steak-and-kidney pies, a tin of beans and a family-sized packet of Smash. Dekka, with surprising acuity, had noticed there was no bog roll in the bathroom, so we splashed out on apricot Andrex and two pints of milk.

'D'you remember Striker, Danny?'

'What, marrer?'

Dekka repeated it. 'D'you remember Striker? Me dog? You know.'

'Yeah, amigo. Course I remember.'

'He looked just like that one, didn't he?'

I looked at Dekka, somewhat puzzled. My right-hand man appeared to have lost his marbles. 'I'm sorry, chav. I'm not with you.'

'The Andrex dog. He looked just like him. Didn't he?'

'The absolute spit,' I agreed. I mean, what else do you say? Dekka nodded and seemed satisfied. Thankfully the topic was dropped.

'Talkin of dogs,' I said cheerfully. 'How the fuck did Keanu Reeves here come to get involved with Miss Loop the Fucking Loop?'

Chico tossed his head.

'OK, she's loca. But she have a lotto money, and she's not a bad girl. She look funny, but she's all right. Anyway, why you complain? You want to sleep on the street tonight?'

Back at Inglebrook Nook, the source of our Juliette's

problems had become all too apparent. In our absence she had shoved the accumulated crap off the table and onto the floor to make room for a bowl of water, spoon, works and the biggest bag of speed my innocent young eyes had laid sight on. One scrawny, stringy little arm was out the jumper and she was busily engaged in tightening a piece of curtain cord above her left elbow.

'About time,' she said, without even looking up. 'I fought you were going to take fow ever, so I started on my own.' She smiled her crazy, lunatic smile. 'But now I have my fwends to help me.'

She looked at Chico. 'Hey, hey, Mr Latino, you know. C'mon baby, light my fire.'

Chico shook his head. 'Ask Danny, he's the expert. He do very quickly.' And, spotting his opening, he went out the door and up the stairs, thus clinching the matter.

Truth be told, I am the expert, and in great demand all over Donny for my speed, professionalism and firm but reassuring touch. Hitting up can be difficult, you see. I mean, have you ever been to the doctor's to give a blood sample? Odds are, especially if you're a woman, that they made a right butchers' outing of it. One student doctor on TV said it was like 'trying to spear spaghetti in a sack', and with women it's even worse. They have a layer of subcutaneous fat which rests beneath the skin and over the veins. On a lot of women you can't even see their mainliner, and you can stab about for ages trying to get a hit. The thing is not to rush it. Feel your way, and don't go in unless you're sure you're on to something. You see loads of people hacking about in a frenzy, just hoping they'll get lucky, which is plain stupid.

Veins are shy creatures, you see. A bit like fawns in a forest. They have to be coaxed and caressed and charmed before they'll appear. First off, you have to be warm. Best thing is when you've just got out of a bath, but obviously this isn't always practical, so make sure you generate what heat you can – long-sleeved jumpers and the like. When the body's hot the veins dilate. The reverse happens when you're cold: they constrict and disappear, huddling back into the muscle and sinew to conserve what warmth they have.

The second thing to ensure is a decent kit. Orange or transparent fine spike, not one of your green- or blue-top hospital knitting needles; these don't pierce the vein, they simply chop it in two. The spike should preferably be new, not only for matters of personal hygiene – if you want AIDS it's up to you, but personally I'm not keen – but because, obviously enough, spikes are a bit like razors: the more you use them the blunter they get. The final thing is attitude. It's a bit like fishing. The little bleeders know you're coming, and they're shy and canny and don't want to be caught. You've got to coax and tickle them up to the surface, and then pop it in when they least expect, and before they have a chance to cringe away and take evasive action.

So that's the set-up. I saw Juliette's arm and sighed. Track marks everywhere, predictably enough; what looked like the beginning of an abscess near her wrist and a classic hot red thing on the inside of her forearm. I touched it and she winced. I knew she would because they hurt like fuck. You get hot red things when you have a hit but the spike slips out halfway through the process. You don't realize and you carry on emptying toxic shit into the surrounding tissue. The following day you get an oval patch on your arm, which is bright red and extremely hot, hence the inventive name we junkies coined. Of course, if you do the job properly, none of this happens, because the toxic shit goes to your heart, brain

71

and kidneys, where hot red things don't show up and therefore don't matter.

I told her to present the other arm, which was in much better shape. Being right-handed, she always landed on her left arm. Her Belsen-like figure also made the job easier – there wasn't any fat for the veins to hide in – and I had the job over and done in minutes. I don't know how much gear she'd put in the works, because it was loaded up while we went to the shop, but it hit her like an express train. Her eyes, which were pale blue in colour, suddenly turned entirely black as the irises expanded with an audible 'ping', and you could see her heart almost jump out of her scrawny chest as it began hammering fifty to the dozen. She tried to speak, couldn't, then, making strange, mewly, choking sounds, got up and rushed to the kitchen sink, where she made retching noises, although of course nothing came up.

'Bit of a fuckin armful there,' observed Dekka. 'What d'you reckon, amigo? Fancy a speedball?'

I looked at Juliette, her spindly frame contorting as she spat bile into the sink. '"Take a Walk on the Wild Side",' I said, and grinned at Dekka. 'Porque no, marrer? Porque no indeed.'

Juliette, with the customary generosity of the totally stoned, who, Christ-like, want the whole world to have a shot at heaven, was happy for us to make free with the speed. This was just as well, as we would have taken it anyway. Chico, being game for a laugh, joined in the fun, and we formed a regular little shooting gallery. I, being the responsible one, mixed the speed fifty/fifty with the smack we'd brought from Donny, and very pleasant it was I may tell you. The only thing that spoiled the effect was Juliette's endless yatting. She talked non-fucking-stop. Like a true speedfreak, it was just an endless outpouring of stream-of-consciousness garbage. The only blessing being that she was mostly too far gone to keep up the appalling 'ickle baby' accent. It was fortunate that we'd all taken up joint residence on cloud nine, otherwise I couldn't have stood it.

At some point later, probably a few hours later, someone suggested going out. The dainty Juliette got on the mobie to Busy Cabs, and twenty minutes later a beat-up Sierra was outside the door waiting to take us to Imps, 'Lincoln's Premier Nitespot', and undoubtedly a total dump.

We all piled in the cab, which dropped us in the shadow of the cathedral, whose imposing Gothic bulk loomed over the crumbling apology for a town like a stern parent disappointed in its offspring. Even though it was well past 11 p.m., Arthur's Round Table Fun Pub was still open for business, so in we went. I think Juliette wanted the chance to show off Chico to the locals; as for us, we were just happy to go where we were taken. It's hard to drink much on speed, cos it closes up your throat, but Dekka has mastered the knack, and Chico and I were doing our level best to emulate him. We were on shorts – easier to get down than beer and less likely to come back up. Being a 'Fun Pub', Arthur's had an impressive list of cock-tails. With the aid of Juliette's financial backing we hacked through a ridiculous selection of pink, blue and green concoctions, full of coloured cherries, chunks of pineapple and floating paper umbrellas. The noise was at a crescendo, chart singles blasting out from the video juke box and teams of aggressive lads and dressed-up lasses all trying hard to pretend they didn't live in Lincoln. 'Nah, mate. Just passin through on me way back to me London flat, like.' In your dreams. The girls were too fat, heels too high, skirts too short, make-up applied in the dark with a builder's trowel. The lads were trying hard to look hard, but merely succeeded in looking stupid. I mean, you can't take it seriously, can you? You have to come from somewhere to be anyone. Everyone knows it. And coming from Lincoln's a non-starter. You can pose around and perfect that dead-eye stare all you like, you'll still be that wanker from Lincoln.

By the time we slid out of Arthur's, it has to be confessed that the grip on reality was slipping. Luckily Imps was only a two-minute walk, because we weren't in a state to get much further. How strange life is, I mused philosophically as we travelled the starlit streets. This time last night we were in the cells. It seemed terribly meaningful at the time, although with hindsight I can see quite clearly that it was just the sort of self-indulgent shite you do think about when you're drunk and actually it means nothing at all. Don't know why I even bothered to tell you.

We made a fair old row, the four of us, as we meandered down the road towards the scarlet portals of Imps. The streets were cobbled, probably because of the cathedral, which made it easy to fall over and our progress even noisier. The stars and the street lights were burning brightly, as brightly as brightly can be, and the cathedral was illuminated in a sulphurous blanket of pale white, which made it melt and shimmer against the orange sky. Our hearts were beating, you felt your ribs might open like the doors of a cage, and this palpitating red thing would finally break its bounds and fly away, free at last from nineteen years of dark imprisonment. We glided down the hill towards the small red door, guarded by two hulking spades in scarlet dinner suits. There was a queue of maybe fifty-odd, shivering in their night-time finery, leaning longingly towards the forbidden opening, desperate to enter the place where all their dreams would come true.

Juliette had changed out of her post-modern anarcho-punk kiddy-combat gear into something she fondly imagined might be construed as sexy. I've seen sexier in the deep freeze at Kwik Save, but let that pass. The kid had a kind of suicidal bravura style, you had to hand it to her. She was wearing a cream bodice top, stiff with embroidery and encrusted with pearls. It sat on what should have been her hips, ending in a central point. It had a low, square-cut neck, and looked like the sort of thing Ann Boleyn might have dandered about in. Unfortunately it presupposed that the girl wearing it had tits, which were meant to swell sexily against the stiff constraints of the bodice, thus setting up an erotic counter-point of the soft and malleable pushing against the hard and unyielding. If you looked at Juliette's neckline you could see the bony sternum pressing through the pale, almost transparent skin. The bodice stood away from her body, almost like it resented the proximity, so looking down you could see the childlike chest, the pinkish nipples, both pierced, resting on the wan plateau of skin and bone. As I said, it wasn't sexy, but it roused in me an unexpected tenderness, a desire to protect this stupid, crazy infant from her own worst impulses – a feeling which evaporated the moment she opened her mouth.

Juliette tripped straight up to the gargantuan spades and flashed a piece of plastic. She was a member, natch enuf, and, smirking at the legions of damned shivering in the queue, we swaggered straight in.

With Chico carrying, Juliette got the beers in and we surveyed the scene. I'd seen it all before a thousand times, but the drugs added a welcome filter of glamour and pleasant excitement. The decor was the usual nightclub red. Large central dance floor, curved staircase at either side, with overlooking balcony and upstairs bar. It looked like there was a smaller, quieter room off to the left and, at the back, a members-only bar, all done out in silver, which coincidentally matched Juliette's shoes. The club was full, and the dance floor thronging with the usual contingent of excruciatingly bad dancers. Lads looking to pull lurked on the margins, scanning for the unattached and inebriated. Half-cut girls hung about in little knots and groups, tittering, nudging their mates and gulping back the ready-mixed pina coladas. The waiters and bar staff were dressed up in imp outfits. They all had little padded red horns, devil eye masks and red satin waistcoats with a black imp holding a trident embroidered on the back. You could also buy a bright red Imps cocktail, which was promoted as being 'hotter than hell'. When you've only got one claim to fame, then you stick to it. Lincoln's Imp is a bit like Wigan Pier: it's not that good, but it's all they've got.

The imp's not even an imp at all, but a devil. He sits, carved in stone, at the back of Lincoln Cathedral, a wee dwarf fiend with massive ears and a bad leg. They say the angels turned him into stone as a punishment. The devil's henchman caught in church. As I said, it's not that interesting.

The nightclub all went by in a bit of a blur. I remember finishing my beer and somehow ending up with an Imps cocktail, which tasted every bit as disgusting as you might suppose. I remember throwing up in the bogs, and I remember Juliette screaming abuse at some blonde girl who was coming on to Chico. I think it was one of the bar staff that started it. That's what Dekka said, and it sort of fits with my partial recollection. But, as I said, it was all a bit hazy.

I remember the club seemed to get darker and hotter. I'd lost contact with the others and was gently leaning against one of the pillars, surveying the dance floor and wondering if I could be arsed to set myself up with somebody shaggable. I decided that, on the whole, the effort probably wasn't worth it. The girls were all Kennel-Club registered, and any attempt to pull would probably involve manifest complications placating tossed-off local lads. The scuffle started low key. I saw Dekka off to the right, shouting. One of the stupidly dressed bar staff was trying to grab his arm, which Dekka kept pulling away. Another, his little satin horns glinting in the laser lights, appeared to be shouting back at Dekka. Sighing inwardly at having to once more hoist the burdens of responsibility upon my weary shoulders, I started to move across, with the intention of extricating Dekka from whatever mess he'd managed to land in.

I didn't move fast enough. I saw it, or at least I think I saw it. One minute Dekka was shouting the odds and trying to shrug off the bloke holding his arm, the next, the other bloke punched him straight in the face. Dekka's nose seemed to burst; I saw droplets of blood and snot showering out, a shining rainbow of scarlet, white and green. For a split second Dekka stood, stupefied by pain and astonishment, then all hell broke loose.

The first punch I threw hit one of the fucking imps on the side of the head and, after that, pandemonium. It seemed like half the club joined in, all intent on murder. I heard glass shattering and I saw or heard Chico, and I remember going down under a mass of trampling feet and Dekka somehow pulling me up again. There was no room to punch any more, and I stuck the nut on some bastard and heard a satisfying crunch as his cheekbone gave way. Even so, we'd fucked it. Arms and legs were everywhere. I was drowning in a sea of hostile, furious bodies, struggling to stay on my feet. If I went down again I wouldn't get up. Then, amidst the mêlée and uproar, I heard the screaming. Thin and high and unrelenting.

When I was younger, one of the lads at school had a lurcher, and we'd go out in the fields round Edlo to hunt with the dog. Once it caught a hare. Oh, she ran like fuck, in great big sweeping circles, but he got her as the exhaustion and fear slowed her down. As he started to rip and tear, she screamed, thin and high, like burning wire passing through your heart. I never went out in the fields again. I dropped the boy with the dog and found the boys with the drugs. But I never forgot her screaming. She screamed right through my dreams for years.

Now it was Juliette screaming, her mouth a dark hole in her chalk-white face. She was screaming her head off. Screaming our salvation. I think they stopped battering us just to shut her up. No-one could stand that, like nails dragging down a blackboard, or biting down hard on silver paper. It just wasn't tolerable.

Somehow we ended up outside. The scarlet spades chucked us onto the cobbles and then impassively went back to the job of guarding hell's gate. Someone, Juliette I suppose, must have called a cab, because I remember crawling onto the back seat and feeling the stickiness of Chico's blood as I collapsed against him.

The naked, swinging 60-watt in Juliette's front room revealed the full extent of the damage. Dekka was the worst. His nose broken and flat on his face, still pouring with blood as his amphetamine-crazed heart pumped away nineteen to the dozen. His earring had somehow been torn out in the ruck, leaving a gash from which blood poured in narrow rivulets onto his collarbone. His eyes, probably as a result of the initial blow, were swelling visibly.

Chico's face wasn't too bad. He'd caught a blow that

78

had grazed his cheekbone and taken the skin away, but it wasn't serious. Unfortunately you couldn't say as much for the rest of him. He'd been jumped from behind by one of the hulking bouncers and had spent a good few minutes on the floor having the shite kicked out of him. Already stiffening up, he could barely stand straight. His back and chest a mass of rising bruises, where various steel toecaps had thudded home. It was apparent he'd broken some ribs and, to complete the scene, he had a fairly bad gash just above his left elbow. Compared to my amigos I got off lightly, my sufferings amounting to no more than a badly cut bottom lip and general bruising and misery. I pointed out to Dekka that this was mainly thanks to his intervention in dragging me back up from the floor. He tried to say 'nada, marrer,' but his face was so swollen he could hardly speak. There was nothing for it, the elfin princess called another cab and we trooped off to the local casualty.

After waiting a mere four and a half hours amidst the usual assortment of oddments and weirdos, the four of us staggered back out – bandages in place, noses reset, stitches done, painkiller scripts in hand – and made for home. Juliette had come down from her speed about an hour into the waiting and had become pinched, with-drawn and utterly silent. As the cab drove through the chilly, grey, dawn-streaked streets she began to cry. She made no noise, but her scrawny little frame started to shudder and shake. I thought for a terrible moment she was having some sort of fit, which, as she had the house keys and the money, would have been the final agony on this grim night, but then I saw her face and realized she was sobbing. To my utter amazement, Chico reached out for her and wrapped her in his arms. 'Tranquilo, me ninya. It OK. Tranquilo, me honey. Es OK.' She curled her tiny body inside his arms, so it looked as if he was nursing a child, and her sobs subsided. Chico refused to catch my eye.

It was gone six thirty when we crawled into our beds. Juliette had a stash of valium, which was handy cos, despite our exhaustion, the speed was still in our systems, making the pulse rates jump and pinning the eyes open. The downers must have done the trick, because I was gone within seconds of touching the pillow. The last memory I have is of Dekka breathing noisily through his mouth at my side.

It was three in the afternoon when I woke. Dekka was still dead to the world and the rest of the house was silent. I checked the hot-water situation, and then, giving thanks to a merciful God, showered the accumulated mud, blood and gore of last night's festivities from my aching bones. I'd stiffened up in the night. My cut lip had swollen, making me look like a *Baywatch* babe who's overdone the collagen, and my kidneys were hurting, whether from the kicking or the speed I wasn't sure, but who's splitting hairs. Once partially resurrected and dressed I checked the drugs stash. It looked none too hot. Two days, maybe. Three if careful.

There seemed bugger all to do except watch telly and wait for the others to surface. Fuck it, I thought. I wanted out. I wanted to breathe a bit, free of the clouds of dog hair and eczema scurf rising from the smelly bodies of Dandy and Beano, or whatever Juliette's fuck-stupid dogs were called. As far as I could judge no-one had fed, walked or otherwise tended to their simple canine needs since our arrival some twenty hours previous. Tough being a dog, eh?

It took me about half an hour to walk into town. It was mostly uphill, and I took it slowly, enjoying the cold sunshine and clean air. When I got to the town centre there was really only one place to go, and I bent my joyful footsteps accordingly.

Close to, it seemed even bigger. Huge and golden, floating above the city as I climbed, higher and higher, laboriously upward. When I got there I stopped. It waited for me across the square. It had waited for a thousand years, another ten minutes wasn't going to matter much. Massive, its solid body rising as if from the very bones of the earth. Yet for all that heavy tonnage, the megaweight of stone pressing downward on groaning foundations, the effect of the thing was to pull you up. Tracery and soaring lines and flying towers and vaulting spires. Your eye travelling ever upwards as this huge conglomeration of stone gathered itself to leap to heaven.

For a few minutes I stood and watched, gobsmacked by the aspiration, the enormity of it all – or maybe just feeling the after-effects of the kicking I'd taken the night before. The huge gate was open, a stream of people scurrying in and out. It was mostly tourists and schoolkids on trips. There was even a busload of Japanese, which I thought dead impressive. I must have been there about ten minutes in all, and the cold was beginning to get to me. I decided it was time to make a move and began to walk down to the gate. It was as I was walking that I clocked her. I was legging it down to the gate, dodging through the Japs and the kids, and something just slipped past the corner of my eye. I turned my head to see better, then stood absolutely still.

It was a girl in a blue cardy, walking away from me, down towards the town centre. There must have been fifty yards or more between us, and I only saw her from the back, but I knew. I knew it was Eleanor. I just did; I was

81

certain of it. I started running full pelt, trying to get to her, trying to reach her, and almost went straight under the wheels of a massive green-and-gold coach that pulled straight out in front of me. Not even pausing to insult the driver, I skidded leftwards and detoured round. She'd vanished. The road in front was empty. I looked round, trying to see where else she could have gone, and walked a few uncertain steps forward. There was nothing to be seen. If she had been here, she'd gone, disappeared. Maybe I'd made a mistake; the hangover, plus speed, plus battering had probably sent me a bit off kilter. Best just to keep tranquilo; easy to make mistakes when you're knackered.

I walked back the way I'd come and stood once more in front of the cathedral gate. It had been her. I knew it. Sure of it. And some day I would find her, as sure as my name was Danny Mac, I would find her. In the meantime the cathedral loomed above me, an endless stream of people flowing in and out of the gate. I took a deep breath and moved.

Inside, it took a minute or two to adjust. The light was dim, filtered through the high-up gimlet windows, but it was the size that caught me off guard. I walked straight through, up the central aisle, ignoring the kids and the tourists. The air was cold and clean, eddying round the vast space and up to the unseen heights. A few, very few, were praying, kneeling, echoing words that had hung in the air for 900 long years. I wondered if He was listening, or if He'd ever listened. Had they shuddered and twitched here in 1348 with their heads bowed and their hearts beating? Eyes darting nervously, trying to spot the symptoms. Ears pinned back to catch the tell-tale coughing, praying to an unheeding God that this terrible scourge be taken from them.

82

They died horribly, you know. And they didn't call it the Black Death; that came later. They called it the blue fever. Same result, though. Interestingly enough, it didn't just stop at people. Dogs and cats and sheep – killed the lot, and not a nice way to go. If you had to pick the fatal disease of your choice, bubonic plague would not be it. Physical agony complete with mental torment. 'Norra lorra laffs,' as Cilla might say.

I'm interested in plagues. AIDS is interesting – doomed youth and all that. And that moment of truth. All those if onlys. Not possible with everyone, I grant you. But I bet a lot of them can look back, as the KP blossoms on the skin and the blindness and incontinence set in. Yeah, I bet a lot of them can look back and think, If only. If only I hadn't gone to that pub, that club, met that person. What if I'd stayed at home? Gone to Great Yarmouth for the weekend? Watched telly instead? That's the romance of it all, don't you think? That moment. That single, traceable moment when Death tapped at the door. And, despite all the warnings, all the glossy leaflets, all the talk, you leapt to your feet, checked your hair in the mirror, slid back the bolts, turned the key and let him in. Probably even made him a cup of coffee.

Ebola's my other favourite. I wanted to go to Zaire. I saw this fabulous programme on it. It broke out in this shithole of a jungle town. Of course everyone tried to bugger off pronto, but the Government sent in the army. Set up roadblocks and shot on sight. Just like the plague, really. And they didn't have a clue what was causing it. A team of super-brave French and Belgian doctors went in to lend a bit of First-World savvy to the beleaguered locals. You ought to have seen the precautions. When the doctors went into the ebola ward – well, more a filthy room with a few wire cots and mattresses and a lot of dying locals laying about – anyway, you should have seen the gear. Like they were about to leave the module for a walk on Mars. Head to foot in white plastic, with perspex face masks and their own personal breathing equipment. Soon as you touch them, you catch it. When they came out of the room, they walked through a shower of bleach, then, still in their gear, they were confronted by army personnel wielding decontamination spray guns, and they were washed down again from head to foot. Unbelievable, I tell you. Two weeks between transmission and death, and again, a bit of a crap way to go. All your internal organs turn to mush. And because you're haemorrhaging your eyes turn red. Your skin goes a sort of ashy grey, and you get all this frothy scum in your mouth. If you've seen *Zombies, Dawn of the Dead* you get the picture. Only this lot are still alive. Stopped as suddenly as it started, they think the virus exhausted itself. It'll definitely kick off again, though. Take my word for it. Mind you, the Congo, weird or what. They think AIDS started there too. Anyway, if the various diseases don't get you, some loony from the tribe down the road will pick up his machete and give it a go.

On this ebola film, they showed a bloke walking down the street. Being a local, he'd gone to the takeaway to get a bit of scran. Got a newspaper in one hand, wrapped round his food, and was using his free hand to pull bits off to eat. Just like you would after buying a bag of chips on Copley Road. They put the cameras in close up to show his takeaway. It was a rat. Still with the fur and the tail. It was on its back and had been split down the belly, disembowelled and roasted. He'd pulled it open and was happily breaking off bits of meat. And they wonder why they get diseases.

I was up near the altar by this time, and I broke off from

my viral musings because this funny little crip was staring at me. He was a dwarf, no bigger than four feet max, and he was on crutches, because he only had one leg. I know, it sounds like the beginning of some mega-crap joke. 'There was this one-legged dwarf . . .' but it's true. He was fucking ugly as well: jug ears and a fat, squat little face. Not what you might call Mother Nature's favourite son. He saw me look back at him and caught my eye. He was winking at me and beckoning me to come over. I looked at him, puzzled, then he beckoned me again, jigging from side to side, still winking and grinning. I shrugged and started towards him. Just then he turned and ran. Belted away on his crutches, the rubber stoppers making a strange squeaky sound on the stone-flagged floor. When he'd almost reached the door he paused for a second and looked back. He gave a little yelp, then set off even faster than before, disappearing into the light outside.

'Not a very suitable companyero, I feel,' said a voice at my elbow.

'Oh Christ, not you again.' There he was, towering over me, golden hair flopping across his forehead, skin whiter than monumental alabaster and too much fuckin after-shave.

'Had a good night of it, didn't you, chav?' he smirked.

'Not exactly. I've known better. What the fuck do you want?'

He slipped an arm round my shoulders.

'I've come to give you a bit of help. You don't seem to be managing too well on your own. She's watching you, y'know. She's seen it all, amigo, and it's not gone too good.'

His arm felt funny, light and caressing. I felt like I was drowning in his aftershave.

'What the fuck are you on about, chavito?' I asked. To

be honest I wasn't feeling so good and couldn't really cope with this bloke, and his tendency to talk like a cryptic crossword was getting severely on my nerves. I shot a look at the door and shifted my body weight away from him. His grip tightened.

'No, no, me ninyo. Running away won't help. I'd only come and find you again. Listen, Danny Mac. Go south. The dogs are following you, and if they catch up you won't like it. Oh no. Not at all. Go back on the road. Straight, you remember. And don't fuck about. No dandering off here and there. There's another one needed. But let him come to you. You got it, marrer? South. Pronto. That's the lot.'

'Yeah, yeah,' I said. 'Now, do you mind getting your paws off me, cos people are going to talk.'

He smiled. 'If that's what you want, chav.' He took his arm away. 'Feel better now, do you?'

Actually I felt weird. Then he bent down. He really was stupidly fuckin tall. He sort of leant forward, so our faces were level, and looked straight at me.

'Go on,' he breathed. 'What are you waiting for? Get weaving. I'm staying here awhile, but I'll see you later.' He smiled again. 'The eagle and the angel and the ox. Soon the lion will come.'

He gave me a gentle shove and then sort of melted into one of the pews. 'Move it, chav. Standing there with your gob wide open isn't going to knit the baby a bonnet.'

'You're barmy,' I said. 'You know that? Totally fucking barmy. OK, I'm off.'

As I got to the end of the aisle I turned to look at him. He was still in the pew, kneeling now, head bowed and hands clasped. The light seemed to bounce off the gold in his hair and his shirt was so white it looked irradiated. I felt a very strange thing. This emotion which washed through me. I wanted to go and sit next to him and have him hold my hand. Father O'Flynn used to do that. 'Now sit down here, Danny Boy, and hold my hand,' he'd say. And, as I sniffed and snivelled, he'd sometimes pick me up and sit me on his knee. He'd have one hand round my waist, so his arm was there for me to lean back against, and with the other he'd hold my hand. And we would rock to and fro, in gentle rhythm. And we would sing my song. 'Oh Danny Boy/The pipes, the pipes are calling/From glen to glen/And down the mountainside.' He said they'd written it specially for me. One day. One day maybe, I'll tell you about the things we did.

I left the cathedral and walked back in a half-dream. Wasn't feeling too clever by the time I got back to the house. Anyway, once I'd done the necessary and felt more like myself, I sat down with Dekka and Chico and started to talk. My two comrades looked pretty much like shite, especially Dekka, but we all wanted to move. Lincoln was still uncomfortably close to sunny Donny, besides which, the gear stash was pitiable. The general idea was to get back on the A1 and make it down to London. As it was now gone 6 p.m. and pitch black, today was more or less a write-off. Best plan was an early night and a good start in the morning. Everything was more or less settled when Juliette breezed in.

'Hi, gwoovers! How are we all feeling? Ready for adventures in the big bad world? This is my fwend; he's called Mol. We're going to see the Sheriff of Nottingham.'

At this point Juliette started laughing. When she stopped, Chico asked her what the fuck she was on about. The explanation took time and patience, but it transpired that Juliette's short-arse friend had a car and that he was driving to Nottingham to score some speed. She was going with him for more of the same, but, and here comes the important bit, the bloke they were going to see was also a middle-ranking smack dealer. If we took the trip to Nottingham we could make a reasonable score, find somewhere to doss for the night and then hit the M1 for our trip to London the following day. Sound as a pound, in my book.

'What about the dogs?' This from Dekka. 'Shouldn't you give them some food and take them for a walk or something?'

'Shit!' yelped Juliette. 'My poor darling baby pupwups. Isn't Mummy very, very bad?'

Rusty and Dandy stood up and began to look interested. In the event, our departure was delayed for nearly an hour whilst Dekka and Juliette took them for a walk, fed them and generally did lots of canine fucking about. I made a mental note to keep Dekka well away from any future doggy interaction: it was both embarrassing and time-consuming. Not a happy combination.

Finally we got into Mol's car, a slightly weird old black sedan affair, which looked like he'd borrowed it straight from Al Capone. It was big, though, you had to give him that. Juliette sat in the front, with the three of us sprawled on the leather bench seat behind. Fortunately, Mol appeared to know where he was going, because Juliette was well and truly away with it. We must have looked fuckin ridiculous. Juliette was wearing some blue velvet affair with a hood, and she'd tied fistfuls of scarlet and blue ribbons in her hair. Red eyeshadow and blue lipstick completed the picture. Mary, Mary, quite contrary. She was sweet and brave, you know. But absolutely fucking barking. As for our mate, Mol, he wasn't much bigger than Juliette, had to sit on cushions so as he could see through the windscreen and drive the fuckin car. And dressed in a funny little suit, with this Russian cap thing on his head. It had ear flaps which tied under the chin. Mol didn't say much – not surprising with Juliette around. But he seemed in a good mood, nodding and smiling as we bowled along the A46, and occasionally promising that his man sold really shit-hot gear.

I don't know how long we took, hour and a half maybe? Juliette made a half-hearted attempt to navigate once we got into the Nottingham suburbs, but Mol wisely ignored her. Soon we were back on home turf, back amongst the badlands, with the high-rises rising all around and the crappy little shops covered with graffiti and iron grilles. The car stopped and we got out.

'Up there,' said Mol, winking at us. 'He lives on top of the world.'

We looked upward, following the pointing finger, to three impossibly tall and thin blocks huddled together.

'Two months ago,' said Mol, 'a lad was drinking with his mates in the local there,' he nodded to a flat-fronted pub set in the foot of the nearest block. Sure that we'd got the drift, he continued, 'Anyway, they'd all had a lot to drink. When the pub chucked out around midnight, well, one drunken lad turns to his mate and says, "I bet you a pound you daren't jump off the top."'

Mol pointed upwards again. It was maybe twenty storeys.

'So six of these lads took the lift to the roof. And the boy said to his friend, "Is the bet still on?" And his mate gets out a quid, and says, "You can see the colour of my money, right enough?" So the boy says, "You're on." Picks up the quid and puts it in his pocket. Then he jumped.'

'What happened?' said Dekka.

'He screamed as he went down,' Mol said. 'No, not screamed. More like a shout, I suppose. His fall lasted about three seconds. He must have twisted in the air, because he landed on his back. Snapped it clean in two. He survived for sixteen hours in the hospital. They gave the quid to his parents. Towards the funeral I suppose. He was seventeen.'

'How do you know all this?' I asked.

Mol winked at me. 'I was there, old lad. I lost a quid.'

chapter four

IT WAS THE TOP OF THE WORLD. THE NINETEENTH FLOOR. The rest was as expected. Tim was a slight bloke, who might once have had pretensions to being middle class. Curly, pale-reddish hair. His house decoration courtesy of too much acid and too much E: swirly pictures, smiley faces and magic mushrooms covered the walls. Tim was very stoned, as he had every right to be in his own house at eleven o'clock at night, and he just pottered about making stupid stoned remarks, whilst his wife, Yvonne, got down to business.

We all hit up in the front room. We watched the video of *The Blues Brothers*, which in my opinion you can't enjoy properly unless decently smashed. Then we hit up again. Mol had a bag of speed and was doing the honours for Juliette. Me, Dekka and Chico stuck mainly to the smack, interspersed with occasional speedballs. Normally I don't like speed, but there was so much about it was hard to refuse. Mol seemed to have mountains of the stuff, and every time I looked up he seemed to be shovelling more of it in Juliette's arm. We were all pretty far gone. Tim put on another vid, but I can't remember what it was, then a buzzer went off.

'It's three o'fucking clock,' said Yvonne. 'Some people have no bloody manners.'

She grabbed the intercom, listened, then buzzed the lock. The door opened and what looked like Ruud Gullit's younger brother walked in.

'This is Mikey,' said Yvonne. Mikey grinned affably, then sat down next to Yvonne. This night was rapidly turning into a complete fairy story. Mikey was in business, you see. The crack business to be specific. He'd come to do a bit of trade and join in the party. Best time I'd had in years.

'Danny, amigo mio,' said Dekka. 'This is fucking A-one totally great.'

'Couldn't agree more, chav.' I looked at Dekka and laughed. He laughed back at me. Chico was laughing too.

'Hey, companyeros, don't leave me out. We are los tres. Para siempre.'

Chico held out his hand, I joined with mine, then Dekka. Los tres. That was right. Somebody had said that, hadn't they? Couldn't remember where, though. Couldn't remember much if truth be told. I had a vague idea that me an Chico hadn't always been the bezza mates we seemed to be tonight, but what the fuck? At the moment I loved everybody, especially Dekka and Chico, cos they were me marrers. We were all so happy. Juliette was laughin her head off, talking to Mol non-stop. She was stroking Chico's leg with one hand and Chico was smiling, the beautiful mouth curved upwards, eyes half-closed. Tim had given up with the vid and was totally obsessed with the hi-fi. Knee-deep in a pile of CDs he was searching for favourite tracks, cueing them up like a pro and calling out for requests. Mol suggested another hit, joshing at Mikey to stop being so mean with the crack, and grinning and winking at us all. I wondered why he'd kept his hat on, ear flaps and all. It looked fucking stupid.

I mixed my own gear and used my own works. I thought I'd been careful, but it hit me like a train. For a few minutes all I could do was sit very still and gasp, then I came to and everything was back under control. The room was a blaze of activity. A turmoil of hypodermics, spoons, silver paper and balls of Kleenex with blots of blood, which seemed to bloom and spread like flowers.

We were all completely off on one, in one of those totally brilliant euphoric time capsules, each utterly tripped out by the wonder of existence. This is why it happened, I suppose. If things had been different, less totally good, if we hadn't each been consumed by our own personal miracle, we'd have noticed in time. We would, I'm sure. We would have done something. But we never got the chance.

Chico said it first. He was sitting next to her. His voice was soft, uncertain, not sure of what he was seeing.

'Danny, there's something wrong. She can't breathe. Danny, come here.'

Juliette had gone blue. She was really blue and making this awful gulping sound, thrashing and sucking to get air into her lungs. She looked like she was fitting, but her eyes were wide open and the expression on her face was terrible. It wasn't the classic smack OD, because she didn't like heroin and hadn't taken any that night. It was something to do with the vast quantities of speed and crack she'd poured into her arm and lungs, until her central nervous system had gone apeshit. Her heart and brain were racing too fast for her lungs to keep up. Her eyes were black with terror and amphetamines. I felt panic wrapping round me.

I heard myself shouting, 'Where's the phone? Phone the fucking ambulance. Somebody phone the fucking ambulance.'

Everybody was talking and moving at once, like those nightmares when time goes funny and the chaos is in slo-mo. Like the needle had stuck, I was yelling over and again for the phone. Chico was trying to pull Juliette to her feet, but she kept collapsing back onto the settee. Tim was still standing by the hi-fi, saying nothing at all, and over all the pandemonium I could hear Yvonne screaming, 'Get her out of here. Get her out of here. Get that bitch out of my house.'

'She's fuck dying, you cunt.' This was Chico. 'Phone the ambulance. She can't breathe. She's going to die.'

'That's your fucking problem. Get her out. Get her out. She's not fucking going over in here.'

I started to grab the phone. Juliette was making a rattling sound in her throat, her body jerking across the settee. Her eyes were fixed. Yvonne tried to pull the receiver away from me and I shoved her off. I dialled 999 but nothing happened. Juliette was convulsing. Like she was under water, her mouth was wide open, her face full of panic and horror as she tried to drag the air into her body, tried to force the oxygen through the no-go zone the speed and crack in her system had created. What the fuck was happening? The line was silent. Fucking silent. What the fuck was going on?

'Get her out!' Yvonne was howling in my face. In one hand she held a piece of wire cord. 'I've cut the fucking phone, you twat. Get her out. She's not dying in here.'

I hit her, straight in the face, as hard as I could. She saw it coming and partly dodged and rode the blow, but I still felt the moment when my fist connected. 'You murdering cunt,' I said. 'You murdering cunt.'

94

I think it was Mol who opened the door and started to drag her out, but I can't be sure. Dekka had her under the arms and we managed to half pull and half shove her into the lift. Despite her tiny size, as a dead weight she was still hard to handle. When we got to the car, Dekka and the Mikey bloke had to carry her. Chico got in the back and Mol drove. I went with him in the front.

'Hospital,' I said. 'Where's the fucking hospital?'

Mol shrugged. He was still calm, still rational. 'You'll have to tell me. Not my town, mate.'

'Next to the castle. Drive out of here, turn left. I'll show you. What you waiting for? Move it, man, move!' It was Mikey.

The car shot forward, Mikey leaning on his elbows from the back seat, giving directions. I could hear Chico talking to her, telling her all the sort of shit you hear in the movies. 'Hang on, baby. It'll be OK. I'll look after you. Take it easy.' He even said he loved her. Which, as we all know, wasn't true. But it didn't matter, cos she couldn't hear him. She was rattling and gasping, her eyes wide open and pleading, her hands curved rigid. The black car was screaming through the city streets, following Mikey's directions.

'How long?' said Chico. 'How far? She's going to die. Where's this fuck hospital?'

'Five minutes,' Mikey replied. 'Nearly there, man. We're nearly there.'

But not near enough, because she gave up on us. She went into a sort of seizure. Chico tried to hold her. Her back was arching and her legs kicking, and Chico had his arms around her middle, trying to hold her against him and stop her damaging herself. Then she started making these awful choking sounds. This terrible gargling deep inside, like she'd gone under quicksand, looking for air

95

but filling her mouth with mud, sand and water instead. Then nothing much. She stopped making all this horrible noise. Her body relaxed and went quiet, and her eyes didn't seem as agonized, mad and staring. 'OK,' Chico whispered. 'That's better.'

I suppose in some ways it was better. No-one admitted anything, but Mol slowed the car and Mikey stopped screaming directions. We headed out of the town centre, Juliette lying across Chico's lap. No-one said anything at all.

The first person to speak was Mol. He pulled up and got out the car, leaving the door open.

'What you waiting for, lads? Drop her here and we'll be moving.'

I looked out the window. It was still very black and hard to see. Nobody spoke or moved. I got out the car. It was the town tip. That's where he'd brought us. Notts County Council refuse dump.

'If we just roll her down there,' he continued, 'probably be four or five days before they find her. And we'll be well out of it.'

'We can't leave her here,' I said. 'You can't honestly mean to leave her here? With the rubbish. She isn't just rubbish. You can't . . .'

'Up to you, sunshine,' he replied affably. 'I'm not tooling round much longer with a body in my motor, I'll tell you that for free. And I'll tell you another thing. I want out of this little scene, and quickly, so why don't we just roll her over there? She's dead, old lad. It doesn't matter any more.'

'No,' I said, and turned and got back in the car.

Mol followed, got behind the wheel and drove on. Then he made the position clear. He wanted Juliette's body out of his car. Very quickly. Then he would drive us anywhere in Nottingham we wanted to be, then he was going home to Lincoln.

'You can't say fairer than that, now, can you?' he asked. And I suppose he had a point.

In the end Mikey told him where to go. There's a park on the edge of the city. Well, half park, half open ground. The River Idle, a tributary of the Trent, runs through the park, with willow trees lining the banks. It's a favourite place for the youth of Nottingham. In summer they hang out there, drinking cider, smoking dope, listening to music and swimming on warmer nights. 'We could leave her there,' said Mikey, 'under the willow trees. The police will think she'd been out with her boyfriend, or to a party. Just another overdose. Nothing to connect it with us.' I thought about her parents. What they would feel when they found out. Bit late to worry about that now. Should have kept an eye on her, shouldn't they?

'What's her second name?' I asked Chico. He didn't know. We looked in her handbag. She had a laminated student card. She was a first-year doing fashion and design, I think. Her name was Juliette Robinson. In the photograph she was smiling – black eyeshadow and bright red lipstick, a kiss-curl stuck down on her forehead.

We stopped by an iron gate, which was padlocked.

'It's OK,' said Mikey. 'You can get through down the side.'

Dekka and Chico took her, with an arm round each shoulder, their hands locked under her thighs, so she was sort of sitting between them. Luckily, rigor mortis hadn't set in, so her body was still malleable. As they picked her up her head sagged downwards, her neck unable to sustain the weight. We found the way in quickly under Mikey's direction, then we started across the field towards the river bank.

97

'Why are we poncing about like this?' Mol asked. 'Why don't we just leave her by the hedge?'

I was beginning to hate him. He was her friend, for fuck's sake. No-one answered. We just kept walking, and Mol fell in behind us, sighing as if his patience was being tried to the absolute limit.

The withered winter grass was wet beneath our feet, and we slipped and slid our way across the ground, which got boggier as we approached the water. It was cold and very bleak, but you could imagine in the summer sun you would see things differently. Half a dozen willows leant down towards the river, which was shallow and clear, with a stony bottom. There was an arching, blue-railed footbridge about fifty yards downstream, and Mikey said the water was deeper there.

When we got close to the edge, Dekka and Chico, panting with effort by now, set her down, and she lay curled on the grass, her skin freezing to the touch.

'Where shall we put her then?' Dekka asked.

Nobody spoke. 'Chico?' I said. If anybody had responsibility, it was him.

'Under the trees,' he said. 'The trees will hide her. Shit, amigo. What a fuck mess.'

We carried her cold, stiffening little body a few yards further, parting the hanging, naked willow twigs, and laid her on the ground. Chico used his thumbs to push the eyelids down over her terrified, black-eyed stare. She lay curled on the bare earth under the winter tree, her legs tucked up beneath her, her blue velvet cloak lying like a flag behind her, the hood down, showing the ribbons in her hair.

Mol began to walk back towards the car. 'Best of luck, darling,' said Mikey, then turned and followed. Dekka hesitated, then went after Mikey. I stood by the body, head bowed. Beside me, Chico crossed himself and said something under his breath; he crossed himself a second time and touched my elbow.

'Come on, amigo,' he said. 'Vamos.'

Across the field the car lights were on and we could hear the engine. We started to run, and we left her there in the cold and dark, left her all alone, and tore across the field. Our business was with the living.

'Well, lads,' said Mol. 'Quite a night. Where would you like to end it?'

'Drop them at my gaff,' said Mikey. 'They can crash there.' He turned and scanned the three of us. 'Unless you've got other plans.'

It was something of an understatement to say we had no other plans. Once again following Mikey's directions, Mol tooled the sedan through the grey-streaked streets of Nottingham. He was still chatting away and happy as Larry. He was beginning to really piss me off. I didn't like his coffin of a car neither.

In the half-light it began to rain. Slowly at first, with big, fat, heavy drops, which became smaller and quicker. I wondered how long she'd keep dry. She would just lie there. The tree would protect her a little bit, but eventually the rain would find a way through. The ribbons in her hair would become muddy and flattened, leaf mould and bits of twigs and dirt would catch on her clothes and insects would smell her out, attracted by the slow scent of decomposition.

They say they get inside your coffin eventually. That no matter how much you dosh the dinos for oak and mahogany they eventually bore their way through. And what then? Crawling slowly over your corpse, looking for the best bits, exploring all the little nooks and crannies. Chewing through the clothes, burrowing in the flesh, laying eggs and hatching maggots. Until all that's left is bones and hair. I don't know why, but apparently they don't go for hair. It's supposed to go on growing after you're dead. Not for ever, natch, but for a week or so.

Was that what was happening to Juliette? How long before the beetles smelt her out? Their claws catching on her tights as they moved up inside her skirt? Maggots crawling across her ribs, like a car bumping the sleeping policemen, and slugs and snails leaving a trail of glistening silver slime across her nipples? Perhaps there was a spider sitting inside her mouth, which must by now be quite dry of saliva. Woodlice crawling in her hair, burrowing in her inner ear. What would happen if they went up her nostrils? Say something fairly small, like an earwig, wriggled up her nose. How long before it encountered obstruction? Before it couldn't go any further? Where does the nasal passage go to anyway? I think it goes to the brain, or down to the throat, depending on your direction. I remember at school being told that the embalmers prepared Egyptian pharaohs for mummification by inserting a silver hook up the nasal passage and fishing out the brain.

We should have taken her to the hospital, I know that. Even after she was dead. But we couldn't, could we. We'd have been totally and utterly shafted – in the cells on a charge of Class A drugs, supply, possession, manslaughter, murder, accessory. Her family had money. They'd have seen us crucified. You know what it's like when some lass with well-off parents cops it. Flog a tenner tab of E to some solicitor's daughter, and if the silly bint drops you're looking at fifteen years. HE DEALT IN DEATH the tabs would scream, whilst they go on about how the dopey bint who's just croaked it was bound to have won the Nobel Prize and been a supermodel, if only she hadn't given you a tenner.

We couldn't have done much else, you see. And we had tried to save her; we had tried. Anyway, it's over now. What the fuck does it matter.

By the time Mol dropped us at Mikey's place it was early morning. It's the worst time of the day. Everything grey and desolate, the drugs wearing off, and reality looking as crappily real as only reality can. Five a.m. is the most common time of death. Now there's a surprise. Mol was humming under his breath as he pulled up in the car. As we started to say our goodbyes a phone began to ring. Mol dived inside his jacket and fished out his mobie. 'Bit of a night, boss,' he said. 'Yeah, no sweat. I'll be back in time for breakfast.' He popped the mobie back in his jacket and smiled at us.

'This is where we say goodbye then.'

'You cunt,' I said. 'You fucking dwarfish bastard. I'm going to kick your fucking brains out. You've had that fucking phone all night. You had the phone in the fucking flat, didn't you? You could have called the ambulance, couldn't you? You just let her die on purpose.'

Mol shifted away from me, hands held up, head shaking from side to side.

'Calm down, Tiger. None of this is anybody's fault. You can't blame anyone. Not Tim's wife – only doing the necessary – and not me. She would have died anyway. We all know that. Looking for death was little Juliette. I forgot I had it. Bit of a panic in there, after all. Completely slipped my mind. But it wouldn't have made any difference. You know that.'

We clambered out in silence, but your man Mol was buoyant. Entirely unaffected by the trauma of the night, he gave us a cheery thumbs-up and disappeared into the dark. 'See you again soon, lads,' he called just before we shut the car door. No-one replied, but it didn't seem to bother him.

No-one spoke in Mikey's house, either. He wandered about, dumping sleeping bags and armfuls of blankets on the front-room floor. He made a big pot of tea and silently pointed to the milk and sugar. He put a loaf of Mother's Pride next to the toaster, then nodded to the corner stairs.

'I'm going to bed, guys. Bathroom's up here. Door on the left. Door on the right is my bedroom. If you get cold, there's a gas fire in the front room. See you later.'

After Mikey's departure we had our tea. It tasted normal, tea-like, which I was grateful for. Then we arranged the motley assortment of bedding and lay down. Yeah, I know. I know what you're thinking. We should have looked after her. We knew she was bonkers and we should have kept an eye. Well maybe, but it's too late now. No point crying over spilt milk is what my mum used to say.

Mikey woke us at half two in the afternoon. He was up and showered and wandering about in his Y-fronts showing off his muscles. What is it about smilers? They say we're all the same, but that's obvious bollocks. Take Mikey's physique, which he was keen to share with the rest of us. Anyway, never mind, because our attention was distracted from Mikey's convincing impersonation of Mr Universe by the sound of the front door being battered in.

The battering continued, accompanied by shouting. Mikey went to the door and looked through the spyhole. He beckoned to me and, very quietly, I walked up behind him, and put my eye to the hole. There were two men outside, behind them a car in which other people were sitting. The men were both in their early twenties, heavily built and powerful with short, razor-cut hair. One had a spider's web tattooed on his neck. Clearly suicidal in this area of Nottingham, they were shouting, 'Open the door, nigger,' and hammering with their fists. I stood up straight and took a swift look at the door. Like any self-respecting crack dealer, Mikey had a steel-reinforced door with double locks.

Mikey looked at me and raised his eyebrows. I shook my head emphatically. Following Mikey, the four of us tiptoed out of the front room into the kitchen. Mikey signalled for us to stay put, then silently climbed the stairs. His bedroom was directly over the front room and the bathroom was over the kitchen. The back door opened onto the backyard. The back wall was about ten metres away, and it had a narrow wooden door which opened onto a jennel. Mikey had covered the door and wall in razor wire and electric fencing. No-one could get through there in a hurry. The hammering on the door had reached crescendo level. Chico, Dekka and I were gazing up the steep narrow stairs whence Mikey had disappeared when we heard the sound of a sash window being pulled up and Mikey's sleepy, irritable voice: 'What the fuck's going on? Can't a man get no sleep in this world?'

More shouting followed, although we couldn't hear what was being said. I didn't need to hear the words, I'd know that voice anywhere in the world. Then Mikey replied, 'Listen up, man. I live here on my own. The only other people who stay in my house are my brother and my woman, and neither of them have any business with you.'

More shouting and noise. Another bout of hammering at the door. Mikey again: 'OK, my friends, I'm gonna tell you a couple of things. Give you some education. My brother Laurence ain't here; he's down London. My woman ain't here neither. I am here. My name's Mikey,

I'm here. I'm here alone, and I'm tryin to get some rest. That's the first thing. Second thing is, I don't take kindly to strangers hammerin and screamin on my doorstep, and I don't take kindly to being called nigger by shite like youse. So, my friends, if you want to walk out this neighbourhood in one piece, I suggest you leave now. If you want to stay, then stay. I'll be right down, and me and the other niggers on the street will come out and have a nice discussion, like.'

Silence ensued, then Mikey came down the stairs.

'You hear what they said?' he asked.

I didn't really need to hear what they said, and when Mikey told us it came as no surprise. They were looking for three lads from Donny. These three lads had been grassing to the police, they said. Caused a lot of trouble had these three boys, then legged it. Done a runner and vanished. They'd heard that three lads were staying with Mikey, hence they called round. You see, these boys were wanted back in Doncaster. They'd got a bit of explaining to do. If by any chance Mikey did run across them, well then, he should tell them to go home. He should tell them that Gary Gibbson and Paul Tickle want to see them. Want to see them quite badly.

We made some more tea to calm our nerves and sat down with Mikey.

'Weird guys,' he said. 'And who's the fucker with the voice? Has someone chopped his bollocks off? Real weird it was.'

I looked at Dekka and half smiled. Gibbsey's rusty, squeaky schoolgirl's voice was not a safe topic of conversation in Donny. Taking the piss out of Gary Gibbson was like volunteering to sign your own death certificate. 'Well?' said Mikey. I shrugged. There didn't seem much point in pretending, so we told him more or less the whole story. We told him about the late-lamented Teapot and Mr Gary Gibbson and crew, and we told him we were off down the smoke, with a deep and heartfelt desire to put the aforementioned well behind us.

'OK,' said Mikey. He looked round at the three of us and gave us a slow grin. 'I'm going to make you an offer you can't refuse. If you guys would care to hop into my motor in a couple of hours' time, and if you're prepared to make a charitable contribution to the petrol and driver's running costs, then I'll give you a ride to the smoke and get you away from the gangstas on your tail.'

'Why would you want to do that?' I asked. My natural belief in the ultimate goodness of humanity had never been overwhelming.

'Decided this is a good time to visit my bro,' said Mikey, stepping into a pair of drawstring trousers with enough material in them to clothe the rest of the street should they have chosen to get in there with him. 'I ain't seen Laurence for a couple of months, and besides' – pulling on a T-shirt resembling a small tent, with the legend 'OJ' on the front – 'I'm sorry the bitch is dead and all that, if she was your woman' – this to Chico, who looked at the floor and then looked away – 'if she was your woman, I'm really sorry. But the bottom line is any stiff is bad news. I don't want the po-lice anywhere near me. I don't want your white-boy posse after me neither. So I'm going to get myself outta here. If I was a total, double-six, mega-cunt, I'd leave you and fuck off solo. Which would be the sensible thing. But I have some self-respect, and I think your Mr Gibbson needs a lesson in good manners. So I'll help get you outta here. But I want the petrol money up front, now.'

'How much?' I said.

'Twenty quid between you. In fact, make that twenty-one. Seven each. No arguments that way.'

Dekka nodded at me and fished in his pocket. Chico, who seemed to be operating on some sort of autopilot, handed over his share in silence.

Mikey counted the money, then nodded. 'OK. I've got arrangements to make, business stuff. I need to see a few people and set a few things up. I'll be back inside the hour. I might have a couple of mates with me. Look through the spyhole before you let me in. Right, I'm off. My mobie number's above the fridge. If I'm not back in two hours, ring.'

We spent the next hour loitering miserably around Mikey's flat. Dekka watched *Man About the House* on Sky Gold. Chico sat in silence. Every car engine, every footstep on the street outside was Gibbsey and Ticka coming back for a rerun of *Teapot: The Movie*. I went upstairs and looked out Mikey's bedroom window up and down the street. I went down to the kitchen and looked out the back window. I couldn't sit still. Hurry up, you dozy black bastard, for fuck's sake. This was doing my head in. I decided to take a dander outside, take a recce out the back. Check for possible escape routes. Whatever.

It took me several minutes and quite a lot of hard work to get the back door open, which gave me some comfort. I also noted the steel-strengthened hinges and the protective metal security gate. My professional respect for Mikey went up a notch. The backyard itself was a bit of a tip and nothing to write home about. A small shed affair at the far end. Loads of junk lying about.

'You didn't listen to my advice, and now look what's happened.'

I was so shocked I fell over the stairs which led from Mikey's back door into the yard. Luckily there were only three. I looked up to see Mikey's next-door neighbour, a chubby middle-aged bloke, leaning over the wall. He gave a supercilious sort of smile. I recognized him immediately.

'Well, fuck me sideways. You're the cunt from the caff.'

'There's no fooling you, my young friend. Remarkable powers of observation. Sadly your ears are not as needle-sharp as your eyes. You didn't listen, did you? My advice went unheeded.'

'Look, chavito,' I said, 'why don't you just fuck off out of it? I don't want your "advice" as you put it. Don't give a fuck. You know nowt about me, so don't try and start comin like me dad.' Why I said this is anyone's guess, me dad having fucked off pronto the moment Mam passed on the happy news that little Danny was on his way. Mam still remembers his name, though I don't carry it, and if she's drunk enough, still goes on about how 'special' he was. Oh yeah, Mam, really dead special. Wouldn't know the cunt if I fell over him. Anyway, back to tubby git next door.

He stood on his top step and leant on the wall with his elbows. 'Listen if you can. What you hear will be of benefit. You must resume your journey. Death and despair follow at your heels and will soon outrun you. Yet hope remains and a gleam of light still shines. Follow the straight road south. Do not delay, do not turn aside.'

'You obviously think all this fuckin riddle-me-re stuff is dead impressive,' I said. 'But it's all bollocks to me, amigo. You're wasting your breath.'

He shook his head. 'You are not lacking in wits. Why else was the task assigned to me? If persuading dumb beasts were the matter in hand Francis would be here in my stead. You should recognize a compliment when you see one.' Then he smiled. 'But you haven't remembered me yet?'

I shook my head. 'Total blank, chava.'

He rested his elbows on the wall and peered down at me. 'It will come to you.'

'I can't wait,' I said.

A funny whirring noise came from somewhere in his backyard. I stood on tiptoe and could just see this funny-looking kid in a go-kart. Well, I say kid because he was kiddish, although he was a bit big. Maybe he'd just had a prang, 'cos there was blood, but I couldn't see where from, he was at the wrong angle and too far below me. The kid started making funny snuffly noises, like it hadn't learned to talk yet.

Tubby had one last shot. 'Remember, the straight road. Any error will prove costly,' and with that he turned aside to help the kid, who was, in my opinion, not playing with a full team. I went back inside. I was totally fucking sick of nutters.

Mikey turned up about twenty minutes later with one of the brothers in tow. Dwayne, as they called the unlucky bastard, was to hold the fort until Mikey's return. In ten minutes we'd left Dwayne in possession of Mikey's crack empire and were piling our bags into a red BMW that had seen better days. By this point it was well dark and all I wanted was to get my arse out of Nottingham.

At first, when Mikey drove past signs for the M1, I thought he was being a canny local and taking a short cut. Later on it became dismally clear he was headed elsewhere.

'Kin'ell, chav,' I said eventually. 'What's going on?'

'Bit of business, man. Loose ends. Won't take half an hour.'

We took an underpass that led onto a dual carriageway skirting the city centre. We passed the station, then turned off by an ice rink and began cutting through backstreets. It was cold and the wet streets reflected the lights. There were a few people about: girls standing in little knots, hanging on corners; men walking with heads down and collars up. Mikey stopped the car, put the headlights on full beam and hit the horn. Two lasses, one black, one white, immediately moved towards us at a sharp clip, wobbling slightly on their heels as they tip-tapped across the street. They reached Mikey's window and leant down, the black girl in front. Both were smiling, but you could smell the fear on them. Fear, and maybe something else: anticipation? Dread? Excitement? Who knows.

'It's mah main man,' said the black girl, teeth flashing. 'Has Daddy got some sugar for his best baby girl?' She was so close she was practically climbing inside the car. Eyes wide and mouth slightly open. She wore purple lipstick.

'Get out my face, Delilah,' said Mikey. 'Back off some, girl, and you and skinny-ass bitch listen up and listen good. And if I think your listening is up to standard, well, your good daddy might just see what he can do.'

She didn't need telling twice. Delilah pulled her head out the car window, then she and the white girl crouched down by the door, faces level with Mikey, expressions of rapt attention. You might well be asking why Mikey had slipped from native Notts into a poor approximation of New York rap. No mystery, you see, he was largin it, being the big show boy, telling the girls who was the boss. Spades do this all the fucking time. Yeah, me last contact with the sunshine of Jamaica was when Granddaddy got on the boat back in 1957. Yeah, born and raised in Balby, Donny, South Yorks, GB. Yeah, nearest I've been to the Caribbean is looking at the Bacardi ad on telly, but that doesn't stop me talkin a lot of I & I shite when the mood takes me. Gets fair on me tits, I have to tell you.

'I'm taking a small trip outta town, like,' said Mikey. 'I'll be gone a few days, no more. While I'm gone, Dwayne takes over. While I'm not here, he is me, you follow?' The girls nodded silently. 'You give him exactly the respect you give your daddy, that clear?' More nods. 'So that means business as usual. No putting out the slack because I'm not watching over you. I expect my usual money good and waiting, and I don't want to hear any half-arsed excuses about being two hundred down because of this or that bollocks. Do we understand each other?'

'Every word clear as the day,' said Delilah. Skinny Ass nodded.

'I don't hear you say anything,' said Mikey. 'Praps you're confused?'

You could see the tightness play across her pallid face. The words came out quiet but audible. 'Yeah, Mikey, I understand.'

'OK.' Mikey reached into his pocket. 'Time for the presents.' The girls bent forward, their faces thrust towards him. 'Oh, I forgot.' Mikey brought his hand out empty and grinned. 'I've saved the important stuff till last.' Utterly still, the girls dragged their eyes from his pocket and listened. 'Now, as I'm away, I don't want anyone getting restless, don't want anyone fancying a change, don't want anyone coming over all independent, like. Am I really clear on this one? Like crystal clear?'

'Baby, are you crazy? You think I'd ever throw you over. You think I'd look at another—' Delilah's sentence came to an end as Mikey grabbed her by the back of the neck and banged her head hard against the edge of the window.

'Don't talk to me like that, you stupid bitch. You don't have no options on throwing me over, you silly tart. You work for me. And if you ever forget that, you'll have a face full of acid. Do you read me?'.

Her forehead was already swelling where she'd nutted the car, but credit where it's due, she kept her wits about her. 'Yes, Mikey. I understand. I know where you're coming from.' Mikey turned to Skinny Ass and raised an eyebrow. 'Yes,' she said, 'yes, I understand. I'm clear. Yes, Mikey, I understand.'

Mikey smiled. 'Good girls. OK, here come the sweeties.' He handed out three rocks apiece. 'And don't say Daddy isn't good to you.' The girls were grinning now. Genuine smiles of thanks and happiness. They both kissed him. 'When you run out, you go to Dwayne, but don't get greedy now. He'll be keeping a tally. OK, my babies, go and get some money earnt.'

They smiled and waved and said thanks. Delilah told him to have a good trip and be careful, and to be sure to get back soon. Skinny Ass said to take care, then they picked their way over the puddles back across the street. Skinny Ass wasn't much, about seventeen, pallid with blond hair and a thin mouth, but Delilah had some class. A real body on her, that one. One of those brilliant black girl's asses, high and round and hard, like an apple. She was darker than Mikey, who was half-caste or thereabouts, and there was something about the way she showed her teeth when she talked. I've never had a black girl, you know. D'you think they're different? I thought about asking our mate, Mikey, but decided to wait until we got to the smoke. I didn't want to be chucked out the car if he took it badly.

We were back on the ring road and then tooling off towards the M1. 'Ow far to London, amigos?' asked Chico. 'Ow long?'

'Christ,' I said. 'It talks. It moves.'

'Shut the fuck,' replied Chico, amicably enough. 'Ow far, mi amigo?'

'Two hours, max. It's a piece of piss,' said Mikey. He looked at the dashboard clock. 'Bit a luck we'll make it for last orders.'

111

We shot down the wet, black road, putting the miles between us and the psychos, moving further and further away. Mikey drove fast and well, doing a ton with no apparent effort, the braids on his head stuck out like a mane and his broad hands were tight on the wheel.

I bet you've gone off our Mikey, haven't you? I bet you were just coming over all cosy, enjoying a happy little glow of racial harmony, and then he went and spoilt it all. Well, what the fuck did you expect? Girls don't stand on the streets in the rain for the fun of it. You have to force them to do it. Keep them at it. Especially a classy bint like Delilah. Give her half a chance and she'd be eating your balls fried on a plate. So you keep them down. I have to say, all told, they looked in pretty good shape for a pair of crack-addict street whores, which I think reflects pretty well on Mikey's management skills. Do you think he fucks them? Not sure meself. I mean, the black girl was well fit, but I'd worry about catching something. Even if she always, always uses a rubber. Even if she resists every single time, no matter how skint, when a punter says, 'Double money for no johnny,' and believe that and you'll believe anything. But for the sake of argument, lets say she does. But it's not just the big stuff like AIDS and syphilis, there's scabies, crabs, herpes and God knows what else. You'd always feel she was a bit ackie, wouldn't you? A bit second hand, soiled goods, reduced to 30p in the charity shop, all proceeds to Oxfam. Nah. Don't fancy it much. She's all yours, Mikey.

Chico was in the front, beside Mikey, and me and Dekka sat behind. About ten miles out of Nottingham Dekka had fallen asleep, slumping annoyingly on my left shoulder. I kept trying to shove him off, but every time I did he mumbled a bit and flopped back. Eventually I gave up and left him to it. He must have been dreaming, cos his eyes were flicking back and forth below his lids and he kept making funny squeaky noises. Once I thought he said, 'Please, no please.' But knowing Dekka it was probably 'Peas, no peas.' I wouldn't say my marrer mayor was thick, but, as he would be the first to admit, I'm the brains of this outfit.

Mikey had put the motor on cruise control. The motorway was pretty clear and we just carried on surging quietly forwards. Occasionally some tanked-up nutter or hyper-stressed sales bloke would shoot past, but in the main we were undisturbed. I saw a sign saying, 'London 77', and then looked out the window at the car passing in the outside lane. It seemed to slow as it drew level and, unbelievably, miraculously, so entirely out of the blue, I saw her face.

Her long dark hair fell past her shoulders, and in the pitch dark I couldn't make out who she was with, who else was in the car. She was in the front seat, and she turned full face to me and seemed to spread her arms, and as I stared, transfixed, she smiled and my heart felt like it had burst inside me. I was flat against the car window, leaning towards her, longing for her. She was the lily in the field and the stars in the sky. The car began to pull away and she turned back towards me. She did; she turned her head for me and she kept smiling, and she was brighter than the sun.

And then the car was gone, moving ahead, straight as an arrow, and I could see no more. The darkness returned and the new moon shone pale and white above the orange glare of the streetlights. I felt strange inside, sort of warm and sad at the same time. I couldn't understand, you see. But there was no-one to ask.

When I was little, every time I got the chance, I used to run across the road to the presbytery. Sometimes, when me mam went AWOL, I'd stay all night. And if I didn't understand, Father O'Flynn would explain. 'Questions, Danny,' he'd say, 'so many questions.' And then he'd pick me up, sit me on his lap and smile. 'I'll tell you what, my son, we'll see what answers we can find. But,' and here he would lean his face closer to mine and whisper, 'I'll start by telling you a secret, but keep it to yourself. The secret is, my boy, that there are many more questions than answers.' He used to say that questions were bold and brassy, always drawing attention to themselves, always shouting and showing off. But answers, he said, answers were shy wee things. Sometimes they hid in books and sometimes they hid inside our heads or our hearts, but it was never easy to find them. You had to search quietly and carefully, otherwise they'd run away.

I'll tell you something, something I've not told me mam, or Dekka, or anyone. I think I loved him. He used to wear an old cassock, rusty black with age, buttons down the front. When he picked me up, I used to bury my head under his arm and curl up my knees. I'd shut my eyes and the world would go away, so all I could hear was his low voice quietly singing. 'I'll give you one-o/Green grow the rushes O.' Eventually I'd join in: 'Five for the symbols at my door/And four for the gospel makers/Three, three the rivals/Two, two the lily-white boys, clothed all in green-i-o/One is one and all alone/And ever more shall be so.' All the old songs. We'd sit and sing for hours. Every time he tried to stop, I'd beg for 'just one more, Father. Only one more, please.'

I wanted so much for him to think well of me, I used to lie in confession. 'Bless me, Father, for I have sinned. It has been seven days since my last confession.' School made us go every week, you see. Then I'd come out with a little list of minor misdemeanours. Sin of pride – showing off

114

because I'd been picked for the football team. Sloth – left my homework two days running. I couldn't bear to tell him the truth, couldn't confront him with the crap reality of my life. Stupid thing is, he might not have minded. But I couldn't take the risk, you see.

'*Agnus Dei, qui tollis peccata mundi.*' Can that be done? Father O'Flynn used to say mass in St Peter's, and we'd all go from school. That was my favourite bit. All kneel for the *Agnus Dei*. 'Lamb of God, who takes away the sins of the world,' and then we'd all join in: 'Have mercy on us.' The sins of the world. Can you imagine how many? What does He do with them? Can they be deleted, like on-screen mistakes? Or are they all logged, docketed and filed. Cross-referenced, so you can look up M for murder, or W for West, or G for Gloucester, and you'll find the duplicate? And do you have to truly, honestly, repent before He gets the sin, otherwise you get to keep it? What would you do with the sins of Fred and Rosemary West? I mean, you wouldn't want them hanging round the house, would you? '*Qui tollis peccata mundi.*' What's He done with Freddie's sins? Although, seeing as he topped hisself, Fred and the entire parcel are probably not His responsibility.

Interesting that stuff, I thought. Inter-breeding you see. They're all at it in these rural shitholes, nothing else to do of an evening except fuck your sister. And it's interesting what we can achieve when we push ourselves, isn't it? You know, when we really try. I mean, look at Freddie. Total no mark. Crap job, crap house, crap clothes, crap car. You couldn't accuse him of overachieving. But then there was the other Fred, not the amiable, lumpy, dim bloke the neighbours knew, but Fred the master-murderer, who kept it up for over twenty years. Did over his first wife, his kids, anyone daft enough to stay in his house and, if supply was getting low, went out and found them at bus stops and the like. Can you imagine if Fred had put all that thought and energy into his career? He'd be managing director of ICI by now.

Sometimes I think about those girls and it frightens me. I can touch their terror, their claustrophobia and disbelief. Helpless while those two lumbering animals called the shots. I'm not usually bothered by these things, but this one got to me. I saw something on telly about one of the girls. She was a decent lass, a student, and religious as well. He taped her face up and gave her a straw to breathe through, and when he'd finished he buried her, head down, in a sewage drain. 'And I hope she died quick/And I hope she died clean/O young Willy McBride/Was it slow and obscene?' When her family finally got her back, twenty years on – three cheers for the police and a bouquet of roses for the social services – they reburied her, or what was left of her. Her sister put all this stuff in her coffin. Favourite books – she was studying medieval art of all things – mementoes from her bedroom, family photos and a pair of fluffy bedsocks. The sister cried about the bedsocks. She said Lucy used to get cold feet.

chapter five

FIRST THING WE DID WHEN WE GOT TO LONDON WAS have a jag. By the time Mikey was over the M25 we were beginning to feel the need, and he didn't need much persuading to stop. We went to this big pub. A gabled affair called Swiss Cottage, which did a passing fair imitation of a real Swiss cottage, except that it was stuck in the middle of three dual carriageways, which slightly detracted from the Alpine ambience.

We got the drinks in, then went in twos to the bogs. It's always a pain having to hit up away from home, but what else can you do? Once the four of us were feeling human we had a serious chat. The plan all along had been for me, Dekka and Chico to doss at a place in North London. There were a couple of Donny lads there already, and Dekka had a sort of open invite as they were mates of his bro. We intended to give it a couple of days to get our bearings and then take it from there. Obviously the ever-present problems of money and drugs would have to be attended to eventually, but we were sound enough on that score to be able to lie low for a day or so. The hope being that, if we gave it a couple of weeks, the police would get their act together, Gibbsey and Co. would be safely locked up and we could return to the land of our birth.

Mikey told us he was off to stay with his brother, who lived off Ladbroke Grove. He gave us the address and his mobie number, and we gave him the address of the squat and brought him another beer to say ta. He told us to keep in touch, but he needn't have fretted. I was relying on Mikey and brother Laurence for London drug contacts, so the likelihood of us never meeting again was slim. We were halfway down our second beer when time was called, and ten minutes later Mikey was tooling into the distance in the red BMW, and we three companyeros were standing outside Swiss Cottage tube station trying to figure out where the fuck we were going.

Dekka had an address: 13 Green Lanes, Hackney. So where the fuck was that? In the end the bloke in the tube station helped us out and sold us three tickets for Manor House station. He told us it was near there, and to ask again when we came out. He also told us to go to Finchley Road tube, which was just across the dual carriageway, and to change at King's Cross. We did as we were told. I don't like it when I don't know where I'm going; makes me feel stupid and unsure. At King's Cross people kept cannoning into the back of us as we stopped to read signs. Cocky fucking Londoners, who do this journey every day of their lives. I hated them.

Anyway, we weren't as green as we were cabbage looking, because we got the right train, and tooled up the Piccadilly Line with lots of other deadbeats, heading out to the places where people with any choice in the matter don't want to be. Manor House station was on a crossroad. Another whacking great dual carriageway running from north to south, intersected by Green Lanes, running east to west. There was a massive pub, wittily called the

Manor House, perched on the corner, and a bunch of dodgy-looking spades hanging outside it.

'What do you think, chavito?' said Dekka. 'Which way?'

How the hell was I supposed to know? Anyway, I made an executive decision and took the road left. To my relief, number 13 appeared about fifty yards from the junction. It was a big old detached house, with a flight of steps leading up to the front door. Stuck in the sea of mud which once might have been a front garden was a transit van with 'North London Posse' painted on the side. Next to it were two beat-up motorbikes and what appeared to be the wreck of an old Triumph Herald. We clambered up the front steps and leant on the bell.

The door was answered by a bloke in his fifties. He had cropped grey hair with three beaded plaits hanging down the back of his neck. He had bare feet, filthy jeans covered in writing and felt-tip drawings and a baggy purple T-shirt. 'Hi, my friends, how can we help you?'

I looked at Dekka and Dekka looked at me. No-one said anything. I took a deep breath.

'Are Terry and Jez around?'

'Sorry, my friend. They left. Left about two months ago. Gone to Wales, I think.'

Oh, just wonderful. Oh, fucking marvellous. Freezing me bollocks off in the middle of London, nearly one in the morning and nowhere to go. I looked at our decrepit crusty friend, forced an ingratiating smile on me clock and gave it me best shot.

'It's like this, you see. We're from Donny. Doncaster. And we're down in London, like. Anyways, we got this address from Terry and Jez, and they said, like, any time we're down, we should drop round. So we thought we'd take them up on it, like. Maybe stay a couple of nights.

Had no idea they'd left, and now we're pretty stuck. I mean, I know it's a bit awkward, but any chance of staying, just for tonight? We don't expect much, just some floor to kip on, but we're a bit stuck, you see.'

Decrepit crusty considered the matter. Told us his name was Trevor. Trevor Forever. Said that we could come in, but he would have to convene a 'house council' – whatever that might be – to decide if we could stay or not. I could clearly see that trying times lay ahead, but beggars can't be choosers, so in we trooped.

It was a tip. I mean a total tip. It smelt of damp and decay. Broken radiators hung off the walls, and a half-empty bag of cement lay at the bottom of the stairs, and, judging by the little light affair that Trev the mega-plonka was carrying, no electricity. I looked back at Chico and Dekka and curled my lip. Sharing my disgust, they returned the gesture. 'Decide if we could stay here?' Fuck me, they ought to fucking pay us for the privilege. Trev was still leading the way up the endless stairs. Stupid hippie cunt. What was he doin, pissing around like this at his age? I ask you. I mean really. People like that should be shot.

He led us into a big room, which had a TV at one end and a pool table at the other. The crumbling walls were pasted with flyers for toss-awful local bands and various posters defending the right to party, asking for the legalization of cannabis and banging on about single mothers and the SWP. Marvellous. Round the telly a few people were sitting on a battered settee watching some vid or other, the TV being hooked up to some big battery affair in the corner. Two blokes with coloured hair were playing pool. The floor was covered with ashtrays, glasses, newspapers and piles of unidentified shite.

Trevor Forever pointed to a couple of beanbags and

suggested we sit down. He gave us a beer apiece and then went off to convene his house council. The two lads playing pool said a vague 'hi man', but otherwise we were totally ignored.

'Mierda,' said Chico in my ear. 'Mierda mayor, Dannito. These fuck cunts from another planeet.'

'Esso es, chavito mio. Lost the plot big time. Listen, what we goin to tell them?'

'What about?' said Dekka, which was a bit on the slow side, even for him.

'About why we're here, fuckwit.'

'Sorry, marrer,' said Dekka. 'Wasn't thinking. But spot on. We can't tell this shower of weirdos about Gibbsey; they'd fucking wet themselves.'

'So we just come for small 'oliday?' said Chico. 'A leetle treep.'

I sniggered. Sometimes Chico sounded really daft. 'Yeah, amigo, "a leetle treep", as you say. That'll do.'

'Fuck you, gringo,' Chico said. 'But serious, companyeros, that's all we say?'

Dekka and I nodded. 'It'll have to do,' I said, 'cos it's all they're getting.'

Two minutes later Trevor Forever was back, with a trail of grotty-looking crusties behind him. You're not going to believe this, but the twat actually rang a little bell and shouted, 'House council.' We really are playing at being grown-ups, aren't we? Anyway, Trev was obviously numero uno in this gaff because the boys downed pool cues, the telly was switched off and everyone shifted enough debris to sit down in a circle in the centre of the room. We stayed skulking out the way on the beanbags, but Trev, obviously a true democrat, beckoned us forward, and a few more ashtrays were shifted so we could join the magic circle.

121

Trev introduced everyone. The two boys with the green hair were twins, called Tariq and Leon – middle-class tossers staging a ten-minute rebellion against Mummy and Daddy. I made a personal promise to kick their stupid white, even teeth down their throats before I left. If they were so keen to experience life on the edge, then I'd be pleased to give them a helping hand. There was Karen, dismal fat bint with whining toddler; a Cornish bloke with curly hair, called Barry; and a Dutch couple, called Johan and Eva. This cracking little group was completed by Kieran, half asleep and totally stoned; Tip, scrawny and ferrety; and a girl called Kim, who wore a zippy blue-and-white top, had short, dark hair and looked about fifteen.

Trevor, in his self-pronounced role of facilitator, introduced everyone, then asked us to 'tell us a little bit about yourselves'. Oh, for fuck's sake. Dekka shot me a look of pure horror. 'Claro, chav,' I muttered, then took a deep breath and opened my gob. I decided to speak for all three of us, for the very good reason that I was the least likely to fuck up.

'Hi,' I said – 'Hi', can you imagine it? – 'My name's Danny, and these are me mates Dekka and Chico.' Dekka and Chico smiled. Chico looked like a Hollywood star; Dekka looked like a psychopath.

'We've come down on a trip from Doncaster to meet Terry and Jez. Didn't realize they weren't here any more. We're only here for a couple of days, but we haven't really got anywhere else to go. It'd be great if we could just doss down for a couple of nights.'

Trevor Forever then went round the entire group asking what everyone thought. It was fucking endless, all of them blathering on about nothing for a good ten minutes apiece. The only exceptions being Kieran, who was asleep, and Kim, who was too young to hack it, and just said in a strangled voice that she thought it unfair to chuck us out. Hurray for Kim.

Johan, fucking clog-wearing Dutch bastard, wasn't keen. 'If you have come down to see your two good friends, what is the point of your staying here? I mean, I think you will like to go to Wales to find Terry and the other boy. Yes?'

Smart-arse cunt. 'I see what you mean, Johan,' I said, favouring him with my most brilliant smile, 'but the idea of the visit was to come to London. Tez and Jez are mates of Dekka's brother, like. And they always said we could stay any time, so when we got the money together, we thought, why not? But there's no point in going to Wales, cos we didn't come to see Terry and Jez; we came to see London.' I gave another smile; this one was smaller, self-deprecating. 'Y'see none of us as ever bin south before, and we wanted to see what London was like.'

This master stroke brought a murmur of sympathy. But our tulip-growing friend didn't seem impressed. It was all looking a bit touch and go.

By this time it was well past half-two in the morning, so they put it to the vote. Chico proved his worth, as all the girls voted for us to stay, including the lovely Eva. Johan, looking mucho pissed off with his other half, voted to turn us out, as did the wanky twins. Kieran abstained due to unconsciousness, Barry voted against and Ferret-face voted for. That left the thing tied at four against, four in favour. Complicated, democracy, innit? This was Trev's big moment. He announced, as house facilitator, he had the casting vote, then he rang his bell again and asked for silence, whilst he called on the 'spirit of the house' to guide him. I know it beggars belief, but the rest of the wankers actually took this mega-shite seriously. Trev sat cross-legged, hands on knees, and shut his eyes. I looked swiftly

123

at Chico and Dekka, then looked at the discarded pool cues, handily placed just to our right. They got my drift. Our new friend Trev had better say yes, otherwise it was straight into the ultraviolence. I closed my hand around my now-empty beer bottle. Six against three. I didn't care, we'd fucking kill them. Suddenly I realized Trev had snapped out of the meditation and was talking to us.

'. . . so as long as you're prepared to abide by house rules and make a contribution in terms of house labours, then we'll let you stay, at least for two nights.' He gave a big smile, like he'd just offered us the crown jewels on a silver plate. 'Ta very much,' I said, feeling a wave of disappointment. I'd been looking forward to sticking my bottle straight in his smug face.

Trevor then closed the house council and offered to show us where we could sleep. We went up two more mini flights of stairs to a small attic room, which was full of boxes. Trevor told us to move the boxes onto the landing, whilst he fetched the bedding. He returned, helped by Karen the fat bint, carrying a load of sleeping bags, duvets and the like. Trev disappeared again, whilst Karen hung around trying to be helpful and smiling at Chico. Trev came back with a piece of tatty red cloth, which he fixed up across the window as a sort of curtain. He also had a sheet of paper, which he handed to me. The house rules, no less. 'Cheers, Trev,' I said. 'OK, see youse in the morning.' Trev wondered if we'd like him to stay and go through the rules with us, to see if we could 'identify any points of conflict'. I said it was probably better we went through them carefully in the morning, as we were too tired to concentrate properly. This satisfied TF, who mercifully fucked off, dragging Karen with him. The minute they got out the door I chucked the house rules straight into one of the remaining cardboard boxes.

'What a shower,' said Dekka. 'I tell you, mi amigo, I couldn't stand more than two days here.'

'Why this Trevor not at 'ome with 'is familia?' enquired Chico. 'He's old man. What he do here? And you see the cunts play the pool? Fuck wankers, like Dekka say. He's right, Dannito, two days enough.'

'I'm with you every step of the way, companyeros,' I said. 'I think los tres should get out of this dump, pronto. What say we ring Mikey tomorrow and check out our options. By the way, Chico, don't know what you're complaining about. Only been here two hours, and already you've got a lovely chicitita sniffing round your bedroom.'

Chico grinned. 'No gracias, hombre. I theenk Karen more for you. She look a bit like your girl at home. What her name, Regi?'

'Fuck off,' I said. 'Reg might not be top-line shaggability, but at least she's not fucking fat. But seein as you mention it, amigo mio, I thought our Karen looked the spit of that big lass from Hyde Park you used to poke.'

Chico affected total bewilderment. 'You know who I mean, Dekka,' I said. 'Come on, marrer. She used to sit and stare at him with her tongue hanging out. Big lass, blondy-brown long hair. Had a white jacket with fur round the collar.'

Dekka's face suddenly lit up. 'Mandy,' he howled. 'Bandy Mandy. Of course I fucking remember.'

Dekka and I were almost crying with laughter, and eventually even Chico joined in. He agreed that Bandy Mandy was not exactly the high point of his shagging career, and in return we generously pointed out that lots of thirteen-year-olds make mistakes, and they can't be held responsible.

'So what do you reckon to the others?' I asked.

'Eva,' said Dekka. 'Bon-bon bonita. But cloggie boy was beggin for a slap.'

'Wasn't he just?' I agreed. 'Sooner we're out of here the better. Only problem is, where do we fucking go?'

'What about this Mikey?' Chico asked. 'We try for him manyana?'

Dekka and I both shrugged. 'Aye,' said Dekka. 'Have to see what the brother's like, and take it from there. She was all right,' he added. 'The young lass, the one who stuck up for us.'

'I've seen worse,' I agreed, trying surreptitiously to secure the best of the bedding for my corner of our little shelter from the storm.

Despite being on the floor, it wasn't too bad really. Trev had provided loads of sleeping bags and stuff for us to lie on, and if you wiggled about a bit it was possible to make quite a comfy little nest. I felt myself slipping into unconsciousness, like a newly launched ship freed from her moorings. 'I name this ship HMS *Danny MacIntyre*. Good luck to her and all who sail in her. Hip, hip, HOORAY, hip, hip, HOORAY, hip, hip . . .'

It was about midday when we surfaced and returned to the land of the living. If anything, the squat looked worse in daylight, and a more depressing dump it has never been my misfortune to visit. For a start there was no hot water, which was annoying, and the bog didn't flush, which was disgusting. Did this crew enjoy living like animals? Praps it made them feel closer to nature or something. Tossers.

We made ourselves some tea and went and sat in the big main room. Hardly anyone was about. Someone was playing what sounded like Prodigy at top volume, which hammered through the house and made watching the TV difficult. Shut your gob, Keith. I don't care how fuckin angry you are, I'm trying to watch *Grandstand*. The only other person in view was Kim, who was towing a big black bin liner, into which she was throwing empty cans and bottles and the general debris of the previous night. In the daylight she looked even younger than before. Thirteen or fourteen maybe, fifteen max. She didn't say much, just 'hello', and then carried on with her stuff. Dekka was right, she was actually quite passable, although a bit gawky for my taste.

She towed away the now full bin liner, and you could hear the empty bottles clattering as she dragged it down the stairs. Two minutes later she was back with a brush-and-pan affair, going round sweeping up all the ash and tab ends and God knows what else. Complete waste of time, of course, but maybe it made her feel useful.

We spent about an hour just sitting around, drinking tea and smoking, which was totally boring, but no-one could think of much else to do. Kieran ambled in and passed a spliff, and was joined by Barry and Tip. Nobody said much.

'Let's go out,' Dekka said. 'This is doin my head in.'

'Good idea, marrer mio,' I replied. 'Chico? You coming?'

The three of us hauled ourselves up, collected the drugs stash and made for the door. Even walking the streets was better than hanging around this dump. As we clattered down the stairs, Kim came out of a little room off the landing and followed us down.

'You goin out then?' Dekka asked her.

She looked startled for a moment, then nodded. 'Yeah. Just down to Fin Park. Nothing much.'

She told us that there were some shops and pubs and stuff down the road, and that she'd walk down and show us the way.

'Great,' said Dekka.

'Yeah, that'd be cool,' I said. 'Ta.' Chico said nothing, just smiled. Usually that was more than enough.

We walked alongside a waterlogged park with the thunder of London traffic accompanying us. Suddenly Dekka burst into song.

'I saw a mouse/Where?/There on a stair/Where on a stair?/Right there/A little mouse with clogs on/Well I declare/Going clip clipperty clop on the stair/Oh yeah.'

Coming up in the opposite direction were Johan and Eva. Dekka started again.

'I saw a mouse.'

'WHERE?' yelled me and Chico.

'There on a stair,' carolled Dekka.

'WHERE ON A STAIR?' me and Chico.

'Right there.' Dekka pointed at the advancing Johan. They were almost up to us now.

As they passed, we all joined in the finale: 'A little mouse with CLOGS on.'

He didn't say anything. Well, what could he say. Just carried on walking with a tight-arse expression on his face.

All three of us cracked up. Sometimes the simple pleasures are the best. 'Nice one, marrer mayor,' I said. 'Nice one.' I heard a funny breathy sound and looked round. It was Kim. She had her hand up to her mouth, but was laughing fit to wet herself. She finally got a grip, then half smiled at Dekka.

'Yeah,' she said. 'Nice one. Pair of stuck-up knobheads, they are.'

We carried on walking for another five minutes or so until we hit Finsbury Park. It's nowt to write home about. Not much money or much flash about, but different from Donny. Really different. The people for a start. Like some fucking refugee-camp overspill. Every shade you can think of. Snatches of foreign language, stuff in the shops you've never seen before. Kim told us little bits. Showed us the Arsenal shop by the tube, which was of note only for future wrecking expeditions. Showed us the Greek food shops, and the Indian sari shops, and a caff which she said was cheap and quite good. And she told us that they had a big Irish do in the park every summer, which you could hear from the house.

'I want some food, amigos,' said Chico. 'I'm fuck starving.'

Me and Dekka agreed, so we all trooped back to the 'cheap 'n' good' caff.

'OK, then,' said Kim. 'I'd better go. I'll see you later.'

'Aren't you hungry?' I asked.

'Nah. Not really. I'm—'

'Come on, you daft bint,' said Dekka. 'It's my treat, right? Get some scran down you.'

She hesitated, then shook her head. 'It's all right. I can't let you pay for me.'

'You can,' said Dekka. 'Why shouldn't I, if I want to? It's me own money.'

She grinned at that, and with all of us agreed we settled down at a table and gave full attention to the menu. Chico ordered steak pie and chips; I had shepherd's pie, peas and chips; Dekka, who can eat like a fucking horse when the mood takes him, had double cheeseburger and chips; and Kim, after a bit of pushing, had cod and chips. Plus four mugs of tea and four Cokes. Luxury or what? Sometimes, just sometimes, you have to say it, life is sweet.

The caff was sound. It was warm, the food was decent and it didn't cost an arm and a leg. I felt better with some hot scran in me belly. More ready to face whatever life had to chuck at me. I mean, you've got to have the basics in life: the drugs and the drink, tobacco, tea and sugar to get you on your feet in the morning. Those are the must-haves, but occasionally you feel yourself running down, like a motor in need of a full service. At such crisis points it's amazing what a decent pile of hot scran can do for you. It can really set you up. Gets rid of that hollow feeling, that cold, sicky, wasted feeling you get sometimes. They ought to have me on the adverts, didn't they? 'Dashing Danny Mac says you can beat the heroin blues. Just neck a massive slab of piping-hot shepherd's pie.'

'Wait a minute, amigos. I've finished my fuck cigarettes.'

'Here, Chico,' I said, 'have one of mine.' He was already out of his seat.

'No, s'OK, chavito. I have to buy anyway.'

'It's just across the road,' said Kim. 'You can see it from here.'

We sat finishing the dregs of our tea, waiting for Chico's return. Suddenly the door of the caff burst open with a violence that made my heart lurch. It was Chico. He stood in the doorway for a moment, grinning all over his face. He had something in his hand, which he started waving at us, and he was shouting and doing dance steps. He pirouetted the length of the caff to our table. Then he grinned again. 'Yes,' he said. '*Ave Maria.* Yes. Viva, viva, viva. *Ave Maria, Gracias a Dios.* Yes, amigos, yes. Yes.' He was still dancing and laughing. Then he cleared a little space on the table and plonked down the ticket in his hand. 'Mira, amigos, mira. Look this.'

It was a Lottery Instant. Chico was always spending on the 'lotteria', as he liked to call it. I was fond of explaining to him, via the science of probabilities, what an utter waste of time and money the whole thing was. Except it wasn't. Because lying there on the table was a sight more beautiful than the flight of angels. 'Over the Moon', said the ticket, beside a picture of a laughing cow bouncing on a space hopper. Next to the cow were six numbers, and three of them said exactly the same thing: £1,000. Chico had just won a thousand quid. Unbelievable.

We went crackers. Completely crackers. We even left a £5 tip in the caff. Madness or what? Then we pelted out in search of a post office so Chico could claim his dosh. Following Kim's advice, we came back past the Arsenal shop, down the tube, one stop and out onto the Holloway Road. Then we were jogging up the side of yet another dual carriageway – London's fucking full of them – crossing at the traffic lights, past a few cheapo clothes shops and into the big-style PO. Of course there was a fucking queue, which meant another ten minutes of purgatory, whilst Chico read the rules and the small print on the back for the thousandth time. Then he arrived at the front and reluctantly passed the ticket across and waited whilst the postie bloke disappeared with the world's most precious piece of cardboard.

It seemed ages, but he finally came back. Chico was waiting by the serving window, and Dekka and I were crammed in on either side of him. We stood transfixed by all that money, and watched the bloke count it out in clean tens and twenties. He put the cash in two plastic bags, £500 a piece. The bags were dropped into the serving drawer on his side, then he pushed it through and Chico picked them up. And that was that. We were loaded.

Natch enuf we went to celebrate. We took a taxi with Chico's new-found wealth and went to Camden. I can't remember what the pubs were like or what they were called, we went to so many. The afternoon became a blur of laughing, drinking and shouting. It was soon dark, and I'd more or less lost track of time. I wasn't even very clear where we were. At some point we settled in this pub. We'd had a ponder and decided that, seeing as Chico had some dosh, we needn't worry too much about eking out our stash. Fuck it. Blow it all tonight. We're celebrating, aren't we? Tomorrow we could phone Mikey and go and score. I mean, we're in fucking London, right? If you can't score smack here, where in the world can you? Chico said he'd made up his mind. He was going to give me and Dekka a hundred apiece, because we were his companyeros. We shook on it, then Dekka said he wanted to say something. 'It used to be me and Danny,' he said. 'Chavers together for ever. Two against the world. But now it's not two any more. We've been through it, the three of us. And now it's los tres.' Then he said sorry to Kim for leaving her out. But she said no sweat because this was very serious stuff and she knew it. Like I said, we were pissed.

We went down the bogs to do the drugs, as per usual. When I've finished the shepherd's pie ads, I could do a TV series, *Bogs I've Hit Up In, Danny Mac's British Tour*. The good burghers of the Camden Licensed Victuallers Association were obviously aware that their bogs were being used for purposes other than shitting, because the cunting landlord had removed all the toilet seat lids, plus the tops of the cisterns. To complete his anti-drugs crusade, he'd cut off all the sink taps and dyed the bog water dark, ammonia-smelling blue. Yeah, very clever mate.

Dekka had to go and fetch Kim and get her to check out there was no-one in the girls' toilets. Then she kept guard whilst I shot in an collected half a pint of cold water. It really was a mega pain in the arse all of this. Because of the landlord's fucking vandalism there was nowhere to cut up the gear. No flat surface to chop on. We ended up having to use a clean piece of floor. The whole thing was a time-consuming fuck-up. Even after the hit it wasn't over, cos we ran out of water and had to get Kim back to do the business. I needed the smack just to get over the trauma of getting it in my system. What a load of bollocks, I ask you. I mean, as you can see, it didn't stop us. Nothing could stop us. It just made the whole operation even more tiresome, dangerous and dirty than normal. Well done, mate, a real triumph in the drugs war. I felt like going over in his fucking toilet just to spite him. DONNY BOY IN DRUGS DEATH. Well, on second thoughts, praps not.

Anyway, after the toilets travesty we decided to take our custom elsewhere. We staggered off and shortly found another pub. Happily Camden seemed to be full of them. The one we ended up in, the Hogshead, was crammed with crusties. In one half, some sort of ultra-dire pub band was doing its soundcheck and warming up for what was obviously going to be a mega-shite performance. Luckily, you couldn't hear them too well from our end, so we got our drinks and settled down to watch the local kids honing their predictably crap pool skills.

We were happy. In fact, we were having a pretty good night of it. Chico, still laughing and doing the odd salsa shake, was explaining that tomorrow he was going to ring his mother and tell her he was sending a present. She could buy a plane ticket and go to see her sister in Madrid, buy a new dress, or go out for a really posh meal, or get some gadget for the caff, which had something to do with potatoes, but Chico wasn't very clear on that. Dekka, meantime, was getting more than friendly with Kim. I'd noted fairly early on that whatever pub we stumbled into they somehow ended up sitting together. Now Dekka had his arm along the back of her seat.

I was a tad surprised by this. Dekka's never been much of a one for the girls. Not much interested really. I mean, he's always had a girlfriend, some half-presentable bint hanging around in the background, but it's never been a priority for him. Dekka's one for the lads. He likes playing pool, drinking lager, watching the match on the telly, going out with his mates, getting loaded and having a ruck on a Saturday night. He was straightforward, was our Dekka. What you see is what you get. A big, strong, hard lad. A sound mate and a good laugh on a night out. That's about it. So, as I said, this comin on to Kim business was a bit of a surprise. She seemed to be actually encouraging him, which was fucking amazing, but there you go. Young love, magical innit?

Anyway, Chico and I carried on drinking, then we played a bit of pool. We were taking on the crusties for a fiver a go and winning hands down. To those that have shall be given more. Then, out of the corner of my eye, something caught my attention. Standing alone, at the side of the bar, was a tall thin bloke. He was watching us, and as we moved round the pool table his eyes followed. He just stood there, perfectly still, staring; the expression as empty and flat as a shark in the water. He was beginning to get on my tits and I dead-eyed him a couple of times, but to no effect. He just kept on watching, leaning against the bar in his long dark coat.

Eventually we won the game, and decided to get off the table, having scooped a respectable £25. I went back to join Dekka and Kim with Chico and asked if anyone fancied some chips, because I was going outside for a quick dander to get some speedy scran. No-one was interested, so I was away and over the road to a dodgy-looking kebab joint. I took the chip packet and strolled around outside. I suppose it was freezing, but I was drunk enough not to care.

We were quite near a canal, and I walked up to the

bridge and looked over. The water was dark and thick-looking. You wouldn't want to fall in there. Not like Teapot. He must have made quite a splash. I wondered if he'd been alive when he hit the water. Surely not. He'd have bled to death long before that. What the fuck made Gibbsey do it? I mean, what was the point?

Y'know, I saw something on telly this morning about Third World poverty. There were all these Indian blokes with various deformities, and they were having to beg, cos the DSS ain't up to much over there. Disability Living Allowance? I don't think so. Anyway, the camera panned across to this guy, and I thought I was going to be sick. He was kneeling in this little home-made cart affair. It was made out of bits of old wood and only about a foot off the floor. He was leaning forward and paddling with his hands to make the cart move along. He moved the cart up to the camera, and as he came closer you saw why he was kneeling in the cart. And when I saw the bone stumps sticking out, and the open, toothless mouth, I thought of Teapot. Thought of DI Stockwell and those fucking pictures and the horror at the heart of all this. And I very nearly chucked up.

I dumped the remainder of my chips and started to walk back to the pub. There was a tall guy waiting for a bus, and he was staring at me. They were all at it tonight. I mean, I know I'm well worth a second look, but this was getting ridiculous. As I drew nearer, the tall guy waved and smiled. Then I smelt the aftershave.

'It's you again,' I said.

'Too right, chav,' he replied. As he came forward, under the streetlights, his hair shone like gold. He must colour it; that sort of shine wasn't natural.

'I saw her again, you know,' I said. He nodded, but remained silent. 'I saw her in the car,' I continued. 'She

135

knows who I am, doesn't she? She looked at me. She turned her head and smiled at me.'

'Yes, chav,' his voice was soft. 'She knows you. Knows all about you. She even knows your name.'

I could feel a stupid smile spreading across my face. It must have been the drink. 'She knows my name,' I said.

He smiled back and nodded. Then the smile slipped and he tensed and turned round, scanning the road behind. 'This is a bad night, marrer mio,' he said, and beckoned me towards him, into the shadow of the bus shelter. He put his arm across my shoulders and inclined his head. His breath smelt of flowers. 'Listen, amigo, and listen carefully. Go back to the pub, find your companyeros and go home. This is a bad night to be out.'

'What are you on about?' I asked. 'None of this bollocks makes any sense.'

'Oh, I think you'll find it's sound advice,' he said quietly. 'Just take my word for it. Go home, amigo. And tomorrow you have to move. Manyana you find the lion. Esso es, chavito. Look, my number's up.'

And so saying he skipped on a number 9 bus and disappeared into the night. He even had the gall to wave to me out the back window.

It must have been the drink wearing off, cos suddenly I quite fancied going back. I was tired and felt a bit ackie and wasted. We'd been at it for hours, and it was probably time to turn it in. I walked back to the Hogshead, and decided to tell Chico and Dekka that one more pint would do me.

I walked in to complete pandemonium. The band had packed in, and a tape had been put on at top volume. Chico was dancing with a girl whose long black hair almost reached her waist. Loads of other people were shuffling around to the music and a gaggle of crusty girls were doing a sort of conga round the pool table. Dekka was nowhere to be seen, and I had to check the place twice over before I found him. He was sat in an alcove with Kim on his knee, and he looked like he was swallowing her tonsils. So what the fuck was I supposed to do? In the circs there seemed only one sensible option. I bought a bottle of Becks, and sat down and waited.

I didn't see him, but I heard the shout. 'Ey up, old mate. Fancy seeing you here.' It was Mol, the shortarse with the hat. He limped over, plonked himself down on the seat next to me and poked me in the ribs. 'If it isn't the tiger cub himself. Young Danny Boy.'

'Fuck off,' I replied. And meant it.

Mol seemed to think this was a huge joke. He laughed a lot and poked me in the ribs again. Then he straightened his hat and told me I was 'a right one'.

'Yeah, aren't I just?' I said. 'Sorry, can't hang around, we were just off.'

'Off where?' he asked.

'Oh, to this mate's gaff,' I replied.

'Near here, is it?' asked Mol.

'Yeah,' I said vaguely. 'Not too far.' Why didn't he just fuck off? I couldn't stand the stunted little bastard.

'So where are you staying?' he pressed on. 'In Camden? Or somewhere else?'

'What is this?' I said. 'Twenty bleeding questions? Look, next time I'll try to remember me postcode, but right now I'm knackered, and seeing as they've just rung time, I'm going to say ta ra and go and grab me marrers.'

Mol winked at me. 'If you want your marrers, Danny Boy, you'll have to move it. They're coming with us. We've been invited to a party. Can't promise it'll be as shit hot as our last little get-together, but we'll give it our best shot, old mate.'

I didn't bother replying. I got up and went straight over to Dekka and tapped him on the shoulder. 'Oy, lover boy, I want a word.' Dekka dropped Kim and came up for air. He looked flushed and very pissed and his eyes were glittering.

'Alrate, chavver. Where you been? Listen up, Mol's here.'

'I know,' I said. 'I've just seen the little toerag.'

'Oh, come on, he's not that bad. He's given me and Chico a wrap of coke. D'you want a line before we go to this party?'

'I don't know,' I said. 'I was thinking of going back and getting me head down.'

'Nah,' said Dekka. 'You can't do that. It's only eleven. I'm not hanging round that dump a minute longer than I have to. Have some coke; you'll be right.'

I looked across at Chico. He was still with the black-haired girl and obviously totally off his head. The girl was running her hands up and down his chest. I turned back to Dekka, then looked at Kim. Her face told the story. The stupid bastard had given her a line of coke; probably the first she'd ever had. What a total fucking waste of gear. I lost my temper.

'You got the coke wrap, Dekka?' I said coldly. Too drunk to notice my tone, he nodded and passed it over. 'How much has she had?' I said.

'Oh come on, chav,' said Dekka. 'It was only a line. Not much. She wanted to try it.'

'So you gave her some before I'd had my cut. Very nice. Listen, chav, these are our drugs. Us three. You don't share them with any passing bit of skirt. I thought you fucking knew that. And as for you,' I said, looking at Kim, 'if you fancy getting into gear, well go and find your own. Keep your sticky little fingers out of my stash, otherwise you'll be really fucking sorry.' I was so angry I wanted to hit her, which was stupid, because one line wasn't a big deal. But that's how I felt.

'Tranquilo, chav,' said Dekka. He looked hurt and embarrassed and bewildered. 'I'll take Kim's line out of my take, claro? It's no big deal.'

I nodded and felt a bit ashamed. 'OK, marrer. Forget it. Let's go to this sodding party.'

Of course, once I'd done the coke I felt considerably better. So much better, in fact, that when Chico grabbed my arm and told me Mol was giving us all a lift to the party, I got in the car without a murmur. Dekka, Kim, Chico and the girl with the hair were fellow passengers. Mol, his feet barely reaching the pedals, tooled off across London.

After fifteen minutes or so we crossed the river. To the left was St Paul's, a great, golden cross on top of the dome. The river was all lit up, steel posts with big balls of white light marching down either bank, and boats with strings of party lights and big fuck-off buildings with laser and neon. It was the width and the space of it all that took your breath away. Through my cocaine eyes it looked fabulous, unreal city, like something out of a book. What business did I have being here?

I was sitting in the front with Mol, and as the car sped southwards I asked him where we were headed. He said it wasn't far now, and as I looked out I could see the landscape fading, the buildings getting shabbier and the shitlands starting. Twenty minutes later we were there.

'OK, lads,' said Mol, climbing out of the car. 'Here we go.'

chapter six

IT WAS A GREAT PARTY. LOADS OF DRINK, PLENTY OF drugs and lots of totally wasted girls just waiting for someone to take advantage. It was a couple of hours before I even came up for air, and when I did I couldn't find Dekka or Chico anywhere. I was still looking when some vaguely posh girl I'd had a grope with earlier shoved a bottle of vodka in my hand and, holding on to the shoulder of my jacket, towed me into one of the bedrooms. There was no lock on the door, but she didn't seem to care. She was the first girl I'd had since Reg in Donny, and that seemed like a lifetime ago. You might have thought all the drink and drugs would have put me in the nice-try, three-out-of-ten-for-effort category. But not a bit of it. Shagged her arse off, didn't I.

When I finally rejoined the fray, Dekka had reappeared. He had his arm round Kim, who looked fuckin dreadful. Her eyes were like piss holes in the snow, and her face was dead white. When he saw me, Dekka dragged her over.

'Danny, chav. I've been lookin fuckin everywhere for you. She's bin sick. I think I ought to tek her home.'

Looking at Kim I could see Dekka's point. It was on the

tip of my tongue to remind him that I'd wanted to go home three fucking hours ago, but I managed to stop myself. As someone once said, no-one likes a clever cunt. There were only a couple of lines of coke left, and I was shagged out, in every sense of the word.

'OK, chavver. Look, we'd better find Chico. Any idea where the fuck he is?'

Dekka hadn't a clue. I told him to stay put in a corner near the bogs and to look after Kim. I told him not to move on any account, and that I'd find Chico and be back pronto. We agreed we'd have to take a taxi back. Probably cost an arm and a leg, but we weren't exactly awash with options. Coming up to two in the morning, and no idea where we were, except that it was nowhere near Green Lanes. Having seen Dekka and bint safely deposited, I set off in search of Mr Latin Lover.

Chico was nowhere to be found. The place had seemed quite small from the outside, but once you got in rooms seemed to appear from nowhere, all of them crammed with people. I just couldn't find him. I even pulled the duvet off an ultra-pissed-off pair of party funsters, but it wasn't Chico. At first I was irritated, then angry, but after half an hour or so I began to panic. I checked back with Dekka a couple of times, but he'd seen no sign. Kim had been sick again and was hanging on to Dekka's arm like she was drowning. 'I want to go home,' was all you could get out of her. Yeah, me too, but where is fucking Chico?

It was on my third sortie that I bumped into him. I'd gone downstairs, to the basement, and he was standing in the doorway. Tall and thin he was, in this Seventies-style long leather coat, greased-up black ringlets hanging down his back. He was semi-leaning on the door frame, totally blocking the way, the way through. I pushed past and he

141

told me to watch myself. Then he caught my sleeve and pulled me back.

'No-one taught you any manners?'

'Spot on, mate,' I replied. I couldn't be bothered with it. I had to find Chico. I pushed on, but he still had hold of my arm.

'Well, I think good manners are important.'

'Yeah. Sorry, mate. I'm in a hurry.' I jerked my arm to get rid, but he still held on. So far I hadn't looked at him. My eyes had been fixed ahead, searching the blackness of the room behind for any sign of me marrer, but even with the jerk he hadn't let go of my sleeve. 'Look,' I said. 'Fucking pack it in, will you. If I pushed you, I'm sorry, but I'm on my way out. I'm just finding my friend, then we're leaving. So don't fucking start.'

The blow took my breath away. His grip transferred from my arm to my neck, and he slammed me, one-handed, against the wall. Took me straight off my feet and nearly cracked my spine. I couldn't believe how strong he was.

'No-one speaks to me like that. No-one. Do you understand?'

'Yeah,' I said. 'Yeah, OK. I'm sorry.' He was looking at me, his face inches away from mine. It was the bloke from the pub, the one who'd been staring. His flat shark's eyes shiny as wet pebbles. He moved his head back and looked at me as if he found it hard to focus. His grip was still tight around my neck, pulling me onto my toes and cutting off my breath. Behind him the basement was dark, relieved only by tiny orange bonfires, as whoever was in there carried on dancing and smoking in the gloom. His hand on my neck was cold, like he'd been outside or something, and I could feel the cold spreading. For the first time I began to feel frightened. There was something wrong with this bloke, something not normal, a schizo maybe? Or an escaped loony? My breath was getting shorter, and he was still staring at me, like he was waiting for what would happen next. I pulled back my shoulders and dragged as much air as possible down into my lungs.

'Drop it, marrer,' I choked out. 'I'm sorry, OK? I said I was sorry.'

His grip relaxed and I straightened up, then came a voice in my ear.

'Hey up, Tiger, I see you're getting acquainted with my mate. Bez, meet Tiger, our friend from sunny Donny.'

It was Mol, smiling all over his face, nodding and winking, seemingly oblivious to the fact that his best mate had almost killed me. The Bez guy turned to Mol.

'Thank you, my friend, but my own introductions were going smoothly.' Mol nodded, hopping from foot to foot and said, 'Well, I'll be off then.' Bez just looked at him with empty eyes. 'Why don't you do that?' he said, and the next moment Mol had disappeared.

Obviously I was dealing with serious nutter material here. My instinct was to follow Mol and fuck off pronto, but first I had to find Chico. Sometimes I'm just too heroic for fuckin words. I took another deep breath and dug in. 'Look,' I said. 'I didn't mean to be rude, and I definitely didn't mean to piss you off, but I'm looking for me mate. The girl we brought with us is not so good and we need to get back home. So can you just let me through, and I'll find me mate and we'll fuck off and leave you in peace.'

The guy smiled. His teeth were terrible. Nightmare teeth, long and uneven, with cavernous dark gaps. He shook his head, then lifted a long-fingered hand to his mouth. 'Oh, I don't think that's very likely. Why don't you just go back to the party?' As he spoke he was testing his teeth, holding each one between finger and thumb. One of the front ones was loose, and he began waggling it back and forth, pushing at it with his long red tongue. He seemed to have almost forgotten me, but he was still holding my arm, his body interposed between me and the basement room. I felt a sudden certainty that Chico was in there.

'Sorry,' I said. 'It's time to go. So let go of my fucking arm, will you.'

He said nothing. Just stood there smiling, fingers in mouth, his hold on me unmoving.

'OK, you win.' I grinned at him. 'It's a fucking party. Why not enjoy it.'

I turned away to make back up the stairs, and he let me go. I walked up the stairs and round the corner, then stopped dead. Y'see, I knew Chico was in there. I'd heard something while that tall thin fucker had hold of me. Just a muffled noise, but it was Chico, I was sure, and he hadn't sounded happy. I was going to go back and get him out of there.

I tooled back upstairs and found Dekka, still standing by his post. Kim had totally collapsed, and was practically unconscious, with her head on his shoulder. I told him the score and told him what I needed from him. At first he didn't want to leave her, but there was no way round it.

We manoeuvred Kim's inert form to a half-empty corner just off the hall and left her there propped up, then we went down the basement stairs. Bez was exactly where I'd left him, leaning up against the door frame. We went down together, Dekka in front, and as we got to the doorway Dekka lunged at Bez. 'All right, mate,' he cried and threw his arms out. 'Haven't seen you in ages.' Bez tried to deal with thirteen stones of affectionate Dekka and field me at the same time. He got a hand to me, but before he could close his grip I wriggled through and away. I didn't look back. I'd just have to trust Dekka to cope.

I found Chico on a mattress in a pitch-dark room in a far corner. He was alone and crying.

'Chico. Chico amigo, tranquilo. It's me, Danny. S'OK, amigo, what happened?'

Chico put his hands up to his face and jammed his body further into the corner. He didn't know me.

'Chico. Come on, amigo. It's me, Danny, Dannito. Come on, amigo, we've got to go. It's OK.'

I put my hand out to him and he flinched away, curling himself into a ball. He was terrified, absolutely frozen with fear. I took a swift look behind. Dekka was having problems; he and the Bez bloke were wrestling by the door frame, but it didn't look like Dekka could hold it much longer. There were a few other people in the basement, but no-one was taking the least notice. Chico had wrapped his arms around his body and was rocking back and forth. Tears were streaming down his face. I'd kill them for this. I would. I promise you. I'll kill them.

In the meantime I had to get Chico out of this shithole. Crouching down on the floor and speaking very quietly, I took hold of Chico's arm. 'S'OK, ninyo,' I said. 'Come on, Chicito. We're going home.' The word home seemed to mean something. It seemed to break through. I pulled him to his feet and he shrank against me. He was trembling from head to foot. How the fuck was I going to get him past the watcher at the door in this state?

The girl with the hair came up to us as we were halfway across the room. She had a big mouth and her lips were very red. 'What's the matter with your little friend?' she said. 'Can't he take the pace?'

'Fuck off, big gob,' I said. 'I don't have time for this.' She laughed. 'No,' she said, 'you don't. In fact, I think

145

your time is running out.' I didn't reply; didn't waste my breath.

Towing Chico physically across the room, stumbling across prone bodies in the pitch dark, we made it to the door. Dekka had done a heroic fucking job, and was still playing the drunken idiot. 'I know you,' he was crying, arms all over. 'You're my friend.' Bez saw us coming, and for a brief moment the four of us were engaged in a sort of diabolical barn dance, everyone linking arms and shuffling feet as he tried to push us back into the dark. We shoved with all our might to get out of the door. When we burst through I was prepared to have to fight my way back up the stairs, but he just stood there, his long leather coat flapping, his thin mouth in a tight smile.

'Oh well done, Danny Boy,' he said. 'But it's too late. Your time's up.'

Then he turned away and walked into the darkness of the room. There was no time to hang round asking questions. It took me and Dekka to get Chico up the stairs. Every time we passed someone, he stopped and tried to drop to the floor.

'They've spiked him,' I said to Dekka. 'Must ave. Only explanation. Doesn't know me or you or anything. They've dropped a bucket load of acid down him, look at his eyes.'

Dekka nodded. 'We're gonna come back, Danny. When he's right. The three of us are gonna come back and make these bastards pay for this. Christ, I hope Kim's all right.'

She was. Well, sort of. 'Come on,' I said, once we'd pulled Kim to her feet and got her mobile. 'Let's get the fuck out of this unholy dump.' We made for the door. Chico looked a little better. He'd stopped crying and dropping to the floor, and he seemed to know who we were. 'Come on, chavitito,' I said, putting my arm round

146

his shoulders. 'We'll take you home.' Chico looked at me. His face was so beautiful it could break your heart. 'Danny?' he said. 'Yes,' I said gently. 'It's Danny.' Chico nodded. 'Danny, I want my mama. Please. I want to go home.' I nodded. 'That's right, chaver. We're going home. Now.'

We started towards the door. More than anything else in the world, I wanted out of there. I wanted to get as far away as possible. It must have been luck that made Dekka turn round. He'd forgotten his jacket. I cursed inwardly as he disappeared, and we all sat down to wait for him in a room just off the front hall, which was mercifully empty. Dekka wasn't long. Just as he walked in, the words 'right, let's be off' barely out of his mouth, I heard the noise.

The one voice in the world that was totally unmistakable. So that's it, I thought. I'm going to die here. I don't even know where I fucking am, and I'm going to die here. It was Gibbsey.

Him and Ticka were just inside the door. I could hear their voices and they were asking for us. A girl's voice was telling them to come in, saying she'd seen us around. Dekka dived for the door and shut it. 'Come on,' I said, dropping Chico. 'Come on, let's move it.' Dekka and I wedged two chairs against the door and then turned to the window. It was locked. 'Break it,' said Dekka. 'No,' I said, 'they'll hear the noise. Can we snap the lock off?' The two of us frantically started scrabbling at the window. I heard Ticka shouting about checking upstairs. My heart was racing, banging in my chest. I thought about the hare, running in big sweeping circles, screaming, thin and high, as the dog's teeth closed on her belly. 'Come on. Come on, you bastard.' Dekka had ripped the leg off one of the chairs and was hammering at the window lock. It snapped. Dekka looked at me, then leant his weight against the frame. It flew open. We were about five feet above the ground.

'I'll go first,' I said. 'You shove Chico and the lass out after me, then drop yourself.' I was through almost before I'd finished speaking. It was a bit of a drop, but not much.

Chico came first. He was too frightened to jump, but I stood below and Dekka shoved him out. He landed soft, on his feet, and when he stood up he seemed OK. Then nothing.

'Come on, marrer,' I said, mainly to myself. 'What are you waiting for? There's no time. They'll be on us. Come on, you fuckwit.'

Dekka stuck his head out of the window. 'It's Kim. She can't do it. Frightened of heights.'

'Leave the silly cow,' I hissed. 'Come on, Dekka. Come on. They'll kill you. They don't even know her. Come on, marrer. Please.'

Dekka appeared again, this time with Kim. I heard banging. They were at the door, they'd be in the room in seconds. Dekka shot an agonized look behind him. Kim was babbling and crying, 'I can't, I can't, I can't.' Dekka seemed to be trying to say something. I heard a crash, and Dekka said, 'Oh Christ.' Oh, please God no. Don't let it happen. There was another crash and Kim screamed. Suddenly Dekka seemed to make up his mind. He picked her up, bodily, and chucked her out. She landed on her side, rolled and stood up. We all looked up.

Dekka was standing at the window, but he wasn't alone. There were bodies all around him and he was fighting for his life. They were trying to drag him back inside, and he was battling with all his considerable strength to get out of the window. But there was no point, because he was going to lose. A sea of bodies closed round him, hands fastened around his arms, pinning him down, holding him still. They were going to take him away. They were going to do to him what they'd done to Teapot. And I was going to stand and watch it, just like I'd done before.

I was bouncing from foot to foot. I wanted to run away. Take Chico and Kim and get the fuck out of here while I still could. But I couldn't leave Dekka, could I? I mean, he was my marrer mayor. Known him since I was six. My best chav, and they were going to kill him. I knew it. I wouldn't see him again until I saw the pictures. Until some cunt of a policeman slapped the photos on the desk and asked me what I thought. I screamed. Screamed at the top of my voice, 'Help me. Help me. Why does no-one fucking help me?'

And someone did. The last place in the world I'd have looked for it. My screams were drowned in the sirens, and Dekka's fading struggles were illuminated in blue flashing lights as three police cars tore up. For a moment, Gibbsey and crew were undecided. Hold on or let go? They weren't sure. And in that moment Dekka made a dive for it. He did a header through the window like he was coming off the high board in the Olympic pool. When he hit the ground he rolled over and over, then he clambered, very shakily, to his feet. Kim ran to him and flung her arms round him, and he hugged her. But it was me he was looking at. 'You waited for me, chav,' he said.

'Course I did,' I replied. 'Where the fuck would I go without you?'

We turned round and started walking. Me holding on to Chico, Dekka with his arm round Kim. As we got to the end of the road we were stopped by one of the policemen. I recognized him immediately. It was the cunt from the caff, his silly haircut covered up by a Metropolitan Police cap.

'Where are you going?' he asked.

'Home,' I said.

He nodded. 'Do that. Tomorrow you must find the fourth. You cannot remain in the place you have chosen. You must go.' Then he looked at us and reached out. He stroked Chico's hair. 'Children,' he said. 'Suffer the little children.'

Chico didn't cringe away. In fact, he seemed calmer now. The chubby guy laid his hand on Chico's head and said something in a funny language. 'Take him home,' he told us. 'Go back and sleep.' Then a car horn sounded. He turned back to his pigmobile and waved at someone. 'I have to go. Remember, leave tomorrow and find the fourth again.' Then he walked back towards his car. Sitting in the passenger seat was a familiar figure. Odd-looking kid, but I was sure I'd seen him before.

'Come on, Danny. Let's move it.' This from Dekka, and he was right. Not much use hanging about waiting for Gibbsey and Co.

As we walked away, the final disaster of an entirely disastrous night hit home. 'Oh no,' I said. 'Oh for fuck's sake, no.' You must, of course, have seen this coming. As surely as night follows day. I'd been too out of it to think about anything at all most of the time. But I did now. And with a dreadful certainty I knew. Knew exactly what I'd find when I searched Chico's jacket pockets. And I was spot on. Nothing. Nada. Nada de nada. Every single last penny had been nicked, and we weren't about to go back in there to find out who'd done it. I passed on the joyful tidings to Dekka. 'Shit,' he said. A pretty comprehensive response, all told.

Dekka and I pooled our remaining cash. Between us we had £23.72. Not exactly a fortune. I stopped a passer-by and asked where we were. 'Peckham,' was the answer. Did he know how we could get back to Green Lanes? 'Haven't got a clue,' came the response. 'Miles away, innit? Other side of London.'

In the end, Dekka and I agreed that a minicab was the only answer. Kim was being sick constantly and was clearly in a mess. Chico, although improving, was still terrified of his own shadow and hallucinating all over the place. We found someone to take us for £15, which left us with the handsome sum of £8.72. No money, no drugs and nowhere to go. Ain't life grand?

By the time we tumbled back to Green Lanes, it was past 4 a.m. The fucking place was pitch-black, and we had to use Dekka's lighter to see our way upstairs. I left Dekka to deal with Kim, and took Chico to the bathroom. Using cold water I washed his face and hands and then led him back to our room. Dekka told me he was staying in Kim's room. 'She's frightened to be alone, like,' he said, 'and I don't want to leave her.' I nodded. It made perfect sense. She looked frightened and ill and very tired. No wonder she didn't want to be in the dark on her own. Who does? 'Dekka,' I said, 'how old is she? You asked her?' He nodded. 'She says she's fourteen.' I raised my eyebrows and he shrugged. 'Your guess is as good as mine, marrer. See you in the mornin.'

When I went back to the room Chico was in a corner, rocking himself to and fro. One of the real horrors with acid is the amount of time it lasts. Ten, twelve hours, even longer, and one of the jolly side-effects is a sort of speedy feeling, so there's no escape through sleep. I hate the stuff meself. Did it a couple of times and had no fun at all. Got stuck in this fucking fat dealer's house. He'd pushed us into taking a tab, and I'd given in. And did I pay the price for humouring the fat bastard? He put one of his kids' stuffed toys on my lap, and I thought I was going to have a screamin fit. It was a brown fun-fur pony, with stick-in eyes, a grey mane and tail made of that really thick, Seventies-style, fake fur. To my hallucinating eyes the pony came alive and the spiky fun-fur turned into razor-sharp knives. Its white felt teeth were going to bite me and its rolling black-and-white eyes were pure Freddy Kruger. I don't know how long I was frozen there, with that fat fucker laughing at me, but I swore, never again. No, you can stick your mind-expanding, altered states up your arse as far as I'm concerned. And you can quote me on that.

There's some crappy, hippy folklore stuff about vitamin C being good for bringing you down. I'd never believed it myself, but, reasoning that things couldn't get much worse, I took my lighter and went on a recce in the kitchen, telling Chico not to worry, and that I'd be back soon.

Somebody, probably Johan the Tulip and Eva Bonita, had been shopping. The kitchen was full of scran, mostly veggie shite, but within minutes I'd laid my hand on a load of oranges. I rinsed out a mug, peeled three of the oranges and squeezed them in. In the dark I couldn't see to pull out the pips, but I reckoned they wouldn't do much harm. Having vaguely recalled that sugar was supposed to be effective for a bad-trip experience, I heaped in three spoonfuls. Then I found two pint pots, filled them with water and, doing a pretty skilful balancing act, carried the lot back upstairs.

With Dekka gone, the bedding situation wasn't bad at all. I made this huge nest in the corner of the room and then turned my attention to Chico. I sat down next to him and started pulling his boots and kecks off. Once I'd removed his jacket and jumper I tried to get him to take the orange juice. He wasn't very keen at first, but in the end he swallowed it. More importantly, I also got him to neck two of the valium tabs I'd swiped from Juliette. I talked to him and tried to get him to understand what had happened and that it was OK, he wasn't going mad or anything. It was just some wanker who'd spiked him. I don't know if he understood, but he got into bed and lay down quietly enough. I can't explain what it felt like to see him like this. It was horrible, so horrible. I just can't tell you. After we'd been in bed about five minutes I heard a noise. Chico was crying again.

I didn't know what to do. For what seemed an eternity I lay there, hearing his snuffles and cries for his mother. There was perhaps a foot between us, and the distance seemed as wide and impassable as the Arctic tundra. From where I lay I could feel his body shaking with sobs. I remembered how I'd lain in bed as a little kid, wanting me mam to come, but knowing she wouldn't. Wanting somebody to tell me it was all right.

Well, no-one did. And it's not all right. And I don't suppose it's ever going to be. But I couldn't stand any more of this. And who was to see anyway? It was the longest distance, that foot, and when I moved across to him, the noise of the bedclothes was louder than the trampling of elephants. But once I'd started there was no going back. 'Come on, Chico,' I said, and I put my arms around him and pulled him close to me. 'It's all right. I'm here. I'll look after you.' He didn't resist, which I suppose I'd been half frightened of. He curled up against me, his burning-hot face on my chest. And the sobbing got quieter and then stopped altogether. 'It's all right,' I said. 'Nothing can hurt you. Not while I'm here. Come on now. It's OK.' And then I started to sing – very quietly, because I was lying on my back and Chico's head was heavy on my chest. But I started to sing, and Chico hummed along, cos he didn't know the words, but he liked the tune. 'Speed bonny boat, like a bird on the wing/Onward the sailors cry/Carry the lad that's born to be king/Over the sea to Skye. That's us, Chico,' I whispered. 'We're in that boat. You and me and Dekka. Flying over the sea, to a magic island, far away. And they'll never, ever find us.

And in the morning we rose early. Well, we didn't actually. It was well gone half one in the afternoon before any of us saw the light of day. If, by the way, you're hoping I've gone all self-aware and have liberated myself from nineteen years in the closet, well, you're in for a bit of a disappointment. I took care of Chico cos he was poorly. He needed someone to look after him, and I was there. No matter how beautiful he is, I don't want to shag him, and I'm not 'in denial', I'm just telling the truth. I mean, I've nothing against whatever people want to do to each other behind closed doors. Up to them, innit. But the idea of shagging one of them meself. I don't think so. I mean, just look at them. Who'd want to get involved with that crew of mutants? Wannabe girls, wiggling and shouting the odds. Wouldn't touch em with a ten-foot bargepole.

Anyway, in the mornin we all looked a wee bit brighter. Chico was fine, a bit shamefaced about what he might have said or done, which, lucky for him, he could barely remember. He'd gone down the basement with Sindy, the girl with the gob and the hair. She was all over him like a rash, he said, and ten to one it was her who nicked the fucking money. He remembered getting it off with Sindy on the mattress, and drinking cans of Red Stripe, and then the next thing he knew the world started to fall apart.

'S'awful, Danny,' he told me. 'So bad. I got very frightened. I can't leave the corner, because I'm too frightened to move. And the girl, she's such a beetch. She laugh and say things to me. Then she don't look like a girl no more.

154

Her mouth go very big and her teeth very sharp. I can't look at her. And she come very close and talk in my ear. She say terrible things. She say I never leave there.'

Chico's hallucinations had got worse and worse. He had a vague memory of me pulling him out of the basement, and he remembered jumping from the window – he'd seen himself on a cliff top, thousands of feet above the sea and the rocks. Fucking good job Dekka had pushed him. He said that he owed me one for looking after him, and I said 'nada' and we left it at that. He hadn't even realized Gibbsey had turned up, bin too lost in his private horrors to take it in.

'Anyway,' I said, when I'd finished recounting the night's events. 'Thank fuck they didn't get Dekka.'

As if on cue, my marrer mayor burst through the door. 'Look what she's done,' shouted Dekka, 'the little belter.' In his hand he had a plastic wrap; it was full of money.

Well, to cut a long story short, our Kim had proved to be a bit of a star turn. While I was out finding me chips, she'd noticed half of Chico's money practically falling out of his jacket pocket. Being a girl, she hadn't drunk nearly as much as us lot and, mercifully, this was just before Cocaine Mol had arrived on the scene, so our Kimmy was still relatively straight and compos mentis. She'd taken one look at Dekka and put him down as totally wrecked. So she'd got herself up and gone over to Chico and taken the wad out of his pocket. He'd been snogging Sindy the Nightmare at the time, so he hadn't noticed. Deciding, quite rightly, that none of us were much use, she'd shoved the money into the zippy pocket of her kecks, taken a line of coke and promptly forgotten all about it.

It was such a fucking relief, I can tell you; £460 worth of relief. It was the roll Chico had been spending from. It just shows you, there is a merciful God. Chico tried to give

Kim some money, but she wouldn't take it. In the end she accepted twenty because we all pushed her. Dekka was sort of beaming; he had the expression parents get when their kid wins five straight races on sports day.

We packed our bits of gear and phoned Mikey. He sounded chipper enough and told us to get our arses straight over. Dekka fannied about over Kim, giving her Mikey's phone number and address and arranging to meet up. Chico and I said goodbye and left him to it. He caught up as we were walking down to the tube.

It didn't take us long to find Mikey. His bro lived in one of those big white jobs just off Ladbroke Grove. He had a flat on the second floor. Mikey came racing down the stairs, greeting us like long-lost brothers.

'Saw that white-boy posse on the street yesterday,' he said. 'Man did I start to worry. Same two guys. The one with the voice and his sidekick with the fuckin tattoos. They are straight bad news. I dodged into the b2 and they missed me, but they were lookin up and down the streets the whole time. Just on Notting Hill it was. Shit, man, was I glad to hear you when you called. Thought they might have taken youse out and come after me. Went straight back to the flat, got my bro and a few of the boys, and there's six of us, tooled up to the eyeballs, sitting there all night waiting for them. I mean, how'd the fuck those bastards follow us to London, man?'

This all came out in one breathless coked-up rush as he led us up the stairs to bro's pad. Despite the mad delivery, he was talking some sense. I mean, how did Gibbsey know we were in London? Anyway, there was no time to ponder such weighty issues, because Mikey, still babbling on, was introducing us to his brother Laurence, who was sitting on a long, low settee in front of a glass table. To my intense pleasure I noted that Laurie was shaping out five lines of what looked like coke on the glass table top. What a gent. Good hospitality is the mark of true manners, and it doesn't get much better than a free introductory line of coke.

Mikey was talking us up to Laurie like we were his bezza mates and blood brothers. Now this was surprising on two counts. The obvious one is that we'd only known him for three days; the other point is that we're white. Well, me and Dekka; and Chico was dago, not black. The weirdest thing of all was I was pleased. Not just, Oh-thank-fuck-he's-going-to-let-us-stay-in-the-flat pleased, but really pleased. Touched even. I'm fuckin losin it. Must be all the stress.

There was a spare room, with bunk beds and a camp bed in it, which Mikey said was ours as long as we wanted it. After a proper amount of thanks, we dumped our stuff, went back in the front room and sat down to a can of beer and a line of coke. Just the thing to buck up your mood. Mikey repeated his Gibbsey story in minute detail. I told the Gibbsey-arriving-at-the-party story at massive, coked-up length. Laurie obligingly asked how it had all started, so all four of us were able to rant on about Teapot, Donny, Lincoln, Juliette, Mol and all the rest of it. We had a couple of joints and another can of beer, then Mikey put out another line apiece. We had tactfully omitted all mention of Chico's lottery riches in the telling of our tales, but suddenly, impelled by the cocaine generosity, or shamed by Mikey's friendship, or God knows what, Chico came clean. This tale took lots of telling, as Dekka had to point out the utter brilliance of Kim, and Mikey and Laurie had to muse about the possibility of collecting as many of 'the boys' as possible and going back down to the party flat in South London to knock the shite out of whoever happened to be there. A pleasing thought, and one we dwelt on at some length.

'You see,' said Chico, 'I feel very bad. Because I think I have one thousand, then this beetch girl steal my money. But I still have four hundred, and I theenk I geeve some to my mama. I want her to buy a dress, go out, maybe. I don't know. Something nice. But now me, Danni and Dekka, we ave no money and no gear. So we need to find. And I don't know how long before we go home.'

Then he got the cash out of his pocket and tried to give Laurie fifty quid for letting us stay. Laurie looked at Mikey, nodded his head and told Chico he was giving the money back, on the condition he sent it to his mother. Doesn't coke improve your moral sensibilities? Bro Laurie also proved worth his weight in gold by telling us, if it was smack we wanted, he would give us an intro to the Sleeping Giant, who could do us as much brown as we wanted at forty a gram. But we would have to wait till about seven. That seemed sound as a pound, and we all chorused our thanks and gratitude. Laurie put out another line. Chico said he was going to fetch some beers. Mikey and Dekka went with him as an anti-Gibbsey security. Laurie said while they were gone he'd phone his girl.

I took the oppo to have a gander round. It wasn't a bad flat, really, although dead tatty. The front room was huge, with great big windows, flooded with light. All the walls had once been painted white, but they were now very dirty. It was one of those grand old places, with high ceilings and skirting boards a foot deep. There was no carpet, just varnished floorboards, badly in need of another coat, and the kitchen and bathroom were both a bit of a tip. But on the whole it wasn't at all bad. I liked the sunshine and the feeling of brightness it had. There were plants as well – quite big ones, like you get in shops and banks – and all the green looked nice in the sunshine and light.

The boy himself was shorter and stockier than his brother. Head to foot in Nike, short hair with patterns cut in, three earrings in each ear. Not the sort of guy you'd volunteer to mess with. I don't know how long he'd been down in London, but he'd affected a sort of cockney wide-boy patter, which, added to the hundred-mile-an-hour motormouth effect of the coke, made him quite hard to understand. You'd get the general drift, but the details were lost in a welter of speeded-up sound. He was pacing round the kitchen now, yellin down his mobie.

I sat down, then stood up again. The coke was helping – helping quite a lot – but it was unmistakably starting. I was beginning to withdraw, no doubt about it. Five o'clock now, another two hours to go. What a bastard.

Chico, Dekka and Mikey returned at that moment and luckily took my mind off my catalogue of withdrawing ailments. Laurie finally stopped screaming down the mobie, and we cracked the cans and sat down.

We were watching a boxing vid when Mikey's phone rang. It was exactly 5.42 p.m. I know that because I was watching the digital clock on the vid with rapt attention, counting down the minutes till the magic hour of seven o'clock. Anyway, as I said, 5.42 p.m., and our enjoyment of two black guys punching each other's lights out was interrupted by the gentle tones of Mikey's mobie. It didn't ring. Oh no, much too fuckin uncool and ordinary. No, Mikey's phone played the opening bars of 'My Way'. If you didn't answer it, maybe it played the whole song, although technology hadn't yet managed to incorporate ol Frankie Boy's singing. Grateful for small mercies, I suppose.

It was Dwayne, or so I gathered from Mikey's response. Then his face changed and he waved at Laurie to turn the vid down. The four of us sat in silence, listening to Mikey listening to Dwayne. Whatever he was telling him, it wasn't good news. 'When did it appen?' said Mikey. 'He kept her all night? You what? This is fuckin unbelievable.' There was more of this. I looked at Laurie, who shrugged and raised his eyebrows. Mikey was talking about somebody being taken to hospital. 'So how is she now? Nah, don't be fuckin stupid, of course I don't want her back out there.' Then he told Dwayne to take care of the girls. Said he didn't want anyone working without protection. Said that he wanted everything Dwayne could get on the guy. Said he'd be back as soon as, but in the meantime to keep cool. When he was back the guy was dead meat 'and tell her she can come and watch him buy it'. There was a bit more of this kind of chat, then he put the phone down. He looked at us, and all four of us looked back expectantly. 'You're never going to fuckin believe this,' he said.

She'd gone out yesterday, about six o'clock, as normal. Her and Delilah had got the work gear on, and stiletto-tripped down to their usual patch, waiting for the early-evening punters. He'd driven past twice. Circled round slowly, come back, then gone through the same routine again. Nothing unusual in that. Totally normal punter behaviour. Then he'd approached a third time, pulled up bang next to the girls. Hadn't said anything. Just pointed at Skinny Ass and jerked his thumb towards the car seat.

Now psycho punters come with the territory in this line of work, and the girls had their own anti-nutter survival code worked out. Delilah, being the one with the balls, walked forward and told the guy that they did their negotiations outside the car. So what did he want with her girlfriend? Where was he thinking of taking her? And, most importantly, where was his money?

'Dwayne said she was shakin, man,' Mikey told us. 'He said he ain't never seen Delilah scared of nothing in her life, but when she told him about this guy she was shakin.'

He'd been very polite, but there was something wrong. 'He gave me a bad feeling,' Delilah said. 'Like there was a voice in my mind sayin, This guy's bad news.' He hadn't leant across, just opened the driver's window and sat facing straight ahead, so that Delilah was forced to stand in the road to talk. He smelt funny, Delilah said, but then again, so did a lot of punters. If your working whore objected to bad breath and BO she'd be out of a job pretty rapido. S'obvious, innit? If a punter was even half decent, he wouldn't be shelling out thirty quid for a knee-trembler in Nottingham. He'd get it for free down the local meat-market disco. Stands to reason. Anyway, that's by the by. Back to Delilah.

'I want the usual, but not with you, with your little friend,' he'd told her. He'd also told Delilah that he was in one of the boarding-house hotels a few streets away. The sort of hotels that lorry drivers on their way up the M1 use for stopovers. Delilah and Skinny Ass knew them well and had worked in them before, so that was OK. Delilah still didn't like it, though. She still felt something wasn't quite right, so she demanded the money up front. Payment in advance, as a kind of surety. She even hiked up the fee. Told him fifty quid, which was extortionate. She thought, half hoped, he'd tell her to fuck off, but he didn't. Just got a roll of notes out of his pocket, peeled off the appropriate amount, and said, 'Now tell the girl to get in the car.' And, despite all her bad feeling and worry, that's exactly what Delilah did. Skinny slid onto the seat, the central locking clunked shut and the car moved off.

The man turned and looked at Delilah over his shoulder as they moved away. He gave her a wide, slow smile. An evil smile, Delilah called it, and his teeth were terrible.

After two hours had passed Delilah began to fret. Then she caught a punter herself, then another one, and then it was gone ten o'clock and there was still no sign of Skinny. She didn't want to miss the trade when the pubs turned out at 11 p.m., but the bad feeling was growing, so she left a message with a mate, in case Skinny showed, and walked the half-mile or so to the boarding house. They'd never heard of the bloke. No-one staying there who looked remotely like him, no-one who'd brought a thin blonde girl back. There were two other boarding houses in the same street, and she'd checked them both, just in case there'd been a mistake. There hadn't. Delilah rang Dwayne, and Dwayne called up a couple of mates. They fucked around for hours, getting more and more frantic, but found neither sight nor sound.

The next morning Dwayne organized a search party. It was about half four and was just going dark when they found her, more by chance than anything else. She was down by the canal, gagged and trussed up like a chicken.

He'd driven her about a mile away, straight down to the canal, to the old warehouses and unused lock-ups. No-one goes there any more, Mikey said. A pitch-black, deserted dump in the middle of the big city. Skinny didn't want to go there either. She'd tried to get out the car, but it was locked. She'd asked him where he was going, but he'd said nothing, just smiled and showed his rotten teeth. When he'd stopped the car and released the locks, she'd tried to make a run for it. She'd seen the lock-ups and knew what was coming. But it's hard to run fast in stiletto mules, and he'd just laughed at her.

God knows how, but he had a key for one of the padlocked doors, and he'd dragged her inside. She'd started screaming, but he slapped that idea out of her and tied her up. Then he'd walked back out to the car to get his tools. He'd rigged up a swinging, overhead-light affair, then he'd got the knife and pliers out. Holding them, he'd crouched down next to her and explained, very softly, what he was going to do. Whilst he'd spoken he'd stroked her face, his fingers playing lightly over her eye sockets, tracing her nostrils and the line of her mouth. In a whisper, he asked how old she was.

Never the most chatty, Skinny couldn't answer. She said she'd tried to talk, but nothing had come out. He hadn't asked again. He'd stuck the knife up her nose and slit her nostril. When things went quiet he'd asked again. She'd told him seventeen. He'd used his fingers to part her lips. 'I like your teeth,' he'd told her. 'Your best feature.' He tapped on the front ones with his fingernail. Then he'd picked up the pliers. 'Were you a very pretty child?' he'd said. 'All that silky pale hair and soft white skin. And lovely teeth. Like pearls, shining sea pearls from the ocean deep. Such a pretty little girl. Am I right?'

She'd started babbling. Well you would, wouldn't you? He'd told her to shut up, then he'd put his face very close to hers and she'd thought he was going to kiss her, but he didn't, he started to lick her teeth. He took a long time over it, with thorough, delicate movements of his tongue. 'Such a shame to spoil them,' he'd said. Then he put the pliers in her mouth and ripped out two of her front teeth. 'Tell Mikey it's just my little joke,' he said. 'He should choose his friends more carefully.' And that, really, was that. She'd blacked out with the pain. When she woke up again he was gone. He'd cut off all her hair and stuffed her mouth with it, secured by sticky tape. Then he'd left. Got in his car and disappeared.

Dwayne said you couldn't imagine the state when they'd found her. He'd left long strands of pale, bloodied, blond hair sprouting out of her mouth, so she looked like she'd grown a beard. There were bites all over her legs, which turned out to be from the rats, who'd obviously smelt out a handy meal, served hot. They do that y'know. You have a sick animal, specially if it's tied up, and they'll eat it alive. Saw a thing on telly about it. And then, of course, there was the nose. He must have cut the other side when she'd blacked out, because both nostrils were done and spread wide on her face. He'd put some grease in her hair, and tweaked the raggy ends into two points, one on each side of her head. Weirdest of all, he'd taken one of her stockings off and filled it up with bits of crap from the warehouse, until it resembled a long, thin sausage. Then he'd rucked up her skirt, which was short enough anyway, and tied the sausage thing to the back of her knickers, so it looked like she had a tail. And that's how they found her.

We all sat in stupified silence, just looking at Mikey in shock. 'Where's the girl?' said Laurie.

'She's up the hospital with Delilah. Shit, what the fuck is going on? Who the fuck is after me?'

We talked our way in circles for another hour. Mikey didn't owe money, hadn't ripped anyone off, couldn't think who the hell would come after him like this. We were all terrified. If he could do this to little Skinny Ass, what the fuck would he do to Mikey, or anyone with him, when he caught up. The longer we talked, the more an uncomfortable thought kept pushing to the front of my mind. A large part of me was hoping and praying this was some sort of crack-turf war, because, if it was, it was nowt to do with me. But at the back of my mind was a nagging idea, and it just wouldn't go away.

The mobie rang again. 'Yeah?' said Mikey. 'All right, baby. How is she?' It was Delilah; they were letting Skinny go home. They'd asked about the police and Delilah had told them it was all in hand. Skinny had to go back next week to see about plastic surgery on the nose. They'd done emergency stuff on her mouth, but said she'd need to sort the rest with a dentist.

'How's she coping in her head?' said Mikey. The answer didn't seem very cheerful. He told Delilah to tell Dwayne that Skinny was to have anything she wanted, drug wise, anything at all. 'Tell him to ring me if he wants confirmation.' And he said Delilah was to tell the girl he would look after her. 'Tell her to stay home, rest, relax and get herself right again. I'll pay the teeth. They're bad, yeah?' Mikey listened a while. 'OK, baby girl. You stay with her. Forget the work, just stay with her until she's on the level . . . Yeah, yeah. Ask Dwayne. But don't go totally mad. Speak tomorrow. OK. Look after her, you hear? And you take care of yourself.'

He snapped the mobie off. 'Shit,' said Mikey. 'What sort of guy does this? Poor little bitch. Doesn't weigh above seven stone.'

I thought of seventeen-year-old Skinny. Thought of her pale, translucent skin. You could see the blue veins underneath. Her thin, goose-pimply arms, and the peaky little face with its anxious expression. I thought of what she must have felt, tied up and helpless in the corner of the warehouse. I wondered how long I would have lasted in the same circs, as the soft fingers stroked my face, probing and testing. Mikey was right. What sort of man did a thing like this? There was a large part of me didn't want to know the answer.

I took a deep breath. 'Oi, Mikey,' I said. 'Have you asked Delilah what the guy looked like?' Mikey nodded, Delilah had remembered the guy all right. Her description walked straight out of my nightmares. Tall, thin, about thirty. Long, greasy dark hair. Long black leather coat.

165

Terrible teeth. It was him, of course. Who else could it be?

We sat and discussed the implications. Told Mikey and Laurie that it was the guy Bez from the party. Tried to figure out what all this meant and got so frightened we were practically shitting ourselves.

'I don't understand,' said Dekka. 'What's happening? What the fuck is happening to us?'

He got no answer. The TV was turned down, the CD had finished. We sat in silence, looking at each other. No-one said a word.

chapter seven

WE WERE SO UTTERLY GOBSMACKED BY WHAT HAD gone off that it was gone half seven before I even remembered about the drugs. I suppose you'll be tutting about what a self-centred, heartless bastard I am to even think about myself when poor old Skinny's had her teeth ripped out, not to mention the nose job. But that's what you know. I could have been Skinny's brother or nobbio and I'd still have felt the same. You have to get the gear sorted so you can operate. You have no choice. You can't help but think about it, because your mind and body force you to it. That's what being a junkie is all about. The smack comes first, before love, death, *Match of the Day*, or anything else you care to mention. Anyway, that's the philosophy, should you be interested. I'm not makin excuses, I'm just telling you.

I spoke to Mikey and Laurie and asked about the guy with the brown. Laurie nodded and said he'd take me, but it was best if the others gave me their dosh and I bought for all of us. Going mob-handed was bound to unnerve the bloke, and then he might not let us in. Chico, being the only one with any fuckin dinos, splashed the cash, and

Laurie zipped himself into a few hundred quids' worth of Nike accoutrements, and off we went.

Laurie had a metallic green Vitara. Not new, but not that far off. The boy had some class, you had to say it. The minute he turned the key he stuck Buju Banton on the stereo at enough volume to make the car shake, stuck on his Ray Ban shades – yes, I know, it was fuckin 8 p.m. and pitch dark – and wound down the window to allow the entire neighbourhood to enjoy a taste of the Buju man wailing on about 'crossin the mountains and the sea', or some such shite. Then, all set, we tooled off down the road.

The Sleeping Giant lived in Kensal Green, which turned out to be handily nearby. We drove the length of Ladbroke Grove, turned left at the top, then dived off into a series of little suburban streets. Laurie pulled up outside a semi, with a blue Renault in the drive.

'Good sign, man,' said Laurie, pointing at the car. 'Means he's in.'

We rang the bell and stood outside the glass door, waiting. Nothing happened. I looked at Laurie and raised my hand to the bell. He shook his head. 'It takes him a long time to get movin. Give it another minute.' We gave it another couple of minutes. 'Dopey fucker's asleep, innit,' said Laurie. 'Hope we can raise him, otherwise we'll have to think of other angles.' He rung the bell, hard and long, then tried to look through the window. 'Shit,' he said, and beckoned me over.

Through the nets, you could make out a neat and tidy sitting room. Gas fire, pretending to be coal, on full. Fitted carpet. Big, fuck-off three-piece green draylon suite. White 'n' furry rug in front of the fire. Mock-stone chimney breast, with one of those fuck-awful copper hood things. Massive TV, full on. In a chair by the fire, feet propped up on a leather pouf effort, was a huge, inert figure. 'That's im,' said Laurie. 'The fucker's fast asleep, as usual.'

Laurie began banging on the window, whilst I went back and gave the bell some hammer. Laurie shouted through the letter box. We both banged on the window. It took us fuckin ages to wake the dozy bastard. Finally, as we were both banging and shouting at the window, he twitched a bit. Encouraged, we redoubled our efforts. He sat up, and Laurie began waving and shouting, 'Oi, Paul, it's me, mate. Open the door, mate. PAUL! Paul, it's me, Laurie. Open the fuckin door.'

Eventually it worked. He stood up, stumbled about a bit, then headed for the door. It swung open and we walked straight in. By the time we got into the sitting room he was back in the chair by the fire. The room was unbelievably hot. The heat from the gas fire sort of beat at you and took your breath away, and the furniture – the big cushions, hugely padded settee, draped curtains and deep pile rugs – well, that made it all worse. Much worse. And I'm not going to even attempt the fuckin ornaments, all 3,000 of them, because I simply can't fuckin bear to. As I've mentioned before, it's not an easy life.

Laurie had warned me beforehand that it would be a slow process. The Sleeping Giant liked to talk. You got involved in this sad, crappy pretence that you hadn't really come round to buy drugs. Oh no, you'd dropped in because you were a marrer mayor, and wanted his scin-tillating company. You had to have a cup of tea, at least one, and gear could not be mentioned until the tea was finished. Then it was just like a casual afterthought. 'Oh, and by the way, Paul, before I go, hard as it is to tear myself away from your brilliant conversation, and it's a real pity I can't stay longer, you wouldn't, by any chance, and not that it really matters one way or the other, but you wouldn't, out of curiosity, like, just happen to have any gear to sell?' Dear God, give me strength.

I have to admit that Laurie was a total star. We both sat there with our cups and saucers balanced on our laps, gasping for air, me withdrawing to fuck and sweating buckets, and Laurie did the business. He talked about Paul's wife, who apparently was a nurse, which I have to say bodes ill for any NHS patients in west London. Chatted about how Paul's job with the Gas Board was going. Inquired how things were after the holiday – two weeks in Rimini – Paul had flown home on day nine having run out of gear. The wife hadn't taken it well. On and on it went.

I was introduced as a friend of Mikey, down for a few weeks in London. I was now so strung out that I didn't want to talk at all, but I tried to rise to the occasion, and answered questions about Yorkshire Gas. 'No, Paul, don't think I know anyone who works for them.' For fuck's sake, I ask you. My job? Not a lot to tell there. And my girlfriend? I didn't know what to say to that one. Who is my nobbia? Reg? Nah, sweet enough, but basically too crap. Janey? Do me a favour. The girl I'd shagged last night at the party? Didn't even know her name, and don't care, neither. I wanted to say Eleanor, but I daren't. Not only because I'd be lying, but because it seemed . . . well, what? It seemed improper. Rude. You see, I thought about her all the time. What I would say to her, her long dark hair, her arms opened wide for me. But sex? It didn't seem right. I couldn't approach the idea. Couldn't do the usual stuff you do with girls you fancy. Y'know, imagining what they look like naked, what they'd be like in bed. Mental pictures of them taking off their knickers, sucking you off, opening their legs and begging for it. Not with Eleanor. It made me feel almost ill to think of her in that way. Don't know why; it just did.

Anyway, back to the business in hand. Just when I thought I was going to pass out from the heat, boredom and frustration, Laurie made his move and asked the $50,000 question. Your man hummed and hawed a bit, but said, yeah, he could do what we wanted, and then heaved his bulk out of the green draylon and toddled off to get the gear. He really was huge, about six four and built like a brick shithouse. His hands were all swollen up, so his fingers were like bunches of bananas. Laurie said his veins were fucked from too much hitting up, and that thrombosis had set in. His feet were the same, apparently, which is why he wore slippers all the time. Nearly lost a leg two years ago, because he'd started going into his femoral artery – the big one in the groin for those of you who don't know. Anyway, they'd managed to save it, but Laurie said you should see him in summer. He sits round in shorts and a vest, and the state of it. All mottled, Laurie said, with purple varicose veins all over the place, and huge, swollen limbs. God knows how the wife puts up with it.

Finally, he doshed out the gear and the deal was done. I was bad-mannered and desperate enough to ask for the bathroom. I'd brought my works with me and needed a hit so badly I was almost crying for it. The bathroom was spotless, full of huge, fluffy towels and tart's-knicker curtains. I was in and out inside five minutes. Sticking to the etiquette of the thing, Laurie was still chatting on. Having got the gear, we had another ten-minute stretch before leaving. Because we'd come for a chat with our mate, Paul, the gear was strictly sideline, and we now pretended to have forgotten all about it. Of course, having had my hit, I was able to pull my verbal weight rather better. We covered the relative merits of Renault versus VW, and the incredible brilliance of the gas fire, which you really wouldn't know wasn't coal – well, if you were blind you wouldn't – then, finally, Laurie looked at his watch and announced that he really ought to get back, because he'd arranged to meet his brother. He had to shout this information, because there'd been a lull in the conversation and Paul had fallen asleep again. By the time we got out the door, we'd been in there an hour and a half. What a fuckin nightmare.

When we got back to the flat it was nearly ten. I was feeling fairly chipper, though. I'd sorted the gear, most important, and Laurie had said we could use his address to sign on from. We were going to name him as landlord and claim housing ben, which would mean we could give him something for our keep, and top up the miserable dole dinos. I mean, we'd obviously have to think about what else we were going to do for money, but it was something, at least, and would help tide us over until this horror show receded and the fuckin useless police did what they were paid for, and locked up Gibbsey and Ticka. I mean, what are they arsing about at? Fuckin blindingly obvious who topped Teapot. There must be other witnesses apart from us. Fort was packed out at the time. It's just totally typical, if you ask me. Always pokin their piggin noses in where they're not wanted, but comes to something serious and they're nowhere near. Bloody useless, that's what they are.

Anyway, we dandered back to the flat, and I shared out the gear with Chico and Dekka. They didn't seem as relieved as they ought to have been, and nobody was talking much. Then Mikey looked at Dekka. 'Come on, man,' he said. 'You've got to do it.'

I looked at Dekka, then back to Mikey. Both avoided my eyes. Chico was looking at the floor.

'What the fuck is going on?' I said. 'Would somebody like to tell me what's happening?'

Mikey made a sort of open-handed motion towards Dekka. Dekka nodded.

'Chaver,' he said. 'Come into the other room a minute. I need to talk to you.'

I stood up and followed him into the bedroom. I could sense something bad was coming, but I didn't know what. When we got into the bedroom, Dekka closed the door, then he walked over to the window, looked out for a minute, then turned round.

'Chavito, I've got some bad news. I don't know what to say. Look, I'll tell you straight. Chico phoned his mam to tell her he was OK and that he was sending the money, yeah?'

'Yeah,' I said. 'And what?'

'Well, his mam said that your mam had been round the caff, and she asked Chico if he knew where you were, or could get a message to you.'

'Oh, for fuck's sake,' I said. 'Is that it? You know me mam's barking, Dekka. Everyone knows. She's just on my fuckin tail again. I hope Chico said nada. The last thing I fuckin want is—'

'Danny, Danny. Hang on, chav.' Dekka interrupted me. A thing previously unheard of. 'Hold up a minute, marrer. Listen, your mam had been round my house first. She got nowt, but somehow they'd heard that the three of us had bin arrested together. So she tooled round to the caff. Danny, she'd had Reg's parents round the house.'

'What?' I said. I couldn't quite take it in. 'Why? What the fuck did they want? Is she up the duff? They can't prove it's mine.'

'She's topped herself, Danny,' said Dekka. 'She left a letter for you, and another for her dad. She said that she loved you.'

I stared at him. I could feel the blood draining out of my face. Dekka looked back. His pale blue eyes were shiny. He'd folded his arms. I could see every detail of his face: the mouse-brown cropped hair, freckles, thick eyebrows, nose bent by fighting and the unusually pink mouth, which was set in a straight line. Did he think it was my fault?

'What happened?' I said.

'I'm not sure, marrer. It's all come via Chico's mam, from your mam, from Reg's dad. They're burying her on Tuesday. They found her Thursday night; she was hanging from the loft door. Her parents said she'd gone out with a mate on Wednesday night, and she'd ended up in a barney with some girl who said she was goin out with you. The bint chucked a drink over Reg and said that Reg knew shit, cos she was pregnant and it was your baby. I don't know what happened after that, but it sounds a bit of a fuck-up. Anyway, she went back home, said goodbye to the mate and that was that.

'Her parents got worried that she didn't answer the phone, so they went round Thursday night and she was hanging there. They had the coroners on Friday. Suicide verdict. She left a letter for you. Her dad showed your mam. Look, chav, I don't know what to say. It's not your fault.'

I looked at Dekka, trying his best for me, and I felt sick. Because I knew. Oh, I knew all right. I knew what she was like. Knew how sweet and gentle and straight she was inside, and I'd used her. Never no intention of getting serious, never no intention of being right with her. No respect, no kindness, no thought. Just liked the long hair, and the big blue eyes, and sweet, clean little body. Little breasts, with big nipples. Delicate, she was, almost fragile. I told you, didn't I? Like one of those china dolls that cost a packet. No wonder her dad wanted to see me.

What was wrong with me? Why did I fuck up all the time? I couldn't say anything. I just sat down on the bed and stared at Dekka. Then I felt something wet on my face. I put my hand up and wiped it away, but it got wet again.

'It's not your fault, marrer,' Dekka said. 'There's nothing you could have done. She must have been nuts.'

I looked at him and shook my head. 'She wasn't nuts. She was OK. She was a decent lass. Everyone else knows, yeah?'

Dekka nodded. 'What's happening, chav?' I said. 'What's goin on? The world's gone mad. I don't think I can take much more of this. I keep dreaming of fuckin Teapot, y'know. I didn't even like the bastard when he was alive, but now he's dead I can't stop dreaming about him. We should have done something, Dekka. And Juliette, and that poor little bitch in Nottingham, and now Reg. She had beautiful hair, you know. Really thick and shiny. I know she wasn't much, but she had lovely hair and nice eyes. Really big, blue eyes. I mean, she wasn't bad looking really.'

'I thought she was fuckin lovely, man,' said Dekka. 'We all did. We all fancied her. Chico gave it a go when you were off with Janey, but she weren't having none. Like you said, she was a decent lass.'

I listened as Dekka talked. It was like someone had just handed me a pair of 3-D specs and the world had changed. He was right, I suppose. She was beautiful, but I'd been too fucked up to admit it. I mean she'd let me come round and screw her whenever I wanted, so stands to reason she must be crap. I mean nuff said, yeah? Never understood, Dekka now told me, why I wasn't more keen. Too late now though. Could be as keen as I liked, couldn't I? Didn't matter now. She couldn't trap me into marrying her, couldn't corner me by getting pregnant. No, she couldn't get her claws into me any more. Well done, Danny boy. Close shave there. You could have had a lovely, sweet girl, who totally adored you, but that wouldn't do now, would it? I mean, you wouldn't want any of that. What a useless twat I am.

'Was it Janey?' I asked.

'What?' said Dekka.

'The lass who was shouting the odds at Reg on Wednesday night and chucked the drink. Was it Janey?'

'Dunno, chavito. Could ave bin. Chico's mum didn't know who the girl was, but Reg's dad said he'd been told the lass had short blond hair, which dun't sound like our Janey.'

'Oh Christ,' I said. 'I bet it was that silly cow from Intake. The one I used to see in Electric Avenue. Wouldn't leave me alone. Got completely sick of her. Pregnant, she said. Lying bitch. I didn't mean it, you know that. I didn't mean to hurt her. I never thought she'd do something like this. What am I going to do, Dekka? Why's it all going wrong? What am I going to do?'

Dekka walked across and rather awkwardly put his hand on my shoulder. We were as close as marrers can be, but touching wasn't something we were big on.

'It's not your fault. You can't say it's your fault. You didn't know she was going to top herself. You didn't mean to do bad to her. I'm really sorry, Danny. She was a grand lass, but you won't do any good going blaming yourself. Come on, chaver, let's go back in the front room.'

I nodded, went to the bathroom to wash my face, which felt very hot, and then walked in to face the others. Chico came straight over and put his arm round my shoulders.

'I'm sorry, amigo mio. S'not your fault. The chica lose

her head; you can't stop these things. It'll be OK, chavito. It'll be OK.'

I nodded my head and sat down. Mikey said, 'Really sorry, man,' and Laurie nodded sympathetically. I spent the rest of the night getting trashed. Utterly, totally, senselessly trashed. At some point someone, Dekka I think, steered me into bed, took my trainers off and left me to crash out. I lapsed into deep and merciful unconsciousness.

I woke up just gone six. Dawn was breaking and the room was sort of grey. For a second I couldn't remember what the weight in my chest was all about. Then, natch, it all came back. I got up, very quietly, and tiptoed out. Dekka and Chico were sleeping the sleep of the blessed. Dekka, with a quiet, whiffly snore; Chico, his arms wrapped around the pillow, an angelic little smile turning up his lips.

I took the stairs softly and looked around the living room. Mikey had left his keys on the table, so I picked them up and let myself out. Down two more flights of stairs then out the front door. Even in the time it had taken me to get up, it had got lighter. The grey dawn was turning yellowy; it looked like it might be sunny. I started to walk.

I'd dreamt about her all night. Eleanor, that is. Just shows, eh? Couldn't be faithful to Reg, even when she was dead. In my dream Eleanor looked sad. She was standing in a graveyard and the rain was pouring down. The ground was muddy, and I kept slipping as I tried to walk. She was beckoning me towards her, and I was trying to get to her, but I kept stumbling, falling over in the mud. It was taking me ages, but I still kept trying to get to her. Then I noticed that just in front of her was a freshly dug grave. And still she drew me on. And I kept walking, but I knew if I didn't stop I was going to fall in. I was going to take a header straight into that new grave, with the wet brown earth piled up on either side. But worse, the grave wasn't empty. There was someone in there, and he was waiting for me. He was tall and thin. Long black leather coat. Terrible teeth.

I was drenched in sweat when I woke. Hair sticking to the back of my neck, and my chest and back clammy. I needed to get out. I needed some air, and to walk for a while until I felt a bit calmer.

Even at this godforsaken hour of the morning the streets were moderately busy. Poor bastards, tooling off to their sod-awful jobs. No matter how bad it is, there's always someone worse off than you, esso es? I walked down Ladbroke Grove for a while, then turned off left into the backstreets. I walked up the hill, crossed over Portobello and then on again. The streets were nice. Lots of trees, and some pretty little houses, painted bright colours, like at the seaside. I'd kept my mind purposefully blank, but I was half hoping, half thinking, that he might just turn up. He had before, right enuf. So why not now, when I needed him?

I must have walked for an hour, looping round in a wide circle, until I came down a little hill, back into Portobello, and turned to my left into a big square, lined with tall trees. There were big white houses on three sides, and in the middle of the square was a kids' playground, with a five-a-side footy pitch, swings, slide, roundabout and climbing frames. There were benches all round the outside. I sat down. For a while I just stared, semi-sightlessly, straight ahead. Then I remembered something. He'd said if I wanted to find him I should look for him. Ta bom, chav. Well, here goes. I stood up and gazed around the square. Saw nothing, absolutely nada. I walked over and looked up and down the road. Nada. I walked round the edge of the square and checked each

178

of the little side roads and jennels leading in. Nada de nada. 'OK, fuckface,' I said. 'I'm looking, but I can't see anything.'

'That's because you've got your eyes closed,' said a voice in my ear.

I leapt about a foot, but I knew because of the smell. That fuckin aftershave. Should be against the law. It was him, of course. I turned round, for some reason I was smiling. 'It's you, ermano,' I said. 'It's you.' He smiled back and rearranged the endless legs as we sat down on the nearest bench.

'I told you,' he said, somewhat smugly, 'that you'd find me if you looked. Well, chavi chavito, here I am. Kay passer, marrer? Kay passer?'

'You probably know, don't you?' I said. 'You know what's bin happening.'

'No,' he said softly. 'Not everything. I don't know what you know, and that's what I want to hear.'

So I told him. The whole dreary tale, from when I'd left him at the bus stop and went back to the pub. I told him I'd remembered his advice and tried to go home. But I'd not tried hard enough. Told him about the fuck-awful party, what happened to Chico and Dekka's close shave with mortality. I explained about Bez and said what he'd done to Skinny. And, last of all, I told him about Reg. 'So there you go,' I said. 'As they say on the telly, "A lifetime of excitement packed into one weekend." And I dreamt about Eleanor last night, but it turned horrible because Bez was there.'

'No he wasn't,' said Mr Tall and Golden.

'Yes he was, chavito,' I said. 'It was my bleeding dream, so I should know, sisi?'

'You thought he was there, because you're frightened of him,' he said.

179

'So I should have carried on and walked into the grave,' I said, somewhat sarky.

'You could ave walked round it, chav,' he said.

'And to think I wanted to talk to you,' I said.

He smirked and stood up, moving so he was standing directly in front of me, his height meaning I had to practically crick my neck to see his face.

'You know why you wanted to see me, don't you?' he said. He didn't wait for my reply, just carried on. 'You wanted to see me cos you wanted me to tell you what to do. But you already sabey, don't you, chav? You don't fancy it much, and who can blame you. But you know what's got to be done.'

'No,' I said sulkily, 'aven't got a fuckin clue, marrer. Don't know what you're on about. I'm not a fuckin mind-reader.'

He looked down at me and raised his eyebrows.

'Oh fuck off,' I said. 'I don't know what you mean. I've told you twice. How many more times?'

'You'll need to go to the Cross today and get your train,' he said. 'We both know you have to go.'

I nodded. I knew what he meant, right enough, but was dreading it. Shit-scared I was, but it had to be done. Just hoped to God Stockwell wouldn't pounce on me if he found I was back in town.

'Her dad'll kill me,' I said.

He sat down again and put his arm around my shoulders. Like in the Cathedral at Lincoln, which seemed half a lifetime away, his touch was feather light, but very warm. Funny really.

'Don't worry, Danny Boy,' he said. 'It won't be much fun, but you'll survive. Get yourself up there esta notch, chavito. Go back home and follow the coffin. You have to go, me chico. If you don't, she'll haunt you. She'll walk behind you every step of your life. Every girl you take to bed, there she'll be, leaning on the pillows, her long hair tangling in your hands. You have to go back.'

I nodded and got up. 'Best get weavin then,' I said. He nodded and smiled at me, and we began to walk down the hill, back towards Laurie's flat. As we came to the Ladbroke Grove he moved away. 'See you later, chav,' he said and, before I could open my mouth, disappeared up the steps to the tube. I watched him go, his gold blond hair still shining in the early-morning light. 'Fuckin great,' I said, and crossed into Cambridge Gardens. When I got back to the flat they were all still fast asleep.

When I told the others about my plan they thought I'd seriously lost the plot.

'You're crackers, chav,' said Dekka. 'It's not your fault she topped herself. You don't have to go. Her dad'll kill you, for starters. Then there's the polis, not to mention Gibbsey. I mean, he might be down London now, but what if he hears you're back and on your tod? See sense, Danny. It's a fuckin barmy plan.'

Chico felt much the same. He thought we should all stick together, and the idea of me going back on my own, to Donny of all places, was 'loco'. Mikey and Laurie both joined in the chorus.

'OK, OK,' I said, putting my hands in the air. 'I know you think I'm cracked. But I'm going all the same. I've got to. She killed herself cos of me, didn't she? If it weren't for me she'd be alive now. Probably going out with some craphead office worker. Saving up to move to Bessacarr. Thinking of buying their first car. Whatever. Two years I've bin seeing her, off and on. Never even bought her a birthday present. Never even bought her a card, come to that. I've got to go. I'll deal with her da when I get there.'

181

There was more arguing, but eventually they gave up. Mikey even offered to drive me, but I said it was better I went alone. I would have to stay at me mam's, and I couldn't bear Mikey seeing that set-up in all its glory. So we rang up the Cross, and it turned out that if I went in the afternoon I could get a mucho-cheapo, multi-super-saver, aren't-you-just-the-fuckin-lucky-one ticket for the oh-so-reasonable price of £38.50. Return, mind you. What a bargain.

Chico leant me the money and everyone piled in the car, cos Mikey was giving me a lift to the Cross. I felt a bit funny when I jumped out alone, but I told them I'd be back tomorrow night, gave one cool wave and dandered off, jaunty as you like. Second-class smoking was at the far end of the train. I got in the carriage and sat quiet, then the engine started and we were moving. Back to the hills of the North.

Took an hour and forty minutes to Donny. East-Coast-line lectrification, you see. Fastest line in the country, and quite right, too. Just before half five when I got there, and depressed wasn't in it. The whole town looked grey and dark. Dusk had fallen and the streets were full of weary workers staggering home. I went down the underpass, through the Frenchgate Centre and waited outside Tandy for the bus home. I wondered if me mam would lend me any money. A bit far-fetched, I know, but worth a shot all the same.

Thanks to God and his angels, she was out. The house was totally quiet, and I made meself a cup of tea and some scran and had a think. Reg was a Catholic, I knew that. So it'd be St Peter's, stands to reason. I took a deep breath and rang the presbytery. Hadn't rung that number since he was there. Couldn't bear to think of anyone else answering his phone, but there wasn't much option, so I did it.

The new priest answered. 'Yes,' he said. 'Regina's funeral is at ten thirty tomorrow morning. Are you family or friend?' Neither, mate, I'm the bastard who used to shag her. Didn't say that, of course. I mumbled something about being a friend, and he said I would be very welcome. Wasn't too sure about that meself, but there you go. I'd done the necessary now. Knew what I was at. I went upstairs to sort me clothes out.

It took me ages. I wanted to wear a shirt with a black tie, but I couldn't cos I hadn't got a black tie, and all me shirts were ultra cool 'n' groovy down-the-dance-hall-type things. I found the black trousers from me school uniform, which luckily still fitted – bit short in the leg, but not too bad. But what to wear with them? I got so desperate I even risked a raid on me mam's room, but the only black shirt she had was in chiffon, which I thought, especially when you took the diamante buttons into consideration, was probably not what I was looking for. In the end I found a decent black T-shirt – Emporio Armani; I'd lifted it in Sheffield last summer – and my big padded jacket, which was actually dark blue with a white trim, but it was clean and smart and the best I could do in the circs. This done, I had a shower, which, as always, made me feel a bit brighter, scouted a bit more scran and another cuppa from the kitchen, and lay down on the bed to wait for me mam.

Even though I was knackered, I couldn't sleep. I rolled a joint. Mikey had given me a bit of blow before I left – 'Good for the nerves,' he'd said. Eventually I must have dropped off, cos the next thing I knew was the door slamming. Then there was a crash, a man's voice swearing and the sound of me mam giggling. I looked at my watch: 11.45 p.m. She'd been down the Pelican. God alone knows what she'd brought back with her. Suddenly there was a shriek from the kitchen; she'd spotted the dirty plates. 'My baby! My baby's back!' And then there was the sound of feet running upstairs. I rolled off the bed and stood up, took a deep breath and opened the bedroom door. She'd have crashed straight through it anyway, and I preferred to meet her on neutral ground. I hate it when she comes into my bedroom and hangs round the place like she owns it. She always ends up rolling around on the bed, and it's so fuckin embarrassing. Anyway, I managed to get out the door and onto the landing. She wasn't expecting this and ran into me at full tilt. I had to grab her to stop her goin over. Sufferin Jesus, was she drunk. From the smell I would confidently predict brandy and coke, with possibly a few beers thrown in. She threw her arms round me and started crying. 'My poor little baby,' she kept saying. 'My little Daz has come home to Mummy.' I couldn't stop her. She just went on and on. Every time I tried to pull away she tightened her grip. Eventually a shout came from the bottom of the stairs.

'Oi, Deirdre! What the fuck's going on up there? And where's that beer you were getting? I'm fuckin thirsty.'

This brought her to, and she let me go.

'Come downstairs,' she said. 'Have a drink with me and Tony. Where've you been, you little bugger? I've been worried sick about you. Tony'll tell you. Made myself ill, I did. Then I had Mr Clemence round the house. Oh, my poor baby. You don't know, do you? Oh, my tragic little boy.'

She stopped halfway down the stairs and put her hand over her mouth. She was getting ready for a major dramatic performance and I intervened before she could get any further.

'It's OK, Mam,' I said, pushing her on down the stairs. 'I know about Reg. Chico rang his mam and she told him. I'm just up for the funeral. It's half ten tomorrow, at St Peter's.'

184

After this she sort of subsided and went into the kitchen to get the beers, leaving me with the charming Tony. Tony was a bit of a regular round our house. He'd been seeing me mam off an on for a couple of years. Not exclusively, like – there was nothing very exclusive about me mam – but, as I said, Tony was a reg. He was on the dole, and had been for as long as I could remember. Legend had it he'd worked for International Harvesters on the line, back at the end of the Seventies, but since then he'd carefully and successfully avoided any situation that looked likely to bring him into contact with anything remotely related to paid employment. He'd also retained his Seventies hairstyle, a sort of would-be laddie feather cut, which probably looked quite groovy when he was nineteen, but over the last couple of decades had rather lost its gloss. Dekka and I used to amuse ourselves by wondering how he and me mam managed it, because his fuckin belly was so big the missionary position was a total non-starter.

'Thought you'd gone for good,' he said. 'Should ave known you'd turn up again. Your mam's been fair doin her nut.'

'Yeah,' I said. I can't be bothered wasting words on Tony. He's as thick as pig shit for starters, and for seconds I don't like the way he behaves round the house. Like he's got some sort of claim. Even drops occasional hints about him and me mam 'setting up' together, or to be more precise, him moving in here and getting his washing done on a permanent basis. Luckily, not even me mam's that daft.

Anyway, Tony and I were spared more sparkling dinner-party dialogue by the return of me mam with the beers. I'd wanted to talk to her about what Reg's dad had said, but I knew that Tony wouldn't be able to resist chipping in with his take on it all, so I said nowt. Mam wittered on about where had I been and how she'd been at her wits' end. Stockwell had sent some of his minions round the house to look for me, and Ticka, doubtless acting on Gibbsey's instructions, had been round asking after me. Wasn't I the popular one? I kept my answers vague. She wouldn't remember a word of it come morning anyway. Then she started on about Reg.

'Just before I was going out, it was. Lucky I hadn't got the music on, otherwise I wouldn't have heard the bell. Anyway, there he was. I knew something was wrong. Knew it. I've got a sense about these things. It's, like, psychic. I know things. You remember, don't you, Tone, Carolyn's dog? I saw it, plain as day. So I knew.'

At this point Mam favoured her audience with a darkly meaningful look. Tony nodded sagely and I looked at the carpet. Silly old tart. She *knows* fuck all if truth be told. Her premonitions are entirely confined to prophetic dreams, which she never bothers to share with the rest of us until after the event. When Janette two doors down got done by the social, Mam informed anyone who'd listen that she *knew* it would happen. Strangely enough, she *knew* that her mate Carolyn's dog was going to cop it under the wheels of a reversing bin wagon. Hadn't said anything beforehand, natch, cos it would have been too upsetting for poor Carolyn, and – this being the bit she especially likes – 'because fate is written in the stars. It can't be altered'. Over the years I've developed zero tolerance for me mam's telepathic powers, with a particular aversion to her tarot-reading excursions. But what can you do? I've occasionally tried to point out what a complete load of balls it all is, but she's not havin it. What really annoys me is cunts like Tony, who fuckin encourage her. I mean, she's mad enough on her own. Some silly fat bastard geeing her up is definitely not needed. Anyway, dramatic pause over, she was off again:

'I opened the door and he just walked in. Totally silent, he was. I think he was half dead himself. I mean, losing a kid. It's the worst, isn't it? They say you never get over it. He looked awful. White as a sheet, and like his blood had gone cold. "I'm Mr Clemence," he said. Very formal. "I'd like to see your son, Danny." I sat him down and got him a brandy. Said he was all right, but you could see he wasn't. I told him I hadn't seen you since Wednesday morning. I thought you were round with one of your girl-friends.'

You can imagine, can't you? What must he have felt? 'One of my girlfriends', his daughter, dangling from the loft door. He'd told Mam she'd left a note. 'My daughter was in love with your son,' he'd said. He'd wanted to show me what she'd written, but I wasn't there. So despite me mam's best efforts, he'd put the envelope back in his pocket and left. Only stayed about ten minutes, all told.

All attention then turned to me. How had I found out? What had I felt? Had Mam met her? Were we engaged? Mam persisted in presenting me as a tragic Romeo, so unbelievably attractive, so mysteriously unavailable, that beautiful girls went willingly to their deaths, all for love of me. Now, as you will know, I'm not averse to contem-plating my own brilliance, but this was doin my head in. Even worse, she got the CDs going. We had 'Stairway to Heaven', a bit of a Stones medley – 'Angie', 'Wild Horses', 'Sister Morphine' – the last being far more appropriate to me than Reg, who didn't even smoke – and, of course, the immortal Rodney. 'Sailing. La la, sailing,' sang Mam, swaying from side to side. 'La la la laa, di di di.' I kept drinking. There was no chance of sleeping through this racket, and drink was the only way I could cope. Then she hit the Irish songs.

187

'Dance with me, baby. You can't say no. Come on, dance with me.'

She was standing in front of me, her hand outstretched. When I got to my feet the room tilted, and I had to hold on to her until it righted again. She looked into my eyes and put her left hand on my shoulder, then we were away, waltzing three time. 'There's a colleen fair as May/For a year and for a day/I have tried in every way/Her love to gain.' The tenor voice, clear and pure, winding round us like silk ribbon. 'If to France or far-off Spain/She crossed the watery main/To see her face again/The seas I'd braa-aa-ave.' We were both as drunk as can be, but we danced like angels, sweeping round the front room, swinging round and round until the world dissolved. When the song ended and we stopped, I stepped back and gave a half-bow, an inclination of the head. 'Thank you,' I said, and took her hand and led her back to the settee, ignoring Tony, who was looking morose and left out. Then I went in the kitchen to search for more beer.

She must have followed me, cos as I was ferreting in the fridge she touched my arm.

'Danny, are you all right, love? Don't let what's happened . . . well, you know. You're very young. So young. I don't know if you weren't right with her. I don't know what's behind all this, but you've got to carry on. You've all your life left to live. You know what I mean. You . . .'

She sort of trailed off and stood looking at me.

'You're all I've got,' she said. 'I thought something had happened. I was so bloody worried. You're all I've got, Danny. And when her dad came round, I thought . . . I thought so many things. Why didn't you phone? You could have phoned. I couldn't sleep. I sat down here, night after night. I thought, he'll phone, he will. He's all right.

He's always been all right. Nothing can happen to my boy; he's a smart one. That's what I used to call you, remember? Little Smart-arse.'

Tears were rolling down her face, and I did what I've not done willingly for nearly a decade: I put my arms round her. And I told her I was sorry, and that I was going away again tomorrow, but this time I'd phone. And that she wasn't to worry, cos I was fine, and that she was my mam and I loved her. And could she lend us any money?

She lent me thirty quid, and I said 'ta', and that I'd pay it back. Then we got the beers and went back to Fat Tony.

We stayed up another hour, singing our heads off. 'We're on the one road/Sharing the one load/We're on the road to God knows where.' And, of course, 'I've played the Wild Rover for many a year/And I've spent all me money on whiskey and beer.' Very apt. We went through the lot, finishing up with the Beach Boys, with me and Tony doing backing do-wops to Mam's solo. At this point there was a loud banging, followed by a shout of, 'SHUT THE FUCK UP!' It was 3.30 a.m. and clearly time to pack it in.

I borrowed Mam's alarm, which I set for nine thirty, and said goodnight. When I lay down I had to keep my eyes open, cos every time I tried to close them the room span round and I felt like chucking up. It was right, though, to get drunk at a wake, wasn't it? A mark of respect, really. In Ireland they had the coffin open and in the front room, and you could hold hands and kiss them goodbye. Suddenly I sat up. 'I'm coming, Reg,' I said. 'I know I'm much too late, but I'm coming all the same.'

It only took two minutes to pull on my clothes and get out the door. Mam and Tony were dead to the world, so they were no worry. It's no more than ten minutes to St Peter's from our house, up the dual carriageway to Town

Moor, past the Gaumont and down Chequer Road. It was gone four in the morning, and everything was silent and empty. Bits of chip paper were flying like ghosts down Donny high street and the new moon was lying 'in the arms of the old moon, her mother', as Father O'Flynn used to say. I wished with all my heart he hadn't left me. He'd promised, you see. When I was little I used to get frightened that something might happen and he'd go away. 'I'll never leave you, Danny Boy,' he'd said. 'I promise you that.' But he went all the same. I was fourteen. Father Puttman came round the house. Brain haemorrhage they said. Very sudden. No pain at all. Wasn't a young man. After the funeral, Father Puttman came back. I'd been mentioned in the will, you see. Oh, fair gobsmacked they were by that. There were some books, the ones we used to look at together, plus a few more we hadn't got to. His rosary beads and – this took by breath away – the picture. It hung in his room, to the left of his desk, and he used to tell me about it.

It was a copy of a very old picture. Really, really old. Painted nearly 600 years ago, he'd said, in Italy. *The Legend of St Eustace* it's called. When I was dead little I'd liked the colours and the dogs and all the other animals and birds, but as I got older, he'd told me the story, which I thought was brilliant. Eustace wasn't called Eustace at the start. He was Placidus, a young captain in the Roman army, soon after the death of Jesus. In the picture he's riding a grey horse, with a red-and-gold bridle and a harness with great gold bosses going down the horse's flanks. Eustace is wearing brown leggings and this weird sort of furry skirt thing. On top of that he's got a gold tunic, with an ebony-black hunting horn, which is circled all round with gold. But the thing you notice most is this enormous headdress affair. I can't tell whether it's meant to be blue cloth or silver-blue pelts, like wolf skin or silver fox, but it's wound round and round his head, peaked out in front and ending in a long tail down to his waist.

The legend says that Eustace was out hunting one day when the stag he was chasing turned round and stood firm. In between its antlers was a radiant crucifix. Eustace becomes a Christian, but is warned that he will face terrible things which will test his new beliefs to the limit. They weren't joking either. Father told me that first Eustace's beautiful wife was stolen by an Egyptian sea captain, then one of his sons was taken by a lion, and the other was snatched by a wolf. Miraculously they all got back together again. Then, as final proof of their new faith, they faced martyrdom – the entire family – by being roasted alive in a brazen bull.

Apparently, at the time, it was thought to be pretty funny. What you did was build this big, hollowed-out cast of a brass bull. You left a small opening for the mouth and a larger door where people could be shoved into the belly. When the bull's belly was full of people, you locked the door and lit a fire underneath it. You can see what went on, can't you? As the fire got hotter, so did the brass, and the poor bastards inside were soon hopping from foot to foot, and then the whole thing was roasting, so it was like being trapped inside an oven, and every time you touched the walls or the floor it burnt the skin off you. But don't forget the punchline. You see, dying like this took a long time and it was agonizing, and people generally screamed and moaned quite a lot. Hence the mouth opening, which let in enough air to keep the performance going for a wee while, but was also shaped to act as a kind of amp. So when the dying were screaming their last agony, the brass bull appeared to be bellowing or mooing. Hilarious innit? They just don't tell em like that any more.

But the painting didn't deal with all the stuff to come, it was just the moment of conversion. Deep in the dark of the woods, the stag on a small incline above a stream, the bleeding Christ between his antlers, and Eustace, shocked, a hand held up to fend off the vision, but his face enraptured. You can even see the pulse in his neck beating, because he knows he has seen God.

'You see, Danny,' Father used to tell me, 'when we look, we sometimes find things that are very unexpected. Maybe things we wish we hadn't seen. You have to be ready to deal with that.' I've got the picture in my bedroom. There are five, maybe six different sorts of dogs in it – Dekka likes that – and hares and sleeping fawns, and a bear in a cave. There are pelicans – which is a holy bird, because it feeds its young on its own blood and so is near to Christ – cranes, ravens and sparrows. And the green forest floor is studded with tiny pink and white flowers.

I was in front of the church now. No use trying the main door, that would be locked, but I knew about the other one. Hard to find, but not impossible. Sticking close to the side of the building, into the corner and there it is: the sacristy door. I walked very softly. I was drunk enough to do it, but still terrified of being caught. Can you imagine? Front page of every fucking tab in the land – TRAGIC TEEN IS RIGOR MORTIS ROMEO or DESPERATE DANNY SAYS 'BURY ME WITH HER!' Although on the last one there's a fair chance her father will oblige.

Once inside, it was pitch dark. I had to use my lighter to see my way. Through the sacristy, down the passage and out into the side chapel of St Therese of Liseux. 'The little flower girl' he used to call her. She was one of his favourites. She was a nun and died very young. Her statue has her leaning forward in her brown habit, her arms full of pink roses.

I put my hand out to St Therese to steady myself. In front of the altar was the coffin, surrounded by a glow of candles, their light casting a halo of soft steady gold. The church was ready and decorated for tomorrow. Lots of flowers and banks of new candles in Our Lady's Chapel, ready to be lit. Everything ready and waiting to go.

I didn't walk straight to her. I lit a candle for St Therese to say thanks for the helping hand, then I walked around the wall, stopping to say hello. I lit a candle for St Anthony, too. St Peter's has a really good St Anthony; a proper one, with the baby Jesus standing on the open book in his hand, like he's just jumped out of the pages. Then we had the *pietà*, Jesus half the size of the Virgin, which Father explained is the only way you can solve the sculptural problem of getting him laid across her knee. Finally, on the right of the altar is St Michael. He's another good one – armour and wings, and his face, despite the sort of hairdo that would make Mike Tyson look like a bender, is just right. Noble and tough and dead hard, but somehow kind and . . . what? Loving? Whatever that means, but *good* – a real triumph of a face, it is. But there's other brilliant bits. He's got a massive lance in his hand, and the steel-barbed tip is going through the brains of the devil, who's held by the throat underneath St Michael's foot. The devil's face is sort of half man, half goat, but the rest of him is this mega-vile reptile, with these folded-up, horrible green scaly wings and an endless tail, which goes curling round Michael's legs, trying to bring him down, but, natch, no chance of succeeding.

Then I was in front of the altar, and so was she. I don't suppose she'd imagined it like this, but things don't really turn out the way you want them to, do they? I walked round the coffin. It looked like a nice one, although I don't know much about these things. Now that I was here I didn't know if I'd got the bottle to go through with it. I suppose the thing is to just do it. Don't fuck about. I put my fingers under the lid; it gave immediately. I moved from foot to foot to get my balance and took three deep breaths, then I raised the lid of the coffin.

They'd done her hair wrong. You'd think with long hair they couldn't go far wrong, but they'd given her a centre parting. She never had that. Always parted it on the side, so it sort of hung over half her face. Suited her – sweet but sexy – and they'd got it wrong. Made her look different. Her hair seemed to fill the coffin. They'd put her in a white summer dress, long, down to her ankles, but leaving her arms bare. They'd arranged her hair across her throat and over her shoulders. I suppose they'd done that to cover the bruising from the hanging. I was glad, I didn't want to see the mess I'd made. Her eyes were shut and her eyelashes seemed very dark and long, and her skin was as white as bleached linen. Bone white. Whiter than the whitest wash you'll ever get, so white that even the shadows fell back.

I don't know how long I stayed just looking at her, but I knew what I'd come for, knew what had to be done. I reached out my hand. I knew what I would find, but the shock almost stopped my heart. She was cold, freezing cold. I couldn't hold her hand properly, because her fingers were still, and the undertaker, or whoever, had folded them across her breasts, like some fuckin Egyptian mummy. So I couldn't take her hand as such. Instead I curled my warm soft fingers around her cold and rigid thumb. I'd never held her hand when she was alive; this was the nearest we were going to get. Then I told her: I told her that I'd been too stupid to understand, that I'd do anything to be able to have another chance. Told her all the crappy things I'd done and said – the betrayals and the stand-ups, all the selfish show-offs, and the clever little put-downs – and how she'd deserved so much, much better. Told her all me mates thought she was beautiful, and so did I. Told her that she was pure in heart and that she was on her way to heaven. Told her I was really, really, really sorry. But it was all too fucking late.

It's later than you think. Someone said that once, didn't they? When I'd finished talking, I kissed her goodbye. It was like kissing the frost on the windows, colder than the stones. And that's when I think I realized the enormous thing I'd done. She was dead, and stiff, and cold. Tomorrow she would be deep in the ground, then she'd go rotten. Very soon there'd be nothing left at all. And she should have had another fifty years. And OK, it wasn't all my fault. It's a crap thing to do, to top yourself. Selfish as well. And she should have known better, especially than to do it over a cunt like me. But sometimes you can't help what your heart does. I think women worst of all. People on the outside say you're doing the wrong thing, but you don't really have a choice. I know that. And she deserved better.

I closed the coffin lid and left as quietly as I'd come. They were still fast on when I got back home, and in two minutes I was beneath the duvet and sock on. I dreamt about Eleanor and Reg. They were sitting in an orchard, by a river. They were sitting side by side, with their arms around each other, laughing together and eating apples.

chapter eight

THE MORNING WAS COLD AND GREY, LIKE IT HAD TO BE, and I felt like shite, which wasn't a surprise either. The hangover hammering round my head, my hands shaking. I got the clothes on, packed me bag and left a note for Mam. I'd had three cups of tea, which meant nine sugars, four aspirin and two pieces of toast, which had fair choked me. This had all been done in an effort at feeling normal again. It hadn't been much of a success. I looked at the clock: quarter past ten. It was time; it was surely time.

I tried to walk purposefully, but my heart was beating so fast it was hard to breathe. For one wild moment I thought, Sod it. I'd been to see her, hadn't I? Said I was sorry. Done the decent. They wouldn't want me there today, better if I just got on the train. Turn right down the Frenchgate, and all my troubles would be over. But I knew it was all bollocks. I knew, you see, that he'd told me the truth down in that square in London. He knew all right. If I didn't go, didn't face up to it, then I'd never be clear of her. She'd walk behind me every step of my life, whispering her soft reproaches in my ears. Dogging my footsteps with her white dress and purple bruises. And every girl I ever met would be just another go at digging up Reg. I turned left and walked down Chequer Road. I could see the cars outside the church, including the hearse and two black limos. You had to hand it to them. They were sending her out in style.

The family were already inside. Kneeling together in a long row at the front, to the left of the coffin. They'd put flowers on top of it. White flowers, to match her dress, I suppose. I was one of the last to arrive. There were probably about thirty of us in total, which wasn't a bad turnout. But St Peter's usually has 300 for Sunday mass and the place seemed cold and empty. Even the candlelight looked half-hearted, dimmed and defeated by the bleakness of the day. I bobbed down quickly and slid onto the pew. I sat on my own at the back. I wanted a quick exit.

Suddenly the organ struck up and we were all on our feet. It wasn't easy to tell from the back, but I guessed it was mostly family, although there were a few of her mates that I half recognized, and two blokes in suits who were definitely from her work. The new priest was youngish, maybe late twenties, and sounded Scottish. He was nice about her, said he knew her and knew what a terrible loss her family had to bear. He skirted neatly round the suicide – mortal sin and all the rest of it – and concentrated on what he called her 'sweetness of character'. All in all, not a bad effort. Her sister did the first reading. She looked a lot like Reg, but had missed her prettiness, her delicacy of feature. I knew her, of course. Had met her round at Reg's a few times. We didn't get on. She was a receptionist at the Danum, Donny's swankiest hotel, and consequently thought she was a definite cut above. It was all smarmy suits and co-ordinated court shoes and dismal tales of crappy borderline celebs who'd checked in. She was forever telling Reg what a waste of space I was, but I caught her looking a couple of times; she wouldn't have needed much encouragement. The sort of lass who's basically gasping for a good shag.

It was more or less going all right till her dad stood up. I mean, it wasn't the best fun I've ever had in daylight, but I was coping. I'd been worried the sister would clock me, but she'd been too nervous, holding on to the rostrum for dear life, eyes glued to the page in front. I'd slid down in my seat until my head was as low as possible, and I was pretty sure she hadn't caught on. But then up comes Dad.

He was a tall bloke, which was odd, because Reg was tiny. He had a dark suit on, white shirt, black tie. Spotless he was, his hair brushed back, washed, shaved, shoes gleaming. The last thing he could do for her, and no-one could fault him. Immaculate, that was the only word. He didn't read, because he knew it by heart. He looked straight out in front and waited. Waited for the coughing and shuffling to stop. Then, when we were all frozen, caught in the moment, and the silence was absolute, then he began: 'Though I speak with the tongues of men and of angels, and have not love, I am become as sounding brass, or a tinkling cymbal. And though I have the gift of prophecy, and understand all mysteries, and all knowledge; and though I have all faith, so that I could remove mountains; and have not love, I am nothing.' His voice carried over the heads of the mourners, reverberated round the empty seats, connecting past and present, lifting and filling the words. 'Love suffereth long, and is kind; love envieth not; love vaunteth not itself, is not puffed up, doth not behave itself unseemly, seeketh not her own, is not easily provoked, thinketh no evil.' It could have been written for her, and the tears were rolling down my face, unstoppable, as if my heart had burst. And then he looked at me, and he knew, and he said it straight to me: 'When

I was a child, I spake as a child, I understood as a child, I thought as a child: but when I became a man, I put away childish things. For now we see through a glass, darkly; but then face to face: now I know in part; but then shall I know even as also I am known. And now,' he said, and the voice was finally wavering, and he was crying with me, still looking straight at me, the sobs rising in his throat, 'And now abideth faith, hope, love, these three; but the greatest of these is love.'

I didn't see him get to his seat. I was blinded by tears, and people were turning round, because they could hear me; and my crying was noisy, ugly, messy sounds, but there was nothing I could do. Agony and devastation were all around, and there was no release and no escape on offer.

I don't know about the rest of it. Don't know how it went. I remember the music though. 'The Lord is My Shepherd', as they carried her out, the family slow-marching behind the coffin. And now, of course, they knew who I was. The parents, in front, kept their eyes on their daughter's coffin, but the sister looked straight at me, and her face said it all.

As the coffin went out and into the hearse I suddenly realized what the crack was. You see, I hadn't known the form at all. And now I was trapped. My original intention – to do a runner during communion – had gone by the board. So plan B had been to let the family and nearest and dearest fuck off in the cars, then trot off when the coast was clear. But they weren't getting into the bleeding cars. Dad, Mam and sister were standing with the priest by the church door, and a queue of mourners were going past, shaking hands and saying the necessary. The four of them had a perfect view inside. If I got up and dodged out through the sacristy, they would see me and I would look

199

ridiculous. Of course, I could pretend to be overcome by grief and piety, get on my knees and stare up to the altar, rapt and deep in prayer, hoping they'd get sick of waiting and go away. But I couldn't do it, you see. Couldn't do it to her dad. Couldn't leave him standing, on this, the worst day of his entire fucking life. Standing patiently in the cold, whilst the fuckwit who'd pushed his daughter over the edge pretends to pray for her. It was just too crap. So there was only one thing left to do: get up and walk out the normal way, which meant running the gauntlet of Mam, Dad, sister and priest. I was finding it hard to breathe again. My heart had somehow ridden up my throat and I was choking, and my legs had gone funny. When I stood I had to hold on to the bench in front, and I was trembling from head to foot; shuddering, like I'd been dropped in iced water. They were standing at the door, waiting. They must be waiting for me, cos there was no-one else left. 'OK, Danny Boy,' I said to myself. 'Walk.'

I genuflected, still hanging on to the bench, about turned and walked. As I was already at the back there wasn't far to go, but it was like a slo-mo from the movies. Every step took a minute. The four faces at the door turned to me, getting closer and closer, my legs going from under me and my tongue stuck to the roof of my mouth. And then I was at the door and outside, turning to her father, trying to find the words, and she hit me so hard she nearly knocked my head off.

They had to pull her off me. She held fistfuls of my hair, and the nails were going down my face, and I could feel the kicks on my legs and hear her screaming, 'Murderer. Murderer. You fuckin killed her, you fuckin bastard. You bastard. Bastard. Bastard. You killed my sister, you dirty little bastard.' I just stood there as they pulled her off, her dad and the new priest. I think the priest and her mum took her away. I'm not sure. I just stood there, through the lot of it, like I was in a coma or something. Hadn't tried to stop her. Thought it was fair enough, I suppose.

Then there was just me and her dad, standing in front of the church, looking at each other. 'I'm Danny,' I said. 'Danny MacIntyre.' He nodded. 'I know,' he said. 'I saw you in the church.'

'It was my fault,' I said. 'I'm sorry. I didn't know. Never knew until it was too late. But I'm sorry. The lass was lying. I'm sorry. I didn't see. I'm so sorry. I'm sorry. I'm sorry, really sorry, really. I'm so sorry.'

He put a hand out and stopped me. 'Steady on, lad.' He looked at me for a long time and put his hand in his pocket, pulling out a white envelope.

'I thought to myself,' he said, 'I thought, if he's got anything about him, then he'll turn up. She wrote this for you. You'd better take it. Don't come to the cemetery, you'll only upset everybody. But I don't entirely blame you, lad. She took her own life. You never put that rope round her neck; she did that herself. That's what I can't bear. My little girl; she left us all. Left us all behind.'

He paused and shook his head, his eyes focusing beyond me, seeing something far away.

'She was my baby. Her hair was blond when she was little, you know. Only got darker in her teens. White blond, it was, and down to her waist, like a little princess. She was my favourite. We'd take the car out – Moor End, Cusworth, the woods at Sandall Beat – and go walking. Well, not any more. It's all finished now. I thought whoever she fell for would be the luckiest lad in the world, but you weren't even interested. To me she was worth her weight in gold, but you thought she was just another lass. You must have been blind. Couldn't you see how special she was? Can't you see what you've chucked away, you stupid little bugger?'

'Yes,' I said, and the word came out too loud and too angry, and I had to take a breath to steady myself. 'I can see it all now. When it's too fucking late, when it's all messed up and they're just about to put her in the ground. I can see it now, all right. You see, my problem is that I was too fuckin stupid to see it while she was alive. While there was a point to it all. No use saying sorry now, is it? Not now, when she's going six foot under. You see, when she said she loved me I told her to shut up. Thought she was soft, daft. Like you say, just another lass. Liked her the best, stayed with her the longest, but wouldn't admit to myself that that might be cos I cared about her. And I hurt her, a lot. And I nicked money from her and had other lasses, and I didn't care if she knew or not. And I thought all her kindness and all her love was just a pile of weakness and shite. Girl stuff, the sort of crap they all do. And now, when it's too fuckin late, just miles too fucking late, I realize. Realize that I'm a useless cunt who wasn't fit to lick the shite from her shoes. That's why I went to see her last night. I wanted to tell her. I thought she might be able to hear, in front of the altar and that. And that's why I've told you. And you probably want to kill me. And I wouldn't blame you, and—'

'You did what?' he said.

'What?' I said.

'What do you mean, you went to see her? Talked to her last night. What do you mean?'

Then I explained. Told him how I'd got up at four in the morning and come down to the church. Explained about the sacristy door and how I'd lit the candles and opened the coffin, and that I'd talked to her, and then she'd been cold and lovely, and that they should have done her hair properly. And now I really expected him to crack me one. Braced for it, I was. And truth be told, I half wanted it, wanted to be hurt as I deserved to be, and the sister hadn't done nearly a good enough job. But his hands hung loose and open by his sides, and his eyes got brighter and brighter until they trickled over down his face. His blue eyes, like hers, and I was reminded of that last night, the last night we'd had together, when I'd made her cry, and the tears ran in rivers down my face too.

'You did that,' he said. 'You did that for her.'

I nodded, mute with tears, and suddenly his big arms were round me, and we were holding on to each other and my nose was running onto the shoulder of his suit, which, I could smell it, had come from the dry cleaners, and his big hands were patting my back, and no words were spoken because no more could be said.

He handed me the envelope and I put it in my pocket. Then, feeling awkward and unsure, I said goodbye, and he gave me his hand, which is amazing. And we shook hands, and I felt something which is very hard to describe. Because I knew I'd lost Reg, but now it turned out I'd lost other things that I hadn't known anything about or understood at all.

'I won't forget her,' I said, as we turned to go.

He shook his head. 'You will,' he said. 'You probably should. Me and her mother, we're the ones who'll remember. That's our job.' Then he got into the black limo and disappeared behind the smoked windows as the car swung out and onto Chequer Road.

I walked back up Chequer Road, through the Waterdale Centre and into the Frenchgate. It was only there that I suddenly twigged what I must look like. People were staring, and I could see blood on the sleeve of my jacket. I dodged up the escalator and availed myself of

Frenchgate's very excellent toilets ('strictly for the convenience of shoppers and patrons'). Luckily, shoppers and patrons were thin on the ground that morning, cos one look at me and they'd have run, screaming. Reg's sister had done some damage. The blood was coming from my nose and from a scratch that ran halfway down the left side of my face. She'd gone for the eyes, but not quite made it, and the line her nail had cut went from just above my cheekbone to the corner of my mouth. It wasn't very deep and didn't hurt much, but it looked a total bugger. The crying business hadn't done much for me, either. No wonder battered women always look such a fuck. Tears and battering constitute a total cosmetic no-no.

Anyway, restored to near enough my former glory, I emerged from the bogs and legged it to the station. I knew a train would be around cos there's one every half-hour to the Cross from Donny, and, sure enuf, I arrived with just five minutes to go before the 1300 hours departure for 'Retford, Peterborough, Stevenage and Kings Cross. Expected time of arrival 1440 hours'. Ta bom. Ain't that grand. I'd just got enough time to buy meself a couple of cans from the station buffet – cheaper than the rip-offs on the train, who, if there were any fuckin justice, should be arrested and publicly hung for being a bunch of thieving bastards; £1.75 for a can of Strongbow, my arse.

I just made it onto the train, which was all brushed nylon and logo-a-go-go, when the whistle blew and the automatic doors slammed shut. I don't know what made me look out the window. Desperate for a last homesick glance at glamorous Hyde Park flats maybe, who knows. But anyway, I dumped my bag and leant on the door to look out, and I couldn't believe what I saw.

She was standing about five feet away from me on the platform, looking directly at me. Her soft dark hair falling across her shoulders. Her face was gentle and beautiful, and she shone with the radiance of a thousand stars. I grabbed the door handle, but couldn't shift it. The red light was on and I was locked in and she was locked out. The train was beginning to move, to slowly roll down the platform.

I pressed myself against the window and looked at her, and she looked back and gave me such a smile. Such a look and such a smile. And I felt like I was dancing the best dance of my life, and that if I lived for ten times for ever I would never, ever, see anything better than this. Then she was gone. The train picked up speed and that was it. She'd gone.

I stood by the door for maybe twenty minutes, only snapping to when the guard announced we were approaching Retford, and I realized that if I wanted a decent seat in smoking I'd better leg it down there before the train pulled up and a load of scabby Notts bastards clambered aboard. I was too little to take in much of the miners' strike. But I'll tell you one thing I do know for sure, we have some fuckin pride and backbone in Yorkshire, some fuckin guts, and what do those scabby Notts fuckers have? A redundancy notice and a thank-you letter from that old bag Thatcher, that's what.

Anyway, I picked up me kit and shifted it. Luckily the train was brilliantly empty, only about half a dozen in smoking, so I got a whole four to myself. Luxury or what? I spread out my belongings, made my claim and stared ferociously as the Notts lot came shunting down the carriage. Tactics paid off, cos no-one attempted to sit with me. Looking at the empty spaces around I felt, with luck and the right judgement, I might even make it to London solo. When the train was a good five minutes out the station I tooled off to the bogs to do the necessary. This was real pain. First off, I was terrified of losing the gear as the train swayed and juddered. Then, when I'd managed to get it in the works, there was the nightmare of hitting up. It took fuckin ages – the train shooting from side to side, the spike slipping every which way. My fuckin arm was beginning to look like I'd been to Dracula's tea party. Anyway, I got it eventually and weaved my way back to my seat. Actually, I felt knackered. I'd had about three hours' sleep, and I just sat there, sipping from my can and staring out the window.

A few people got on at Peterborough, but not too many. There was a nasty moment when a cunt in a suit started eyeing up my table, but I favoured him with a total dead-eye and stuck my feet on the seat opposite. He got the message and fucked off elsewhere. The only other new arrival was some middle-aged bloke looking after this kid in a wheelchair, and there was a good deal of fucking around as they got settled up the top end in a special seat, which, interestingly, had some sort of security grid, in case the wheelchair's brakes failed. Presumably to stop it rolling down the aisle like a refreshment trolley gone loco. Lots of fun to watch, but tricky on the insurance premium. I looked at the kid in the chair, then looked away again quickly. He must have been in a fire or something, cos his face was enough to make you lose your dinner. He was sort of familiar, probably been on telly in some hospital programme. Maybe an episode of *Jimmys*.

He made me uncomfortable. You know what it's like, you see something horrible, but you can't stop looking. You don't want to do it, but you can't help yourself. This kid was a right mess. The more I looked the worse it got, in the end I couldn't stand it. I got up and moved round the other side of the table, so I was sat with my back to him. Even then I kept wanting to turn round. I wished I

had a paper or had brought me Walkman with me, something to take my mind off the cripple and his fucked-up
face. Maybe he'd been in a car crash and the petrol tank
had exploded.

When the bloke looking after him came down the aisle,
I presumed he was off to the bogs. I presumed wrong. The
minute he slid into the seat opposite – at my table, mark
you, without so much as a by-your-leave – I recognized
him. It was Tubby. Still wearing the hippy badge and still
with the stupid haircut. 'Oh Christ,' I said. 'What have I
done to deserve this?'

'Very little in my view,' he chipped back, sarky as you
like. 'But, fortunately for you, your deserts are not for me
to decide.' He looked me up and down and nodded to
himself. 'It can't be said you are looking well.' At this
point he permitted himself a little smirk. 'But some
improvement on our last encounter must be allowed.'

'Cheers, chav,' I said. 'Sorry I can't say the same for
you.'

'Pride goeth before destruction,' he said, 'and a haughty
spirit before a fall.'

'Oh toss off, you tubby twat,' I said. 'What's the crack
anyway? You come down to sit with me for the pleasure
of pissing me off?'

'For they are a very forward generation,' he said, 'children in whom there is no faith. Listen to me.' Suddenly
he'd stopped pissing about and was meaning it. 'There is
a darkness which may be felt awaiting you. Grave matter
and a deciding.' He looked straight at me, and this was
big-time. 'Do not return to folly as a dog returneth to
vomit. Now is the season to stand and to be strong.'

'I don't understand,' I said. Suddenly I felt very tired.

'Then use the brains that God gave you. You know your
enemy. They have made a covenant with death, and with

207

hell they are at agreement. Again I tell you, now is the season to stand and be strong.'

'Why are you talking to me like this?' I said. 'It doesn't make any sense. I don't know who the fuck you are, or why you keep following me around. I feel like I can't understand anything any more. What's going on? What's happening to my life?' My voice was going wavery. I thought for a terrible moment I would cry.

He smiled, and reached out his hand and touched my forehead, in much the same way as he'd touched Chico on the night he'd turned up in a cop car. Stranger than strange, it was. Hope and well-being flushed through me like a fever, and suddenly the possibilities were limitless and the heartache lifted.

'A light will shine in the darkness,' he said softly, 'and the darkness comprehended it not. I have to leave you now, but you will understand, and you already know who I am, as I told you: Dr Aquinas—'

'Lately travelled from Pisa,' I said.

He laughed. 'Exactly so, exactly so,' but then he caught himself on and turned serious again. 'I cannot save you, Daniel, but I will give what aid I can. And I have set before you life and death, blessing and cursing. Confront abomination; evil multiplies as maggots infesting a corpse. For too long you have walked with the dead.' He nodded and smiled at something over my shoulder. I realized he was signalling to the wheelchair kid. He got up from the table and smiled down at me. 'You must choose,' he said. 'Very soon you must choose.' He looked at me intently, then put out his hand and grasped me under the chin. Holding me tightly, he raised my face to his and spoke directly, only inches between us. 'Therefore,' he said, 'choose rightly.'

My eyes were still locked with his, when suddenly something clicked. 'I know you,' I said. 'I know who you are. Father O'Flynn told me about you. "The most saintly of the learned and most learned of the saints." That's what they said about you. And at school they thought you were stupid, and they called you the Dumb Ox. Then your teacher said, "One day this ox will give such a bellow as will astonish the world." And he was right. The Angelic Doctor, that's another name he called you. You were one of his favourites.'

He nodded and looked pleased with himself. 'You have been well taught, by a sound master. I told you we were acquainted.' Then the train juddered slightly and started to slow, and he became serious again. 'Faith and reason stand divided, Daniel, but with faith all things are possible.'

'This train is now approaching Stevenage,' said a disembodied voice. He turned.

'Before you go,' I said. 'Who's that kid you're with, and what happened to him?'

'Don't you know?' he said. 'Stephen talks of you constantly.'

He walked down the aisle, unbolted the wheelchair and was by the door as the train pulled up. I got out of my seat and watched them go down the platform. Stephen? I didn't know any Stephens, and you wouldn't forget someone who looked like that in a hurry. I mean, Elephant Man eat your heart out, this kid was a serious horror show. But there was something about him. Something made me keep looking at him, some nagging familiarity. I watched Dr Aquinas wheel him off, and just before they turned the corner, the kid said something to the doc and slightly turning his head, so that his face, or what was left of it, was angled towards me.

I heard a thundering in my ears, like the galloping of

hooves. A loud roaring sound, and drumming and a thundering of hooves, and then the ground started to tilt and everything around me began to dissolve into nothingness and blackness. Somebody was screaming. Screaming. Somewhere a boy was screaming, very, very loudly.

A man in uniform was standing in front of me, and I was sitting in another place. There was a glass of water on the table, and I could hear voices. They were trying to speak to me, but they were very far away. 'It was him,' I said. 'I know it was him.' Someone lay a hand on my head and lifted the glass of water to my mouth. 'Drink this,' I heard them say.

We were nearly at the Cross before I came round. Turns out I'd thrown an eppie, and not a small one, either. A real full-tilt boogie job it was. A couple of concerned citizens had rushed to pick me up, and someone else had gone to fetch the guard. I was sorry I'd missed it, cos it sounded mega. The guard had told the senior conductor, who'd promptly put on his gold-braided hat and done an emergency 'is there a doctor in the house?' announcement. No less than three fucking doctors had turned up, and the attention I'd got exceeded BUPA's wildest dreams. Diagnosis was I'd fainted. Isn't medical science wonderful?

Unfortunately, in the course of their ministrations they'd uncovered the track marks on my arms, which had somewhat undermined the sympathy vote. Anyway, despite the revelation that I was a fully paid-up member of the snivelling-junkie fraternity, they continued to look after me, free tea, with loads of sugar, and a cheeseburger on the house. I must admit to being warmed by the generosity of the human spirit.

So by the time we rolled into the Cross I was back on me feet, and firmly refusing offers of ambulances, taxis, or an escort to the tube. I put what I'd seen into a corner of my mind, because I didn't know what else to do with it. I mean, he was dead, wasn't he? I'd seen the fucking pix. Dead, mangled, mutilated, buggered, burnt, castrated, dumped and drowned. Shot as well, come to that. So what the fuck was he doing being wheeled down the platform at Stevenage? I mean, any thoughts welcome, cos I'm losing the plot big style. I flowed on down the tube at the Cross, onto the Metropolitan line and out to Ladbroke Grove. The station names went flashing past – Euston Square, Baker Street, Paddington, Westbourne Park – and I kept repeating again and again the same words, like I could say nothing else. 'I've seen Teapot,' I said. 'I've seen Teapot, I've seen Teapot, I've seen Teapot, I've seen Teapot.'

Everyone but Laurie was out when I got back. He told me that Kim had come over from Green Lanes, but they'd all dandered off down Portobello for a drink. Fortunately, Laurie was heavily involved in a vid of Tyson versus Holyfield and, after asking me how it had gone and if I was OK, he left me to it.

First I got myself sorted. I put every last thing I'd been wearing into a plastic bag, which I put aside for the laundrette. I'd brought more clean stuff down from Donny, which I laid out on the bed. Then I brushed my teeth and had a shave and got into the shower. I didn't just stand there, I washed. Soaping up and down my arms, across my chest and shoulders and doing my armpits twice. I washed my legs, feet and bum, and did a proper job on the tackle. Finally, nicking Laurie's shampoo, I did my hair. Sparkling, I was, from top to toe. I got dry and quickly, rubbing hard with the towel so my skin turned pink, and, as a final touch, I swiped Laurie's deodorant and aftershave. The aftershave was in some mega-expensive bottle and had 'Jean Paul Gaultier' written all over it. I've noticed this about spades, you know. They take care of themselves. Given half the chance they'll spend a fuckin fortune on clothes, cars, jewellery, haircuts, the full shebang. And the results speak for themselves, don't they?

Fat Tony's always mouthing off about what a disgrace it all is. But face it, if you were a lass and could choose between Fat Tony, complete with BO and beer gut, and some black lad, fit as you like and done up to the nines, well, QED, as my history teacher was fond of saying. Race relations in one easy lesson.

Impressive, innit, my far-reaching grasp of the human condition? I went back to the bedroom so clean I felt like I'd been new-born. Clean socks, boxers, kecks and T-shirt, and there I was, a whole new Danny. I smiled into the mirror and did a few steps. 'For he is handsome, he is pretty/He is the toast of London city.' Esso es, muchachos. Esso es.

Although I was tired, I decided I'd go out and see me marrers. I wanted to see Dekka, Chico and, oddly enough, Mikey. Wanted to check everything was OK, wanted to feel the security of being with me chavs. First things first, though. I had something to do.

I'd not forgotten, you see. The envelope had been folded inside my jacket pocket since he'd given it to me. But I'd known I was going to wait. It was a private thing. There was no way I was going to open it on the train. I wasn't going to read this in the company of strangers, wasn't going to have people craning their necks to see what was upsetting me, trying to read the words upside down as they sat across the table. I had no idea what she'd written, but I knew it was between her and me. Her dad had been respectful enough to pass the envelope unopened. Like he'd said, it was addressed to me. Reading it on the train would have been like pulling her knickers down in public. It was for me and Reg, not for other people.

I shut the door, closed the blind and sat down on the bed. It was almost 4 p.m. and the light was beginning to fade. I switched on the bedside lamp. I had the envelope in my hands. It was white, creased where it had been folded up and beginning to mark around the edges. On the front, in a royal-blue fibre-tip pen, she'd written 'For Danny'. The back was sealed down. I got my knife out of my jeans pocket and eased the tip under a corner, then, slowly and carefully, I slit across the top in a neat, straight line.

Inside was a single sheet of white plain paper. She'd used the same royal-blue pen. For a minute I just sat there. I was frightened of what she was going to say. She had written this perhaps ten or fifteen minutes before she did it. It was like looking into the jaws of eternity.

'Dear Danny,' she began. Proper to the very last, even the comma remembered.

'I want to tell you that I love you. You will laugh, but I used to think about our children. What they would look like. How they would be. I always imagined having a boy. He'd have blue eyes and black hair, like you. It's so stupid, isn't it? You always thought I was daft. Well, now you know.

I kidded myself, I suppose. I told myself that eventually I would get through to you. That you loved me, you were just frightened to admit it. I used to think of the nice times we'd had together. This Christmas, do you remember? Sometimes it's like watching a video. I can remember every second, and I run it through my mind again and again.'

Oh yes, I remember. I've got the video, too. Freezing outside, and the Christmas from hell. Mam and Tony totally pissed, pulling each other's clothes off and snogging on the settee. Me, desperate for a window of sanity, off round to Reg's, bottle of vodka in my pocket and the new CDs I'd bought Mam for Christmas. Her face lit up when she answered the door, and her house was like finding sanctuary, clean and quiet and comfortable. A Christmas tree in the corner, and Reg herself, looking like the angel who brings the good news. She must have washed her hair that night, because it shone and rippled and smelled of pine woods. She was set to go out – we were supposed to be off for a drink – and the dress was new, green, like ivy, and clinging as tightly. I was so happy to be out the house, so pleased to see her, that for once I was nice to her. I told her she looked crackin, and asked if we could stay in, drink the vodka and listen to the CDs. Of course she'd said yes, and it had been one of those nights. Drinking and laughing and happy to be together. I'd carried her upstairs – she was so tiny you could pull a stunt like that – and I sang to her. She'd kept giggling, cos I was so drunk I couldn't remember the words:

'She wore no diamonds, no costly jewels/Nor paint nor powder, oh no none at all/But she wore a bonnet, with a rose upon it/And around her shoulders was a Galway shawl.'

And, of course, I remembered.

'I'm sorry,' her letter went on. 'Don't blame yourself. Try to think of me sometimes. I love you, Regina.

And there you have it. Not much to sum up twenty years of a life. No great poetry, no breathless bursts of emotion. Just a note really. 'Back late, don't forget the washing up, going to top myself, ta ra.'

Why did she do it? What made her do that? I mean,

214

she'd had time to think, yeah? She'd written the notes, found the rope, dragged the kitchen stool up to the bedroom landing. It had taken time and effort, but still she'd gone on with it. I couldn't understand, and it made me angry. Angry with myself for being such a selfish tosser, for fucking her up and walking away with not so much as an 'hasta la vista, baby'. But angry with her as well – for being defeatist and apathetic and crap. If she loved me that much, she should have come and found me. If Gibbsey could do it, why not her? She should have fought, tried, not given in. She should have smacked that girl in the pub and said, 'Fuck off, you silly tart. Pregnant? In your dreams, get back to your kennel.' OK, maybe not Reg's style, but she should have fought, had a bit of self-belief. I wonder what she thought of, standing on the kitchen stool. I wonder how long she'd waited, noose round her neck, before she took the final plunge. She shouldn't have done it, you know. She shouldn't have fuckin done it.

I put the letter back inside the envelope and put it in the bottom of my bag. Then I stood up, shook meself and grabbed me jacket. I was off to find my chavers.

It took me a while, cos all Laurie knew was it was one of the bars down Portobello, of which there are no shortage. Finally, on the third try, and about halfway along, I found them. There they were. Chico, with every girl in the place sending sidelong glances and trying to work out if he was famous. Mikey yellin into his mobie, and Dekka with his arm round Kim, looking happy as Larry. The place was crowded and they didn't see me as I walked through the door, which I thought was pretty fucking sloppy security, bearing in mind I could have bin Gibbsey plus death squad, but let that pass. Anyway, I was almost at the table before Chico looked up and clocked me.

'Amigos contigos,' I said. 'Who wants a beer?'

We stayed for a couple of hours, whilst I went through the whole Donny saga, or at least the edited highlights, and they gave me an update from their end. Mikey had been in almost constant radio contact with Delilah, who was providing regular bulletins on Skinny. The news wasn't too good. Her face was a mess and would take some sorting out, but that wasn't the worst of it. She was having screaming nightmares and couldn't be left alone, especially after dark. Which meant Mikey had lost two sources of income in one go, Delilah having given up the street to play full-time nurse to Skinny. Mikey was hardly thrilled, but what could you do? The better news, Nottingham-wise, was that Dwayne was doing the business and behaving like a pro, so at least part of the empire was still intact.

The chitchat done, Dekka got down to the real business.

'We clocked im, chavito. Went out on the town last night for a bit of a looksee and there he was. Didn't see us, cos we shifted, pronto-like, but it was definitely im.'

'Gibbsey?' I said.

'Esso es,' said Chico.

'Who else?' said Dekka. 'He wasn't solomente, neither. Ticka was with him, plus that fuckin dwarf, and a couple of blokes I didn't recognize.'

'Where was it?' I asked.

'Leicester Square,' Mikey said. 'Laurie was goin to take us round a few of the clubs, have a bit of a laugh. We'd been drinking in this bar and we were just outside, standing around, deciding where to go, when Dekka spotted them.'

'We fucked off sharpish,' said Dekka. 'It's weird, Danny. It's like he knows where we're going to be. They were looking for us, weren't they, Chico?'

216

Chico nodded emphatically. 'Verdad.'

'They were standing at the top end of the square and really eyeballing,' Dekka continued. 'It's starting to give me the fuckin creeps.'

'What do you think, amigo?' said Chico. 'What we going to do?'

I stared at the faces round the table. Chico, Dekka and Mikey, all looking at me, and Kim, clinging to Dekka's arm.

'We're going to go and find the fuckface bastard,' I said. 'We're going to go and find him. And we're going to tell him what he did to Teapot and how completely, totally, barking madly out of order he was. And we're going to tell him he's a fucking disgrace, and a murderer, and a rapist, and an embarrassment to Yorkshire. And then we're going to tell him to fuck off out of it and leave us alone. That's what we're going to do.'

They all looked at me, their faces very still. No-one spoke.

'I mean it,' I said. 'I've had enough. I'd rather get my head kicked in than carry on like this. So it's up to youse, but I'm off downtown tonight to find the psychotic fucker, and that shortarse Mol as well. And with a bit of luck I'll do the fuckin pair of them.'

I sat back in my chair, both hands gripping the edge of the table. Still no-one spoke. They'd all dropped their eyes. Then there was a scraping sound as Dekka moved his chair back and disengaged from Kim. Finally, he looked me in the eye.

'OK, marrer mayor,' said Dekka. 'Ta bom. I'm with you.'

I grinned and he grinned back, and relief and gratitude ran through my veins so strongly I could have just hit up. 'Cheers, chav,' I said.

Then Chico spoke. 'Los tres,' he said. 'Siempre. I come too. Let's kill the fuck wanker.'

'And me,' said Mikey. 'We'll sort this together.'

'Ta bom,' I said. 'Amigos contigos, sisi?'

'Sisi,' said Dekka and Chico.

'Sound as a pound,' said Mikey.

I looked around the table and had to fight the urge to laugh. Probably cos the fear and adrenalin were already setting in. It was like a bad rerun of *The High Chaparral*. All we needed was white hats and the sheriff's badge.

We talked for a while about how best to find them, and settled in the end on just going downtown and dandering around. He always seemed to find us, no trouble. Kim was looking at Dekka with gobsmacked admiration. At any moment she was going to say, 'My hero.' Dekka caught my eye and gave a half-embarrassed smirk. I smiled back, it was funny to see him like this, head over heels with a lass. But fair play to him, he was my chaver, and it was good to see him happy.

We called it a day and left the pub shortly after. If we were serious about tonight, there were no points to be earned turning up half-cut. We walked up Ladbroke Grove and put Kim on the tube, and waited downstairs while Dekka said his platform farewells. Then the four of us crossed the road and strolled down Cambridge Gardens. It was cold, and now the light had entirely gone. The trees lining the road were bare and boney, standing against a dark and cloudy sky, yellowed by the city lights. We walked in silence, our thoughts taken up by what was to come.

Laurie had gone out and the flat was quiet. I walked to the front window and looked down on the road below. Standing dead opposite, staring up as I gazed down, was a single figure. Tall and thin, with a long dark coat, which flapped loose around his ankles. It was impossible for him to see me, but nonetheless I moved back from the window, suddenly terrified. My heart was racing and I breathed deeply, trying to steady myself, then, cautiously, I leant forward and looked back down at the street. There was nothing there. I was about to turn away – probably just some bloke, I told myself. Some bloke who lives round here – then I saw the car. Moving very slowly, it was, like it was following a funeral. A great big old-fashioned black-sedan affair; the bloke driving it so short his head hardly topped the wheel, a tall, thin man sitting next to him.

chapter nine

WE SPENT MOST OF THE NEXT COUPLE OF HOURS TALKING through scenarios. Leicester Square, it was agreed, was probably our best bet. After all, he'd pitched up there before, why not tonight? If he didn't show, then we could have a dander round and see what we could see, much like the sailor. Did you sing that at school? 'A sailor went to sea sea sea/To see what he could see see see/But all that he could see see see/Was the bottom of the deep blue sea sea sea.' Even at six years old I thought it was incredibly daft.

I used to like singing lessons, though. Sometimes we did good ones, where the tune and the words were so matched up that it was really spot on. There was one I liked which had two voices. Mrs Ianson would divide the class into boys and girls. The girls sang Polly and we sang Harry. She'd explained that the song was written during the First World War. Harry's been called up and, natch enuf, he doesn't want to leave his girl. He tries to persuade her that it'll be all right if she comes with him. Polly realizes that this idea is a total non-starter and that, though she loves him heaps and buckets, turning up at the Somme with your girlfriend just won't wash. Harry won't give up, though. He keeps on trying, and like Mrs Ianson said, it's incredibly sad, because ten to one Harry got totalled out there in the trenches with the mud and the blood and the gore, and Polly was left crying over his photo. 'A horse I'll buy you, dapple grey, and on it you shall ride/And all my heart's delight will be trotting at my side.' She's tempted, but catches herself on, and tells him no go. 'Alas my love, my dearest, you know it cannot be/I cannot ride with you, my love, to hi-gh Germany.'

Anyway, you'll have to excuse the diversion, or digression, or whatever you want to fuckin call it. Probably due to nerves. If you were getting ready for a run-in with a certified murdering psycho, you'd be prone to the odd digression, I'll tell you.

Bobby Shaftoe was another favourite. 'Bobby Shaftoe went to sea/Silver buckles on his knee/He'll come back and marry me/Bonny Bobby Shaftoe.' Bonny Danny went to fight/His nerves were stretched out fuckin tight/But him and his chavs will be all right/Bonny Danny Macco. OK, it's crap, but it was only off the top of me head.

We also had a long discussion about whether or not to carry. This was a real talking point. I mean, the moral maze or what? If Gibbsey and crew were tooled up and we weren't, well then, we'd be fuckin slaughtered. Serious crucifixion, sisi? On the other hand, carrying in the middle of London was, to put it mildly, mucho peligroso. The cops could be on you at any minute and you'd be looking at serious bother. We discussed the finer points of this for about an hour, and in the end decided against. As Mikey said, when all was said and done, it wasn't our town. If it'd been Donny or Nottingham, then fair enuf. We'd have been out there, baseball bats swinging, Stanley knife tucked safely in our kecks, back-up blade down the side of your rider boots. But we were strangers in a strange

221

land. We weren't sussed to the nuances of the place. And, as Chico pointed out, judging by the amount of polis hanging about Leicester Square, whatever went down would be stopped as soon as it started. And the one thing you don't want is to find yourself gazing at the inside of a pigmobile, wondering just how you're going to dump your flick knife, knuckle dusters and the CS gas your mate brought over from France before you arrive in the station and have a whole pile of new charges added to the collection you're already facing. So that was that. Ta bom. The posse would rely on northern grit, rock-hard fists and mucho muscle. Not to mention as much aggression as you can muster when you're completely shit scared.

Of course, we did what we could whilst keeping legit. Mikey phoned Laurie, who phoned some mates and then phoned us back, and after mucho toing and froing and fucking around, Laurie tooled up with a big plaggy bag containing three pairs of docs and, even better, a bona fide pair of steel toecaps. These went to Dekka, who, when push comes to shove, is probably the best rucker out of the lot of us. Though that leaves out Mikey, and you don't get to run a crack empire by being a soft boy, that I can tell you. Laurie and Mikey also trailed round the house and came up with a wide and varied selection of the crappiest rings you've ever seen. I put two on the middle fingers of each hand, making sure I could still close my fist properly. The other lads did likewise. The point being that whoever you punched would hopefully get his face ripped open, and happily there's no law against wearing disgusting cheapo jewellery.

So there we were, all revved up and ready to go. We sat around trying to watch telly, but were too strung out to do anything at all. Just before ten we started to get serious. First there was the final hit. A medium-sized dose, which leaves you confident and comfortable, but far from smashed. I mean, I don't know if you've ever tried to fight whilst withdrawing, but take my advice and don't fuckin bother. You'll make a total bollocks of it. Motor co-ordination shot to shit, aggression draining out of you and a sort of trembly, tearful feeling which does absolutely nothing for the hard-boy bravado. Obviously, being stoned out your brains ain't much use, either, so you have to watch your measuring pretty fucking carefully.

This all took about half an hour. Then we stood up, as if of one mind, nodded to each other and walked. We went in Mikey's BM, but only as far as Paddington. When there's a ruck in the offing, the last thing you want is your car getting pasted in the general mêlée – makes it odds-on you'll get done for some fuckin silly made-up driving offence on top of everything else. Anyway, we'd planned it like this. You can't perform a screeching getaway through the chocabloca traffic on the Charing Cross Road. You'd probably make better time on your kid sister's tricycle, and – most important, pay attention – once you make a plan, you stick to it. Claro?

So the red BM was left parked down a side street, and we four dandered down the stairs to Paddington. We were buying a single for Charing Cross – a straight ride down the Bakerloo and a five-minute walk from Leccy Square – when Dekka piped up, 'Is this the same station they left him at then, Danny? You know, the real one?'

'Left who, chaver?'

'Paddington.'

'Eh?' I said, puzzled.

'Paddington Bear, you dickhead. I mean, like is this the real Paddington station?'

Sometimes I worry about Dekka, I really do. 'Yes,' I said quietly, hoping no-one else had heard. 'It's the same place.

But he was left on the railway station, not the tube, but it's only next door.'

Dekka grinned. 'That's brilliant,' he said. 'Dead brill. He was sent by his great aunt Lucy from Lima. With a label round his neck.'

'Lima?' said Chico, perking up. 'Sheet. Peru is a bigga dump, and the football team is such big bollocks.'

'We weren't talking about football, you dago twat,' said Dekka.

'Nigeria,' said Mikey. 'Super Eagles. Fuckin sound or what?'

'Shut up,' I said. 'We're supposed to be on a job, not trying for a place on *Question of Sport*. Come on, chavs, get a grip.'

Thus admonished, my chavitos pulled themselves together and stopped talking about fictional fluffy bears or Third World football teams, and by the time we boarded the south-bound tube, we had once again bonded into a feared fighting unit. Or at least we looked sufficiently menacing to cause everyone else in our carriage to discover a new and profound interest in the state of their footwear.

It's a great feeling when people are frightened of you. I don't know if you've ever tasted it, but it's the best. Dropping their eyes to the floor, body language screaming out surrender and defeat. Hoping and praying that you'll pick on someone else, anyone else, but please, dear God, not me. Well, there was more than a touch of that on the tube, and it made us feel better, givin them the dead eye, an slouchin rock'ard. We'd do the bastards. We would. We were going to fuckin kill the cunts.

It was a short ride to Charing Cross, and we leapt off the train full of bravado, trotting along at a sharp clip. Anyhow, we must – or to be truthful, I must, cos I was in the lead – well, I must have taken a wrong turning, cos instead of being on the way-out escalator, turns out we're stood on the platform for the Northern Line. It wasn't the end of the world, and you could see another 'Way Out' sign, clear as day, at the end of the platform, but I was standing still. Looking and reading, telling me chavs to hang on a minute, whilst I tried to take in all this amazing stuff they'd put up. And behind me, in the inter-train silence, the sooty-black tube mice squeaked and gibbered as they searched for crumbs between the lectrified rails.

It was on the walls of the platform, sweeping round as it followed the curve of the bricks. All in black and white, on a sort of laminated plastic. There was loads of writing, with funny old drawings. I couldn't stop looking. She was a Spanish girl, and she must have been really beautiful. Eleanor of Castille. She was married to King Edward I, 700 years ago. The marriage would have been political and arranged, and when all was signed and sealed she would have been shipped over from Spain. Her parents congratulating themselves on bagging the King of England. What about her? I don't know where she sailed from. I guess she must have gone north. It wouldn't have made any sense at all to sail from Barcelona and have to flog all the way round the entire coast of Spain. No, I bet she rode north with her maids and gentleman attendants, baggage and servants and all the rest of it. Starting off in the burning sun, over the great flat plains, and then, as she went further north, the weather got steadily cooler and the rains set in. And the gold of the plains gave way to the green of the high mountains.

The crossing must have been terrible. The Bay of Biscay in some crappy wooden tub 700 years ago. She must have thought she was going to die; the storms blowing up, the boat creaking and tipping, the horses screaming and thrashing in the hold. And all the time not having the faintest clue where she was heading, except that, as sure as hell, she was never coming back. I imagine her like my Eleanor: dark eyes and long, silky dark hair. Edward fell in love with her, adored her apparently. But she died very young – in 1290 it said on the wall – in Harby, Nottinghamshire. God knows what she was doing there. It didn't say.

He had her buried in the grandest style in Westminster Abbey, and had crosses set up at each of the twelve places her body had rested as they carried it south from Nottingham. The Eleanor Crosses they called them. That tosspot vandal Cromwell had them all ripped down, and now only three are left. The Victorians built a replica of the original at Charing Cross, and it stands today, in the taxi yard outside the train station and the hotel.

I read all this like I was mesmerized, and the others had to practically drag me off the platform. I thought it was the most beautiful story I'd ever heard. I wonder what she died of and if she'd had children. Did she keep her maids, so as she could speak Spanish in private? And did she love Edward like he loved her? Did she kiss his neck and call him *querido*? Did she say, '*Mi buen amor*,' and fall asleep in his arms, tickling his chest with her long dark hair? Did she love this green, cold, rain-soaked country, with its hills and forests and long dark winters? Or did she smile brightly and lie? Did she shudder with distaste, teeth clenched and eyes shut tight, as she longed for the sunlight of her home, dark eyes, bright colours and flowers in the night?

My head had barely cleared by the time my chavers had towed me out of the station and up to daylight, or rather streetlight, seeing as it was gone 11 p.m. and pitch black. We were in the middle of Trafalgar Square, and we walked to the lights to make it across and up the road to Leicester Square and our date with destiny. The lights took ages to change and the traffic was completely mad. I mean, gone eleven on a Tuesday night. What are these people at? It defies reason, it really does. As we shifted from foot to foot, impatiently awaiting the advent of the flashing green man, my attention was taken by what was obviously a certified loony. A loony who was riding his mega-crap yammie bike as if Ayrton Senna had been reincarnated. It was a wee red bike, no more than 250 cc, if that, and with his long legs he was ridiculously too big for it. He had on a shiny white helmet, and on the back was a big box that said 'Domino's Pizza'. I watched him come nearer and nearer, as he jumped the lights, cut up taxis and careered round the square with a major death wish. He was approaching our set of lights down hill, zooming past a row of stranded cars at a hell of a lick. Just as he got close, our little green man finally stuttered into life and the lights changed. Two polis in a jam-sarnie squad car pulled up to let us walk, but not your man. Going at God knows what speed, he bounded past the gobsmacked polis, straight through the red light and away down the Mall. Just after he crossed the lights, he half turned, looked over his shoulder and gave me a smile and a thumbs-up. His long blond hair stuck out from under his helmet and the very stars in the sky looked half-hearted beside the gleaming white and gold. 'Well fuck me sideways,' I said. The next thing I heard was the howl of the polis siren, as the two blue boys in the sarnie-car took off in hot pursuit. I started laughing. Really laughing, like I couldn't stop. 'You'll never catch im,' I shouted at the vanishing polis car. 'Not a bloody chance.'

*   *   *

It took us less than five minutes to get to Leccy Square. We stood in the far corner and looked around. 'Sufferin Jesus,' I said.

'Claro,' Chico chimed in. 'So many. Too many. We never find im.'

The place was heaving. The entire refuse heap of humanity had floated in on high tide and dropped onto the iron railings round the middle. There were crappy artists doing mega-crappy pictures. There were South American toerags in ponchos and bowler hats playing wooden whistles. There were Chinese-looking guys doing acrobatics and tatty Arabs playing bongos. It was like some multi-culti version of hell. The shite of every single country in the world, plus some you hadn't even dreamt were on the same planet, the shite of the entire universe, dumped with a 'ta very much, an there you go' on our fucking doorstep. Fuckin Jamaicans drawing charcoals of Princess Di smokin a spliff. Can't they arrest the cunts for stuff like that? Dodgy West Africans with a blanket full of watches, Danish twats – and they have no excuse and should be fuckin shot – I mean, Danish twats offering to braid coloured string and beads in your hair. I don't think so, you silly Scandinavian wanker. Why don't you just fuck off back to the tedious, ultra-affluent dump you came from and stop trying to inflict your piss-awful hippy shite on the rest of us? Bastards or what? Death's too good for them, it really is.

Anyway, Leicester Square was full of them. Plus hundreds of fascinated tourists, plus hundreds of over-excited clubbers and drinkers and cinemagoers. Gibbsey and Co. might be here, or they might not. God alone knows.

'Well,' said Mikey, 'we're here. We may as well give it a go.'

Everyone agreed: no point in standing round like a group of divvys with nowhere to go. We'd look for him. That's what we'd come for. Mikey suggested we should split in twos, take half the square each, then meet back at the Odeon corner, but I completely vetoed this. For a start, we might find what we were looking for, and the idea of running into Gibbsey and gang at half strength appealed to no-one. For seconds, in this heaving morass of humanity there was every chance that if we did split up we'd never see each other again. No, I said. Come what may, the four of us were sticking together.

'Ta bom?' I said.

'Esso es,' said Chico. 'Los quatros, contigos, para siempre.'

'Esso es,' said Dekka. 'Los quatros, para siempre, too right.'

'Mikey?' I said.

'S.S.,' said Mikey. 'Whatever the fuck that means.'

'Come on, ermano,' said Chico. 'You have to say. Say with me. Esso es.'

'Esso ez,' Mikey repeated.

'It's good,' said Chico. 'Now listen and say, los quatros.'

'Loz catrox,' said Mikey.

'Para siempre,' said Chico.

'Para siempray,' said Mikey, really rather well.

'Yes!' Chico shouted.

'Too fucking right,' I said, and did my bit, 'Esso es, los quatros, para siempre.'

'What the fuck does it mean anyway?' said Mikey as we started to walk.

'It means,' I said, 'that we're going to stuff Gibbsey, and the bastard who cut up Skinny, and that cunt Mol, who sat and watched fuckin Juliette die. It means,' I said,

229

pirouetting, and doing salsa steps with Chico, 'that we're going to fuckin murder the cunts.'

'Esso es,' said Mikey and Dekka at exactly the same time. 'Lucky to do that,' said Dekka. 'We should make a wish.'

'What like?' said Mikey.

'Don't be a twat,' said Dekka, affronted. 'If I told you me wish, it wouldn't come true, would it? You've got to keep your wishes secret for it to work.'

'Come on, companyeros,' I said. 'Let's move it.'

And move it we did. We pushed and shoved our way round and round Leicester Square. But no Gibbsey. We went round the outside twice. Nada. Then round the iron railings on the inside. More nada. He wasn't sitting on the grass in the middle with the hippies. Not much of a surprise to be honest. He wasn't hanging outside the cinemas or the clubs. He wasn't trying to buy a slice of pizza for a quid, which is where me chavs had spotted him last. He wasn't in McDonald's, or watching a deranged Brazilian guy walk on his hands. He wasn't queueing for Equinox, or buying an ice cream from Baskin Robbins. He wasn't fucking there.

To be honest, I didn't quite know what to do. I mean, I'd counted on him. For the last week we'd bin legging it all over the fucking country, and wherever we went, there was Gibbsey. Now, the one and only time in my life I actually wanted to see the psychotic cunt, he'd simply disappeared. We turned to Mikey for advice. He knew the score better than the rest of us, cos he'd been down London loads, visiting his bro. Mikey thought we should keep looking. He reckoned there was tons of clubs up and down the main drag and in the little side streets and alleys that made up Soho. Gibbsey could well be about, he thought, and we should give it a couple of hours and take a stroll round. We were prepared and psyched up; no point in chucking the towel and going home.

Agreement was unanimous. 'OK, Mikey,' I said. 'Lead on, cos I'm fuckin clueless round here.' We tooled up the Charing Cross Road and down again. Then we were off into Soho. Why is it, when you see things for real, they're always such a fuckin disappointment? I mean, Soho. I'd always imagined this megaglam mix of posh and porn. Neon lights and beautiful girls and perversions beyond the scope of my nineteen-year-old imagination. Expensive bars, and models, and bottles of champagne that cost more than the social gives you in a year. Golden people spending tons of money and living wild lives. Well, forget it. Didn't even know we were there till Mikey told me. Just half a dozen crappy narrow little backstreets off Charing Cross Road. Tons of tourists, bars an restaurants, and a few sex shops selling the usual dildos, dolls, mags, vids and handcuffs. Bored-looking girls with tired faces and northern accents, trying half-heartedly to entice you into whichever club they were standing in front of. I mean, nowt to write home about. Big style. And as for the posh, the glitz and the glamour. I didn't see it. Must have blinked and missed it. Didn't see Gibbsey, neither.

We checked out the Salsa! club, which had a long queue of euro girls and men who could have been Chico's cousins. We hung round the Hippodrome. We tried Oxygene, and some place up the road, full of spaced-out squatakids. As I pointed out, if Gibbsey had come across that lot it would have been ultraviolence with a capital U, so it was a mite unlikely he'd chosen their club to chill out in. Ambient sounds are not really Gibbsey's bag. We walked up and down and round and round. It was cold and drizzling with rain, and we all got blisters cos we were wearing borrowed boots. I was coming very close

231

to calling it a night when Mikey had another idea.

'Let's go down to Charing Cross,' he said. 'There's a couple of clubs down there and a wine bar that stays open late. S'worth a try?'

'Yeah, chav,' I nodded. 'Owt's worth a try. Porque no?'

We limped off once more down the main drag, turning left by the church just before we reached Trafalgar Square. It was gone two o'clock, though the streets were still busy and the cars were still running. You could see the Charing Cross tube sign, to the left, by a wee set of steps, and beside it the whacking great hotel that fronted the train station. There was a big cobbled apron of ground in front of the hotel, with wrought-iron gates at either end. Taxis drove in one and out the other, and there was a sort of taxi rank to one side. Standing majestically, dead centre as the taxis skidded round it, was my Eleanor Cross.

OK, it was only a Victorian replica, but it was still good. I don't know how tall. Maybe about fifty feet? Dark stone rising to a central spire. In fact, it wasn't a cross at all, more of a monument, or a shrine really. Full of decorations and carvings, and lots of arches and open niches for saints to stand in, although you couldn't tell which ones they were, because it was too dark. It wasn't even in the same place as the original one, either. That had been in Trafalgar Square, at the top of Whitehall. Though neither place had existed when they'd marched in, the muffled drum beating slow time, the men with lowered eyes, and the black horses bearing the body of the dead Spanish girl, the dead Queen of England. In 1290 the top of Whitehall had been bang in the middle of the village of Charing, and this was the last place her coffin had rested before they'd carried her half a mile down the road for her burial in Westminster Abbey. The cross stood for nearly 400 years before the cunting Roundheads ripped it down.

232

No respect and no sense of fucking history. Another 200 years went by, and then the Victorians put up the replica.

Underneath the stone pinnacle, right at the very top, was a sort of protected platform, which was for the largest of the statues. She was looking down, half smiling, arms outstretched. It was the Blessed Virgin, of course, the Mother of God. Our Lady, up there where she ought to be. But it was uncanny, really dead uncanny. Because she looked so much like Eleanor, *my* Eleanor, not the one who died 700 years ago. She looked so much like Eleanor she could have been her twin.

Natch enuf, as I was taking all this in I wasn't standing on the pavement with me gob wide open, like some div of a tourist. No, I was walking with me chavs. We crossed the road and went down a wee side street to the right of the hotel. The street was tiny, but it was obviously latenite-land, cos there were loads of bars and fast-food places open and neon lights and strains of music drifting from the clubs and people generally hanging out.

We walked right down to the end, almost to Embankment tube, and checked out an underground bar. It was weird, had probably been an old cellar or something, cos it was all curved brick walls and ceilings so low you banged your head. There were no lights, only candles, so at first it was hard to see who was in there, but after a couple of minutes it was clear enough. No Gibbsey. Coming out, grateful for the fresh air and the chance to stand up straight, we started back up the road, which had suddenly become completely choca with queers and trannies. Everywhere you looked there were tight white Lycra T-shirts and hair gel a go-go. An the fuckin racket – unbelievable. You could hardly hear yourself think above the whistles an screeching and cat calls.

'They must be turning out at Heaven,' said Mikey. 'Just

across there.' He pointed across the road. Four or five bouncers stood around chatting between themselves as a steady stream of E'd-up disco bunnies tottered out to face reality.

'Not much chance of Gibbsey being in there,' said Dekka.

We carried on up the street and reached the gated-up entrance to Charing Cross tube. We were dawdling, about to cross the road, get on a night bus and admit defeat. I looked across; I wanted one last glimpse of my Eleanor before we went home. She was still there, of course. Standing right at the top, where she belonged. Only the purity of it was all spoilt. Cos some drunken dickhead and his mate were leaning against the base of the monument. I felt myself go tight inside. Disrespectful cunts, I thought. I hopped up the little steps to the taxi rank to get a better look, and me chavs, thinking I was heading for the bus stop, hopped up behind me.

When I got to the top I stopped dead and put my arms out on either side, so me chavs sort of collided into me. Still with my arms out, I backed down the steps, forcing them back with me.

'What the fuck?' said Mikey.

'Shut your face,' I said. 'And don't move. Stay still and keep quiet. We've found him.'

We came to a complete halt as the tide of clubbers heading for the last bus swept round us. I put my finger to my lips, then beckoned. Quiet and wary, Dekka, Chico and Mikey followed me as I crept halfway back up the steps. I turned my head in the direction of the Eleanor Cross, and they followed the sweep of my eyes. Oh it was him all right. Unmistakably him. Dekka was next to me. 'Oh, fuck,' he said, in a voice no louder than a whisper.

chapter ten

WE'D FOUND GIBBSEY ALL RIGHT. MISSION
accomplished. Close to he looked massive. Huge.
The tree-trunk neck settling into the big, square shoulders.
He was half sitting, half leaning on the base of the monument, scuffing at something with the toe of his Reeboks.
Next to him was Ticka, more or less the same size and
build as Gibbsey and as crackpot as they come. Totally
radged was our Ticka, mad as a badger, and half of Donny
had the scars to prove it. The two of them looked exactly
what they were: psychotic hard boys, the sort of lads that
come complete with a government health warning. The
ones you cross the street to avoid. There's only one way
to deal with the likes of Gibbsey and Ticka, you have to
stay away. Don't catch their eye, unless you're on a suicide
bid. Don't talk to them. Don't come to their attention. If
they're in the bogs and you're dyin for a slash, cross your
legs and wait till they've finished. Go without a drink till
they leave the bar. If they look at a girl who's looking at
you, give her the dead-eye and turn away. Don't get in
their way; the price is too high. Yeah, I mean, ask Teapot.
The price is much, much too high.

Staring at the two of them, I wondered what the fuck I thought I was at. But it had gone too far now. It had been my idea and I'd dragged the others with me. I was driving a car with no reverse gear. Straight ahead was the only option.

'Danny, Danny,' Mikey was at my side, whispering in my ear. 'What about the others? Are these two cunts on their own, or what? Can you see anyone else about?'

It was a good point. I nodded to Mikey and started to look around in earnest. Cautiously, I turned my head, checking the gateway and taxi rank. There was no-one I recognized. People were still milling about on their way home, but the streets were emptying and party time was definitely over. I did another recce, checking systematically from one side to the other. Still I couldn't see anything, but I noticed that Gibbsey was also turning his head and saying something to Ticka. The two of them seemed to be waiting for someone, glancing around and searching the crowds.

At that moment a couple in long winter coats came out of the hotel lobby and got in the front cab. Before the second cab could move up to take his place, I saw them. Silhouetted against the brightly lit station windows, their outlines were unmistakable. 'No,' I said beneath my breath. 'Oh bloody hell, no.'

The man was tall and thin, with dark hair hanging in loose curls and a long black leather coat flapping round his ankles. Next to him was a squat little guy wearing a hat with ear flaps. I felt Chico stiffen beside me and he gently touched my arm. I turned to him and nodded. 'I've seen them,' I whispered. I glanced at Dekka and Mikey. They both nodded. Bez had taken time out from my nightmares to appear at Charing Cross station.

The four of us moved together, as if of one mind, into

the safety of darkness and obscurity. We dropped down the steps and bunched up into the deep shadow of the wall and waited. Bez and Mol were moving; walking down towards Gibbsey. Mol was saying something, gesturing with his hands and doing his usual foot-to-foot shuffle. Bez wasn't listening. He was looking around, eyes sweeping from side to side, searching for something he couldn't yet see. Suddenly he stopped, catching Mol, who was still rabbiting on, completely unawares. He stood for a moment, as if unsure, then changed direction, moving away from Gibbsey and towards the steps. Heading straight for us, unhurried, but definite, as if he knew we were there.

Instinctively, in unison, we dropped to a crouch, getting well down, flattening against the protecting wall. As he came steadily closer I began to panic. I tried to keep hold, tried not to give in, but fear was rising inside me like flood water. Chico was beside me, and I grabbed onto his jacket, half hiding my face. Someone else was clutching my leg. We were trembling, huddled together in the deep shadow like children in the dark. He was coming closer, Mol hopping along behind him. Now they were only a few yards away. I could feel the sweat running down my back, and I heard Chico murmuring something too low to catch. Bez paused for a moment and cocked his head, then he began to move again, straight towards us. Utter despair was seeping into me, travelling through my body, carried like a sickness in the blood. My soul was going rotten. I could smell it, sweet and putrid. A soft, pulpy, blackened thing it was, maggot-heaving as it slowly disintegrated and fell away. My soul, dying inside of me. Soon there'd be nothing left.

It was all my fault, all of it, and there just wasn't any point any more. He was coming for me. And now I could see it: the tide rising as he came on. The blood running perpetually, and the hum of wings as they endlessly circled; the buzzing black swarm and the sweet rotten smell of blood. Any second now it would all be over. Somewhere behind me Mikey or Dekka gave a stifled moan. Again Bez paused. He was seconds away, about ten foot from the top of the steps, his shadow almost touching the wall. I shut my eyes and buried my face in Chico's jacket. Any moment now, any moment . . .

'Oi!' Sounding like a donkey with its balls cut off, Gibbsey's squeaky, rusty, schoolgirl's voice rang out across the station yard. 'What youse fucking about at? I thought we were off?'

Bez didn't move. For what seemed like an eternity he remained at the top of the steps, then, suddenly, he seemed to make a decision. He turned and nodded his head in acknowledgement and moved purposely across to where Gibbsey and Ticka were waiting. Then the three of them, with Mol limping along behind, set off.

Not one of us said a word. In the midst of the taxis and the stray clubbers and the late-night drunks, no-one said anything. We remained huddled together, frozen in perfect silence as they walked away. My heart was racing, and I was panting, like I couldn't get breath in my body. When I straightened up, my legs almost went from under me.

I wanted to go home. My courage had shut up shop and caught the early train. I wanted to go home, lock the bedroom door and pull the duvet over my head. I couldn't face him again, not ever. It was too much for me, way out of my league, stupid. It was time to pack it in. The stop for the night bus was just across the road. No more than a couple of hundred yards away. Dekka, Chico and Mikey were all looking at me. Waiting for me. I looked across.

Gibbsey was halfway down the road, with the other three right behind him. Eleanor was still there, gazing down at me, her face tender and lovely. What choice did I have? What else could I do?

'Come on, chavs,' I said. 'Let's get the bastards.' And my voice sounded weak and frightened.

'Yeah,' said Dekka, my marrer mayor, my amigo durande. 'Let's get the bastards.' And the four of us moved forward.

We kept a fair distance behind, watching them as they crossed over the main road, and hanging back as they strolled down a little paved side street that came out almost on Trafalgar Square. It wasn't that easy to keep following. Big knots of people stood about, and couples and groups of drunken lads kept crossing our path and blocking our view, but we stuck to it. They took a diagonal across the square, over the road at the lights and straight through the lions and pigeons in the middle, Gibbsey booting out at the birds as he went. Can't blame him for that, though. They're vermin, pigeons, aren't they? Fuckin flying rats, that's what they are. An when you see them close to, revolting. Filthy dirty and infested with God knows what, and loads of them hobbling about on one leg. They lose them on the tube and lectrified overhead wires. They try and land, and one of their little feet gets burnt off. What a shame, eh? Praps I ought to start up a pigeon charity. I'd need a whacking great government grant, and tons and tons of donated dinos from concerned animal lovers. Then I could build a proper pigeons' hospital, and get a super-qualified expert surgeon to come in and fit little false feet. When my pigeons recuperated and learnt how to use the new foot in a special pigeon gym facility, they'd be ready for a bit of therapy to help them get over the trauma, like. Ta bom. Fucking great idea.

Impressive, innit, how, even at times of trial and tension, I'm still capable of flashes of brilliance.

Anyway, back to the matter in hand. Leaving the middle of the Square, Gibbsey and Co. were over the zebra crossing on the far side of the road. The shadows were deeper there, and the pavement packed with people waiting for night buses. We had a problem. Four lanes of traffic was roaring between us and our quarry, and the only way through was over the zebra, which meant twenty yards of unavoidable exposure. I was undecided, I could just see the back of Gibbsey's head. But the crowds and the darkness were making it difficult, and they were moving further away all the time.

'What you reckon, companyeros?' I said. 'Step out an move it pronto?'

'Esso es,' said Chico. 'No choice.'

Dekka and Mikey nodded assent, so with no more ado we legged it, and in less than ten seconds we were back in the safety of shadows and moving bodies. I stood on my toes, trying to pick out Gibbsey, who was the tallest. I started from where I'd last seen him and scanned up and down the crowded street. I moved to stand on a shop doorstep to get a bit more height and tried again. 'Shit,' I said. 'Fucking shit.'

They'd gone. I'd taken my eyes off them for no more than a few seconds and they'd gone. Dekka shook his head. Chico shrugged. Mikey was still casting about, eyes raking up and down the crowds, but they were nowhere to be seen. I couldn't understand it. They couldn't have just vanished; the bastards had to be somewhere.

'What now, amigos?' Chico asked.

'Keep lookin,' I said. 'You and Mikey look that side, over to the square. Me an Dekka'll cover these bleedin bus stops.'

Everyone nodded and set to. I couldn't believe we'd been stupid enough to lose them. A split second, that's all it took. A split second and they'd gone. It was unbelievable. Ten minutes ago I'd been desperate for them to disappear, to fuck off and never darken my sight again. Now I'd lost them I was furious. I had to find them. I wasn't going to go through all that again. As Rodney would say, 'Tonight's the night.' Tonight I was going to sort it. It couldn't be put off. If I was to go through with it, well, it had to be now. But first I had to find the fuckers.

Dekka and I weren't having much luck. We'd walked up and down the twenty yards of the bus stops twice and seen nothing. We'd looked down the road and across the road. No sign. All the shops and buildings at our back were in darkness, casting heavy shadows. The lack of light didn't make the job any easier. One shop was so dark it was a fucking black hole. I looked at it, then looked again. It wasn't a shop, it was a jennel. A tiny passage leading out to another road, and silhouetted at the far end were four figures.

I grabbed Dekka's arm. 'We've got em. Get Mikey and Chico and catch up with me, I'm not risking losing them again.' Dekka hesitated and I shoved him. 'Go on, chav, pronto. There's no time to argue the toss.'

I slid round the corner of the jennel, hugging the wall, and was immediately covered by complete darkness. They seemed to have stopped to smoke a spliff; I could see the red light dancing between them as they passed it round. Mol got the last hit, and before he'd finished smoking the other three started to move. I glanced round. The chavs would catch me up. Walking on silent feet, I moved into the blackness and followed.

At the far end of the jennel I paused; they were fifty yards ahead of me, disappearing down some steps.

Nervous on open ground, I went after them, taking care to stay well back. At the foot of the steps they turned left, then crossed the road, merging into the shadows of St James's Park. I looked round again. Where the fuck were they? Dekka knew the score. What was keeping them? If I didn't move now I'd lose them. 'Come on, you dopey bastards. Come on,' I said. And then I walked.

They'd been dandering parkside for no more than twenty yards when they were over the road again. They were still moving in the same direction though, so I kept to the shelter of the trees. I kept glancing over my shoulder, looking back, hoping that any moment my three chavs would appear. My three chavs, riding out from the darkness, coming to the rescue. Their shining steeds and silver armour. 'When a knight won his spurs in the stories of old/He was gentle and brave, he was gallant and bold./With a sword by his side and a lance in his hand/For God and for valour he rode through the land.' And there they would be. Dekka, Chico an Mikey. All evil would be abashed and defeated, and every enemy would flee before them. Except they weren't fucking there, horses or no horses. I risked another swift look back. 'Come on, you useless tossers,' I breathed. 'Come on. Rapido, you bastards. Mas an more mas. Rapido.'

I switched my eyes front, pronto. The gruesome four-some were almost at the end of the street, and I wasn't about to lose them again. They turned left and I followed, padding after them as they went over the main road. I hadn't the faintest idea what the fuck they were doing. They seemed to be on a late-night tour of scenic London. Bez was in the lead, and he wasn't just dandering aimlessly. No, he was walking like he had a purpose. Maybe he was thinking of entering Gibbsey for the London Marathon, and this was an early part of his fitness programme. Maybe he was up for being a cabbie and was practising 'the knowledge', fuck knows. Made no sense to me. I just trotted along behind, and hoped to fuck me chavs would catch up before I got murdered.

We came out onto the big square, bang in front of the Houses of Parliament. Big Ben was straight opposite, the beautiful white face lit up and shining. Floating high above us, like the moon's little sister. Gibbsey, Ticka, Bez and Mol went to their right; they were walking slowly but, despite the steady pace, Mol was having a struggle to keep up. The yomp from Charing Cross had obviously been too much for the shortarse bastard. There he was, limping along behind, fucking ridiculous hat bobbin up and down, ear flaps waving in the breeze. Dumbo the midget elephant. A picture suddenly shot into my mind. Lincoln Cathedral, cold and airy, vaults soaring to heaven, and a wee bloke beckoning me, a wee cripple, with a bald head and ears like an elephant. I looked at Mol again, limping along in a hurry, and the words came unbidden, as if someone else had spoken. 'Straight from hell,' I said. 'Moloch, the Lincoln Imp.'

I lingered behind and watched as the four of them crossed over the road on the far side of the square and seemed to come to a halt. Picked out by passing cars, they flickered in and out of visibility, dwarfed by the massive bulk of Westminster Abbey. The great old church crouched behind them, carrying the surety of a thousand years. The white arc of the east door illuminated by floodlights. A whole pantheon of saints and prophets processing around its edges, staring down with disapproval at the horrors in their midst.

The chime was so loud I jumped. Big Ben, striking four. I looked round again. Still no chavs. Where were they? I couldn't do this on my own. Not a fuckin chance. I knew

I had to do something soon, but where were they? I was trying to hold on to my courage, but it was running through my hands like sand on the beach. Come on, amigos. Don't let me down. Dekka wouldn't let me down. Come on, you bastards. Come on.

Big Ben was striking the hours now. BONG!, like on the old *News at Ten*, four times. Four for the gospel makers: Matthew, Mark, Luke and John. The angel, the lion, the ox and the eagle. Four living creatures, each of them with six wings, full of eyes all round and within, and day and night they never cease to sing. Never cease to sing. Fuck it, I can't wait all my life. Never cease to sing. Teapot. See youse later, lads. Never cease to sing. Never cease to sing. I took a deep breath and shouted at the top of my lungs.

'GIBBSEY!' They stopped dead in mid-sentence and four heads turned towards me. I felt the shock of what I'd done, and saw that Bez was smiling. There was nothing for it now. I walked across the road to the Cathedral. 'Yes,' I said loudly, 'you. You, you murdering cunt. I've been looking for you.'

He moved off from the railings and came towards me. We were within a few feet of each other, his pale, psycho's eyes looking straight at me. Ticka was next to him, grinning and flexing his shoulders. I was going to get killed; they knew it and I knew it. Gibbsey nodded and stuck his chin out.

'Well that's funny, you grassin little bastard, cos we've been lookin for youse. So now you've found me, Danny Boy. What you gonna do about it then?'

The weirdness of that voice coming out of such a body was unnerving, as if he'd swallowed a baby and it was squeaking around, trying to get out. He was a good half head taller than me, and at least three stone heavier. Same goes for Ticka.

Father O'Flynn said I was special, you know. Very special, he said. 'You'll show them, Danny Boy, I know you will.' Better to die on your feet than live on your knees. That was what they said, wasn't it? Well, I hope to fuck they were right, because I was just about to find out.

'I want a word, Gibbsey,' I said. 'Want a word about what went down in Donny a couple of weeks back. And I want to know why you an your toerag mates have been chasing us up and down the fucking country.' I was dead meat, and I knew it, but it was too late now.

Gibbsey laughed and put his hand in his pocket. It was a Stanley knife, the tiny, razor-sharp blade flicking out as he slid the catch across. I could feel my insides disappearing. I was terrified I was going to disgrace myself, wet myself, like I'd seen other kids do. Start begging, crying and apologizing. I took a deep breath, trying desperately to get a grip, to hold myself together.

'You know your trouble, Danny Boy?' Gibbsey was saying, moving a step closer, knife resting in his right hand. 'Your fuckin problem is you talk too much. Can't keep it shut, can you? Don't know when to stay quiet.' He grinned at Ticka, and Ticka laughed. Now he'd got something in his hand as well. He was fiddling about, pushing and pulling at a catch on the side of the white pearlized handle. Then suddenly the thing snapped open and locked straight. It was an old-fashioned cut-throat razor. 'Only bought this on Sunday,' said Gibbsey, 'didn't we, marrer?' Ticka nodded and made a few kung-fu type slashes by way of demonstration. 'Cost enough,' Gibbsey continued, 'but fuckin great craftsmanship. So fuckin sharp you won't believe it. Made in Sheffield. Wouldn't mind one meself.'

He turned his attention back to me, face set hard. 'I want to know what you said to the polis in Donny, you grassing little twat. You and your two mates.' He was less

245

than a couple of feet away from me, and it was taking every shred of courage I had not to back away. Still looking straight at me, trying to stare me down. I was trying to work out if I was tall enough to nut him. I was close enough, but I'd only get one chance, and I needed to do serious damage. Break his nose at the least. Better still, break a cheekbone as well. I mentally measured the distance; it wasn't going to work, he was just too tall for me.

When he moved he caught me totally by surprise. Suddenly he shot a hand out and grabbed me by the collar of my jacket, swinging me round and pinning me against him. The Stanley knife was at my throat, the blade nicking in just below my ear. I could feel the warmth of the blood as it trickled down my neck. I kept very still.

'So why don't you tell me all about it, Danny,' he said. 'An don't try anything funny, cos we don't want a corpse on our hands, do we? Mind you,' he continued. 'Church is fuckin handy for the funeral.' I could hear Ticka sniggering, but I couldn't turn my head. Every breath I took I could feel the blade pushing in deeper. I tried to shift my weight, to see what my chances were of getting away from him. I was rewarded for my pains by a tightening of Gibbsey's grip and another puncture from the knife. He was standing behind me, his free hand forcing my chin up and pinning me to him. The blood was sheeting down my neck now, I could feel it. If he went in much further, he was going to get an artery.

'Come on, you little wanker,' he said, 'we haven't got all fuckin night. I want to know what you told your mate, Stockwell. Three of you were up there for fuckin hours, singing your little hearts out. Came for me the next day, they did, an me and Ticka had to clear out of town sharpish. So talk to me, cunt, while you still can. Cos you know what the punishment for grassing is, don't you, Danny Boy?'

Oh yeah, I knew all right. I'd seen the pictures. First they cut your tongue off, then they burn half your mouth away. That'll stop you talkin out of turn.

'Move the knife,' I said, in a voice scarcely above a whisper. 'I can't talk with that thing stuck in me. Move the knife.'

For a second or two nothing happened, then I felt the bite below my ear disappear. I took a deep breath, waited for his arm to drop and turned round to face him.

'OK, Gibbsey,' I said. 'You want to know what happened with the polis. No problem. I'll tell you. I'll tell you everything. Why I was looking for you in the first place really.'

I was bang in front of him, less than two feet away, looking straight into the pale crazy eyes. He still had the Stanley knife in his hand, and I knew he was well within distance. Bez and Mol had moved away, dropping back into the shadows to lean against the iron railings, but Ticka was up with Gibbsey, playing with his razor and grinning. OK, you cunts, I thought. If you want to know, then I'll fuckin well tell you. If that's what you want, then I'll tell you all about it.

'I should start the story at the beginning, shouldn't I, Gibbsey?' I said. 'So bear with me, cos it's a long story. It started on Tuesday, didn't it? We were in the Fort, me an Dekka, Chico and all the others too. Scaz an his bro, Angie, Janey and Teapot. The usual crew. Nowt much happening. Few beers with the mates, a bit of joshing, nowt special. Then you walked in, plus Ticka, of course, and four other lads from the posse. You'd come for Teapot, and he went quiet as a lamb. Knew he was up for a

247

slapping, I suppose. Thought best thing was to get it over with. You remember, don't you, Gibbsey? You remember Teapot? Weedy little fucker, lived near me, down Axside. You came into the Fort, you an your toerag mates. Tuesday it was. Market day. You remember?'

Gibbsey was looking straight at me, his face rigid. There was something wrong with one eye. The lid kept flicking up and down really quick, like he was blinking, but just the one side. I carried on talking, keeping my voice quiet. Looking straight at him.

'You remember, right enough. I know you do. Well, you want to know what happened to me and my chavs, so I'll explain. The polis came back to the Fort that night. It was about ten o'clock, I think. Stockwell it was, like you said. He pulled me, Dekka an Chico. Couldn't understand what the fuck was happening, especially when we got outside an saw the cars. A whole fucking fleet of them they had. An when we got up the cop shop the place was fair buzzin. Well, you know the form; they booked us in, then off we went to the interview rooms. Stockwell did me personally. Fuckin hours of it I went through, and fair bit of slapping about as well. You see, he knew the three of us had been in the Fort all afternoon, and he knew we'd been sitting with Teapot. I don't know who told him, landlord maybe, or one of the regulars. Pub was packed; could have been anyone.'

I took a deep breath, then carried on. 'Anyway, he knew that much, an he knew that a posse had come for Teapot. The other thing was that Teapot's body had been fished out from under the North Bridge not long after. I suppose the pathologist bloke must have had a slack afternoon, cos they already had the post-mortem stuff. That's why they were all hyper – cars an cops all over the fuckin place. Because they knew. They knew what you'd done to him.'

For a split second Gibbsey looked away, shooting a glance at Ticka, and then he was back, staring into my face, our eyes locked together like lovers.

'They kept us in overnight. Well, you probably know that. Got out about six the next morning. None of us had said a word, we said fuckin nada. Didn't see Teapot go, didn't know who took him, didn't know nothing. I can promise you that. Swear to it. OK, so the polis came for you the next day, but come on, Gibbsey. I mean, it's no big surprise, is it? The pub was packed, the fuckin landlord's a grass an we all know it, an when you took the poor little fucker you only towed him straight through the market place, so a few hundred more could see you. I know the polis are crap, Gibbsey, but not that crap. I mean, this isn't your usual local run-in. This is big league; the polis are bound to try a bit harder than usual. Common sense, innit?

'So, I'm tellin you, Gibbsey, we didn't grass. But they pushed us really hard. Tried to shock us into talking by showing us the pictures; pictures of Teapot after they'd fished him out of the water. Really close up and detailed they were. Showing all the stuff you'd done to him. I can't stop seeing them, Gibbsey, do you know that? I can't stop seeing them. I dream about those fucking pictures.'

He moved, bringing his knife up, but there was a lack of resolve, an uncertainty, and I was gabbling, hardly pausing for breath as I spoke. He was going to hear it. If it was the last thing I did, he was going to hear it.

'Do you dream about him, Gibbsey? Does it haunt your nightmares? Or have you forgotten it already? Do you remember him screaming, Gibbsey? Crying for mercy, beggin and pleading with you to stop? Is that the best bit? The bit where he begged you to kill him and get it over with? While he still could, of course. Cos he couldn't do much talkin later on, could he? Saw to that, good an proper, eh? Pleased with yourself, are you? A job well done and all that. Well, let me tell you something, Gibbsey: you're an animal, a bleeding animal. Six of you took him. Six of you for fucking Teapot. The poor little bastard never hurt anybody.'

We were very close now, wisps of our breath intermingling in the freezing night air. One side of his mouth had joined in with the eye, shivering and ticking, and the Stanley knife was loose in his hand.

'So that's why I wanted to see you, marrer. Cos someone needed to tell you. And d'you know what, Gibbsey? When you die, you're going straight to hell, and when you get there, you know what's going to happen? They're going to do to you what you did to Teapot. You'll find out what it's like to be held down and have a broom handle shoved up your arse; you'll be able to check out what it's like being castrated, to have your legs held apart whilst they saw away with a knife, and hear them laugh at your agony and terror. You'll get to know how it feels to have your tongue ripped out and your skin burnt off, and all the other little tricks you got up to in whichever back room you took him to. You'll be able to feel every second of what Teapot felt, every moment of what you put him through. Cos he didn't die quick, did he? But hell's not going to be like your back room, Gibbsey. Close in some ways, deffo, but not the same. Because hell is for eternity. So they won't just do it to you once; they'll do it again and again and again, for ever and ever. An it'll serve you fuckin right.'

Gibbsey just stood there, looking at me, then he turned his head and looked at Ticka. He looked up at the bulk of Westminster Abbey, one pale eye wide with shock, the other eye uncontrollable, batting and flicking like a moth in a jam jar. Every few seconds one side of his mouth shot on a slalom towards his ear, then whacked back to the centre of his face. He backed away from me, shaking his head.

'It weren't meant to happen like that,' he said, the voice still higher, diving an octave to normality, then see-sawing back up to girlhood. 'It weren't on purpose. It just got out of hand. It was an accident, for fuck's sake. An accident.' He turned away from me and walked back towards Ticka.

As if waiting for precisely this moment, Bez stepped out from the shadows, and I felt the air go cold around me.

'Oh, Danny Boy,' he said, speaking in a soft, clear voice, 'what a star you are. A regular little escape artist. Well, if my friend Gary doesn't want to talk to you, I can only think it must be my turn. We have some problems to sort out, as I remember. All a question of good manners really. You see, it was my party.' He paused and smiled. The teeth were worse: rotten black stubs with yawning gaps, the gums swollen, spongy, red and meaty. I couldn't look at his mouth; it made me shudder. 'I'm sure you remember the party,' he went on. 'You seemed to be having such a marvellous time. Quite the life and soul. But then you ran out of stamina, became rather aggressive, began breaking the furniture. Spoilt things for everybody.'

He leant against the iron railings surrounding the abbey and began to roll a fag. Then he lit up and moved in front of me, head tilted as the flat shark's eyes focused on mine.

'As I was saying, it was my party, and you all left without so much as a thank-you, goodbye. And you,' he said, smiling at me, 'and your angel-faced Latin friend said some very unpleasant things to Sindy. Yes, as I said, spoilt the party for everyone, and we'd been so looking forward to it.'

As he was talking he began to walk towards me. Mol hopping along beside him, grinning and nodding. I tried to speak, but couldn't find my voice. I felt heavy and limp, and it was all I could do to keep standing.

'So I thought you might like to come back to the flat with me,' he continued. 'Sindy's there, so you can apologize in person. And then we can all get to know each other better.'

Mol was hopping up and down with excitement, rubbing his hands and cracking his knuckles. 'Oh you'll love that, Danny Boy,' he said. 'Oh yes, Tiger. You're in for a really exciting time.'

'Beautiful teeth,' said Bez. 'Such whiteness, and a natural shine. Almost translucent, like mother-of-pearl. And so very even, so very regular. Don't you think so?'

Mol was ecstatic; he was doing a sort of on-the-spot jig, elbows out and feet tapping. 'Yeah, those teeth are good. Really good. The boss likes teeth. Good, strong, white teeth. Nice, even, pearly teeth. Loves 'em with a passion, he does. Clackers and chompers and gnasheroos. Tickling the ivories. Oh indeedy me.' He winked at me. 'It's going to be a wild night, I can promise you.'

Bez smiled indulgently. 'We'll do our best to entertain, won't we, my friend?'

'Oh yes,' said Mol, pirouetting and jumping on his one good leg. 'And Sindy will help. Oh yes. Sindy likes a bit of fun. Game for a laugh, is that girl.'

I could smell it again, stronger now. All around me – the inescapable blood, pooling and coagulating. And my ears were full of buzzing; the incessant whirr of wings drowning everything as they swarmed in their thousands. I could neither speak nor move. I was in a trance, a coma, and I couldn't shift myself. I tried to turn my head to look for my chavers, even thought about trying to run for it,

252

but I couldn't. Couldn't do it. My flesh draped over my bones like wet clothes on a washing line, sodden, limp and useless, my spirit drowned within me. I was still trying, still fighting. But my struggles served only to take me further under. And all my flailings belonged to the realm of the dead.

'Shall I bring the car round, boss?' Mol was still bouncing and grinning.

'Yes,' said Bez, 'I think we're all ready to go. What's the matter, my friend?'

Mol's face had changed completely. The grin had been replaced by a mask of utter horror. He was shaking and cowering and trying to get behind Bez. Gibbering, he pointed past his boss's elbow in the direction of the abbey. Walking from the east gate, barefoot through the dewy grass, moonbright and more beautiful than the angels, was Eleanor. She came on steadily, until she was directly by us. We were near enough to touch, separated only by the iron railings surrounding the abbey grounds.

Bez turned to face her, and as he did I felt my heart begin to beat and the blood flow round my body. She looked directly at him, her dark and wonderful eyes suddenly terrifying:

'Go back,' she said, 'and take this thing', looking at Mol, who was trying to hide under Bez's coat, 'with you. There is no place for you here.'

Bez opened his mouth to speak, but before a sound came out she raised her hand. He staggered back, colliding with Mol. For a second he went down, grabbing at the railings to break his fall, overbalancing as Mol tangled in his legs. As he pulled himself upright, Bez reached down with his free hand, took hold of the wriggling Mol and flung him sideways. Then he turned back to Eleanor.

He shifted his grip on the iron railings, caught his

balance and, slowly and deliberately, began to climb. As his body rose up he leant forward, stooping above her. Then, when he was almost at the apex, he paused, steadied and, smiling, reached out to take hold.

And now the darkness was absolute. Along the wet roads a red tide was seeping. From the corner of my eye I saw the metallic flash of blue-green wings. Eleanor didn't move. As the long fingers reached for her throat she remained entirely still. He was stretching over the railings, clambering to get at her, the long coat swirling round him like a great black flag. And she was pale and slight as the sickle moon.

'You cannot stand against me. You must stay down.'

When she spoke the world turned over. Crouched at the foot of the railings Mol stuffed his fingers in his ears and whimpered. The stars were shining down on us and the damp night air carried the faint scent of lilies. For a moment Bez hung aloft, then he swung violently back-wards. Grabbing at the railings, clinging on as both hands began to slip. His whole body strained against it, but still he went down. Slowly at first, then gathering speed, sinking finally into a dark heap. He raised his head and his mouth was open, but no sound came out, only blood. He was spitting great gobbets of blood and teeth, and at the sides of his mouth dark shapes were settling and crawling.

When she said he could go, he climbed to his feet in stages, staggering and swaying, the blood still trickling from the corners of his mouth. He stood for a moment, with Mol behind him. Then suddenly he took off, Mol grabbing on to the long leather coat just in time as Bez fair flew, the speed towing Mol almost off his feet. As the two of them moved further and further away they seemed to become insubstantial, fading, as if they had literally melted away into nothingness.

I went down on my knees in front of her.

'Do you know who I am?' she said gently.

'Star of the sea,' I said. 'Seven swords and seven sorrows. A lily among thorns, a spring of running water. Mother of mercy. The flawless mirror. Robed with the sun, beneath her feet the moon, and on her head a crown of stars. Queen of Heaven.'

She smiled. 'Yes,' she said, 'I think you know me, Danny Boy.' I bowed my head, and at that moment I swear I could have outsung the choirs of angels. When I looked up she was gone, but it seemed to me that her radiance shone around me, and beyond the iron railings the wet grass was marked by the passing of her feet.

How long I stood there, stupified and enthralled, I don't know, but eventually I pulled myself together. I wiped my hands on my kecks – they were wet from the railings and sticky with the blood still running from my neck. I had to find my chavs, then we'd go home. I turned round and ran slap into Gibbsey and Ticka.

'Where've they gone?' said Gibbsey. 'Me mates have fucked off. Where've they gone, the cunts?'

'Didn't you see?' I asked, incredulous. 'Didn't you see her?'

'See what?' said Gibbsey. 'One minute they were stood here, next minute they were leggin it down the road and you were messin around on the floor. Dropped summat, did you?'

I shook my head. What could you say? Gibbsey and Ticka started moaning on about having to get back to the flat in Peckham, and what were they going to do now those fuckers had taken off with the car. 'Looks like your prayers have been answered,' I said. 'There's a black cab over there.'

Gibbsey stuck his hand out, and the cab swung round

the square and screeched to a halt beside us. He and Ticka went to get in and then stopped, cos the cab wasn't empty. The driver got out. He was very tall and long limbed, and his golden hair gleamed in the streetlights. He smiled at me, then turned to Gibbsey.

'Want a lift, chav?' he said.

'Aye,' said Gibbsey. 'Two of us. To Peckham.'

'Sound as a pound,' said the golden cabbie. 'Just have to hang on a minute.' He gestured to the back of his cab. 'These two need a hand out.'

The golden cabbie then went round and opened the boot and, after a bit of pulling and tugging, extracted a metal contraption, which he set beside the back door. Out of the other back door came a tubby middle-aged bloke.

'Hey, fat cunt,' shouted Gibbsey. The middle-aged bloke looked round. 'You look really fuckin stupid. A slaphead with a fuckin fringe. You some kind of pervert, or what?'

The man looked straight at him and said nothing. Gibbsey and Ticka were laughing fit to drop.

'Look,' yelled Gibbsey, 'I'm fuckin right. He's got a kid in the car. He's a perve; he's a paedoperv.'

So the three of us were watching as the back door opened and they lifted him out and put him in the chair. It was one of those electro-motorized jobs that can move on its own, like that scientist bloke has; the one that's always on telly and speaks through a computer. Once they'd got him settled, his two helpers moved away, and there was a slight hum as the power switched on and the chair moved forwards into a pool of orange light. The voice when it came was no more than a whisper, like the crackle of dried leaves. The words half formed, struggling to get out.

'Eyo, Gaiey, eyo, Pau; it'sh me.' The chair hummed and

moved forward again, coming to a halt in front of Gibbsey and Ticka.

They couldn't look at him. They kept glancing up then turning away. They just couldn't deal with it. The body was bad enough – the twisted legs, knees and feet all at the wrong angles, and the jackknife in the spine, so he sat hunched over, with his chin almost on his lap. The body was pretty bad, but the face was a million times worse. No ears for a start, and all blackened and bubbling and burnt, and the mouth horribly distorted and sort of pulled apart. No wonder they couldn't look at him. No surprise at all.

He started speaking again, and the two of them stood in front of him, baffled and repulsed. Never famed for patience and sensitivity, Gibbsey decided he'd had enough.

'Look, marrer,' he said. 'I can't make head nor tail of what you're on about, so pack it in, will you, cos we're off home. Save it for the social worker; it's what they're fuckin paid for.'

He made to walk round the metal chair and into the cab, but was stopped in his tracks by the doc.

'Stephen is trying to ask you a question,' he said. 'You will have to excuse him. He's found it hard to articulate properly since losing his tongue. Perhaps I should translate. He's saying, Don't you recognize him? Don't you know who he is? He says that you should. He says he looked just like this, well, apart from the chair, of course, but otherwise, yes, pretty much exactly like this, when you both last saw him.'

'You're fuckin mad,' said Gibbsey. 'All of you. Fuckin looped. Come on, Ticka, we're out of here.'

The boy in the chair began to speak, a torrent of half-formulated sound. The doc nodded his head and patted the kid's arm.

'Stephen says you took him in a brown Sierra, driven by one of your friends. The flat was up in Hyde Park. You took the knife from the kitchen drawer, because your Stanley knife had too small a blade. The new knife was blunt, and after a while Paul Tickle went back into the kitchen to sharpen it, because it was hard to use. He says that you raped him and punctured his bowel. He said you got a tape measure out to see how deep you could push it inside his body. You told Ticka twenty-one inches. He says that a boy with red hair said it was getting out of control and he wanted out. Ticka called him a nonce, and said if he didn't shut up he'd be next. The boy went into the kitchen and made everyone a cup of tea. Ricki Lake was on TV, talking to women who are unfaithful to their husbands.'

Gibbsey had his hands over his ears. 'Shut up,' he said. 'Shut up, will you. Tell him to shut up.'

The chair hummed forward, stopping an inch from Gibbsey's feet. Humping and struggling and thrashing, the kid leant forward and grabbed hold of Gibbsey by the leg of his jeans. With his free hand the kid gestured, tapping himself on the chest, and looking up into Gibbsey's face.

'It'sh me,' he said. 'I'm Seapo, Seapod.' He took a deep breath, using all the strength he had left. 'I'm Teapod,' he said, hitting himself on the chest. 'Loo wha you a done. Becosh I'm Teapot.'

The screaming split the air in two. Gibbsey jerked free of Teapot's hand and looked round wildly. Ticka was already running, running hell for leather straight up Victoria Street.

'Take a look, Gary,' said the doc, pointing at Teapot. 'All your own work.'

'No,' said Gibbsey, shaking his head. He began to back

away down the pavement. 'No, it's not true. It wasn't me. I wasn't, no. I wasn't there, was I? Not me. You can't prove it. It was a mistake. I told you that. I told you.' His voice rose to a scream, 'LEAVE ME ALONE, YOU FUCKERS, LEAVE ME ALONE. I'VE TOLD YOU, IT WASN'T ME.'

He was running after Ticka before the last words were out. Both of them sprinting up Victoria Street into oblivion.

'You're looking well, Daniel,' said the doc. 'Which, it must be said, makes a change.'

'Yeah,' I said. 'Apart from nearly havin me head sawn off I'm pretty plaza.'

The doc told me that they couldn't give me a lift, cos they were takin Teapot home, and I suppose that was fair enough. There was mucho fuckin about whilst they got him settled on the back seat of the cab, and then doc and the golden cabbie set to folding up the electric-chair contraption and putting it in the boot. Whilst they were doin the business, I ducked back inside the cab, where Teapot was. I sat next to him on the wide bench seat. The two of us, side by side. I needed to explain, so I twisted on the seat to face him, which was harder than it sounds, cos his face was such a fuckin horror show. He was looking back at me, and the eyes were still the same: hazel, with sandy lashes. They'd left his eyes alone; and despite the terrible things they'd seen, all the atrocities they'd witnessed, they were still the same old Teapot's eyes.

He was looking at me the way he always used to. The look which said he really liked me, admired me, wanted to be like me. The look he gave when he asked if I'd like a pint, or could he come to the club with me? Or come

259

with me down the park for a game of footie and a bit of a smoke? 'Oh fuck off, Teapot,' I used to say, world-weary, irritated and embarrassed by his devotion. He wasn't good enough to hang round with me. He wasn't hard or cool or clever, or anything very much. Just an eighteen-year-old kid who got on my tits by tagging round after me. But now the world had changed, and I wanted to try and tell him. It wasn't much of an offering, but it was the best I could do.

'I know I was a wanker,' I said, 'that day at the Fort; an before that as well. But that day especially. I should have done something. I should have stuck up for you. Never even said goodbye. D'you remember? You said, "See youse, lads," and we all looked away. No reply. I let them take you and I did nothing. And look at what they did, and I did nothing.'

He touched my leg, very brief and very light, and shook his head. He opened his mouth and took a couple of deep breaths, then he spoke: 'S'low kay, Anny.' He couldn't smile – his mouth was too fucked – but the general gist of a smile was there. You could tell somehow. He touched my leg again, as if for emphasis. 'Yoor ai fren, Anny, ememba? Yoor ai fren.'

I looked at him and tried to smile back – I don't think my effort was much better than his – and I nodded. 'Yeah,' I said. 'I won't forget. We're friends. I know that. Amigos an chavitos.'

He did the smile thing again, and I punched him on the shoulder, very gently, and he gave me a thumbs up and I climbed out the cab.

The doc and our golden friend were waiting for me.

'I've lost me chavs,' I said.

'Nah, marrer,' said Tall and Golden, aftershave knocking me backwards. 'They're on their way. Mira, muchacho, over there.' He pointed across the square, towards the bottom of Whitehall.

'Well, it's off to the opticians for me,' I said. 'Cos I see nada. In fact,' I checked again, 'I see nada de nada. Not one single chav in sight, let alone los tres.'

'Tranquilo, Danny Boy,' he said. 'Your chavs are on their way. Amigos contigos, mas rapido. So no need to fret.' He smiled. 'Anyway, mi ninyo, we're off.' He put his arm round me and the warmth was like the sun on my back. 'Asta luego, muchacho,' he said.

I nodded. 'Asta luego, ermano. Mas an more mas.'

'Goodbye, Daniel,' said the doc, climbing into the cab. He gave another flash of that mega-irritating smirk and leant his head out the cab window. 'Now you must go forward,' he said. 'Go forward and astonish the world.'

'I'll give it a crack,' I said. 'Yeah, Doc, I'll give it a crack.'

As the cab moved off over the wet tarmac, a pale shape appeared in the back window. It was Teapot; he was waving goodbye. I stood in the road until even the red tail lights had disappeared, waving. Waving till my arm was aching.

I heard them coming before I saw them. Down Whitehall, exactly as he'd said. Running full tilt, the borrowed boots slapping on the wet pavement and making a row like you wouldn't believe. Dekka saw me first and shouted at the top of his lungs, and I left the railings, sprinting out from under the shadow of the cathedral, and went to join me marrers.

It wasn't much of a mystery what had happened. It had taken Dekka a minute or two to grab Mikey and Chico, and by the time the three of them had got back to the jennel I'd gone, and no sign of where. They'd looked around, and unable to find me had taken a guess on the likeliest direction, which, natch, was completely the wrong way. Eventually they'd retraced their steps, turned round and set off down Whitehall. By this time total panic had set in and they'd expected to come across my mutilated remains at any moment. Obviously they were pretty chuffed to find me chirpy as a soddin cricket, triumphant and unscathed. Well, a bit scathed, I suppose, seeing as my neck was chopped to pieces and my entire right side was totally soaked in blood from the same. But really it was an all-mouth-an-no-trousers job. One of those things that look dead dramatic, but once you get cleaned up turns out to be nothing at all.

Natch, they were gagging to find out what had gone off with Gibbsey and Co. The Gibbsey part was pretty straightforward, but the rest of it? What was I supposed to say? For a moment I thought about trying to explain, trying to tell them about Eleanor and Teapot and all the rest. But how can you tell people stuff like that? Even your very best and closest chavers, your amigos durandes. How do you begin to tell them?

So I didn't. I glossed it over. Said Gibbsey and Ticka had fucked off, totally spooked by my tales of Teapot. Chico asked about Bez, and I said he'd lost interest when Gibbsey had gone and had just sloped off to the car with shortarse Mol. 'Lost his bottle,' said Dekka. 'Brave enough with little Skinny,' Mikey chipped in. Chico looked at me for a long time and said nothing.

We took a taxi back to Paddington and picked up Mikey's BM. It was dawn by the time we tooled into Ladbroke Grove, and when I fell into my bed I thought I'd sleep for a thousand years.

chapter eleven

SO WHAT CAN I SAY NOW? WHAT DO YOU WANT ME TO tell you?

My name is Danny MacIntyre. I'm nineteen years old. Me mam's an alchy, and me dad . . . well, me dad fucked off pronto before I was even born. I left school aged sixteen with no qualifications; not because I'm thick, but cos I couldn't be bothered, couldn't be fucked to make the effort and didn't see the point. I've got a criminal record. Nothing major: twocking, credit cards – serves the dopey fuckers right. I mean, you apply for a bleeding card, calling yourself Ian O. C. Paisley, just for a laugh, really. False D.O.B., false job (Do I look like a customer-service manager at the Co-op?) and false mortgage. I told them I'd bought me mam's council house. Total joke. Then, next thing you know, the plastic's through the post with a 1,500-quid limit. Well, what would you do? They should have fined the bleeding bank instead of me. Two hundred hours community service that cost me. Fuckin outrageous, that's what it is. (The O. C. was for Orange Cunt by the way.)

Anyway, what was I saying? Criminal record, yeah, but

I kept off the big stuff. It's all juvenile shite. Sort of thing we all do when we're too young to know better. Worst thing I've got is one count of possession: Class A drugs. Smack, of course, but luckily such a ridiculously small amount that not even the wildest stretch of Stockwell's imagination could turn it into an 'intent to supply'. He was well gutted, I can tell you.

It's all wiped in five years, except if you apply for jobs in certain sensitive areas. Pity really, my careers in the teaching profession, police, law and civil service over before they'd even begun. Don't suppose I'd get a job as a childminder neither. Ain't life a bitch?

What else can I tell you? Well, I'm a junkie, which you already know. And most of me mates are junkies, too, and that includes me chavers, amigos verdad. So there's no getting away from it really. I started at fourteen, but I'm not goin into details. I hate it when junkies go public. Posing for the *News of the Screws* with a spike stuck in their scrawny arm and the mandatory expression of snivelling self-pity, with just a touch of defiance. Oh how they fuckin love it, the self-indulgent cunts. It's always everybody's fault but theirs. It was me mam, me dad, me teachers, the social workers, me girlfriend, Aunty Gladys, the bloke at the Post Office who gave me the sack, the bastard doctor who prescribed the gear. Everybody and anybody, but not me. Oh no, mate, not me. It fucks me off, it really does. They take the 500 quid from the newspaper or the telly company and off they go, displaying their scars like bleeding beggars, talking about hitting up in their feet, or their necks, or their dicks. I even heard one fucker tellin some tosspot TV bloke that he used a vein in his fuckin eyeball. 'That's how desperate Carl has become,' said TV bloke. Bollocks, mate. Carl's puttin one over on you to get his stringy corpse on the telly, and the eyeball's double insurance that he'll trouser the 500. It makes my blood boil, it really does. They give decent junkies like me and me chavers a bad name, and it's not even interesting. You've heard it a thousand times before, and it's nothing but the same old story.

One day I'd like to stop. But not tomorrow, or even this week. To be truthful, I'm scared shitless. The physical side, withdrawing and the rest of the nightmare, it terrifies me. A couple of lads I know in Donny have been through it, and it sounds like bleeding agony, but it's more than that. It's the mental stuff, all the psychological misery. 'Like swopping your colour TV for black and white,' one of the lads told me. He said post-smack, everything looks dull and flat and dead. You just can't summon up the interest any more. Can't even find the energy to get out of bed some days. You see, it's not an easy gig. Yeah, I'd like to come off someday, but not yet awhile, not yet.

An now's not a good time. Show me a doctor, social worker or lawyer, and I could give a fuckin crackin speech on the stress I've been through these past two weeks. It'd be stupid to add to that by trying to come off gear. That's my take on it, anyway. You can suit yourself.

Do you know how often I think about Reg? So many times, every day. When she was alive and I was seein her, barely gave her a passing thought. Dead, she's taken up permanent residence inside my head. Got a mortgage with the Halifax and bought a neat little semi, situated somewhere just behind my forehead and above my eyes. I see her in the coffin, and in my dream, eating apples. I see her every time a lass with long hair swings down the street. When a girl laughs with her friends, I turn round, because it might be her. And everywhere and always I see those china-blue eyes, edged all round with dark lashes, like the Victorian dolls; the ones that cost a packet.

Reg is the only girl I've ever been serious about, although I've had fuckin hundreds, and now she's dead, I don't really know. Because I know what I did, there's no escape from it. So at the moment I'm not up for it, girlwise. Not interested. I just keep thinking of her, thinking of her and wishing she hadn't done it.

Anyway, what's the use? 'If wishes were horses, beggars would fly,' as me mam would say. Other people say 'beggars would ride', but mam's version is better: more poetry in it.

I keep thinking about things. Whether to stay here or go back to Donny. And what I'm going to do. I want to be famous, to do something so big and special the whole fuckin world sits up gobsmacked. But I don't know how to swing it. I mean I'm good at footy – school team, town youth team (kicked out for drugs) and all that – but good's as far as it goes. Star of the local pub team, maybe, star of the England team, definitely not. I can't sing and I don't want to be in some poxy fuckin band. At five ten (ish) I'm too small to be a model, and I haven't got the muscles for it. I mean, the face is bonny enough, but you have to be six plus for the catwalk, or so Chico says, and he should fuckin know. So what are the alternatives? I mean, tell me, just what does a poor boy do?

I'd like to be a doctor, a specialist, then I could waltz around saving lives and looking mega-important. I'd specialize in tropical diseases and be a world-respected authority. Then when they had outbreaks of green monkey fever and lassa fever and ebola, I'd be on TV, giving my expert opinion, before fearlessly putting on my space-age protective clothing and going out there to save the benighted darkies. The tabs would give me front page, BRAVE DANIEL GOES INTO LION'S DEN, and I'd be modest but determined. I might even do a bit of table-

266

banging, like that arsehole Bob Geldof, and say, 'We need your money to save these tragic people. Just give us the money!' Then I'd get a knighthood, which I'd give back, making a speech about the suffering of Irish Catholics and their long torment under the yoke of British and Unionist rule. Unless Ireland was already free, in which case I'd accept, but only on behalf of my colleagues and as a tribute to the spirit of the people I'd just saved.

There you have it. My future career entirely mapped out, save the odd qualification here and there. I don't know, you see. I really don't know. Things have changed and I can't just go back, but goin forward, well, it's not so simple. Half the time I don't know where I am at all.

You see, I know I've got two or three years at most. Two or three years, largin it with the lads. Shoutin and showin off, givin people the dead-eye, ripping off stuff from the shops, rucking on a Friday night. Going down the posh end with Dekka for a spot of B&E when the money gets tight. Up to Elland Road on a Saturday, if we've got the dinos. Doing gear, joshing with my chavers, shaggin a few lasses (once I've got over Reg), people pointing at me in the market place, saying, 'That's Danny Mac.' Being a figuera, dandering around town and feelin fine.

Ta bom. But in three years I'll be twenty-two, and so will me chavers. And there'll be other nineteen-year-olds. Then the amigos will start going steady – I mean, look at Dekka and wee Kim – and everything will drift apart. And I'll be stuck in the corner of the Fort, nursing a pint and selling gear cut with aspirin to aspiring sixteen-year-olds. It makes me go cold, I tell you. It makes the hairs on my arms and the back of my neck stand up. I don't want it. I don't want to be crap and old and finished when I'm twenty-two. All the glory days well behind me.

It's so tight, you see, our time of triumph, so quick to

end. We're like those mayflies, or whatever you call them. Ugly beetle things, crawling about in the mud at the bottom of the pond. Then, one day in May, they find the stalk of a water lily or reed or something, and clamber up out of the muddy water and into the air. They shed their ugly black skin and emerge like tiny angels, beautiful wings of fine white lace and long delicate feelers, with slender bodies. They spiral up into the spring air, sleek and lovely, flying so fast and so fine. Fighting for mates, trying to fuck as much as they can while the going's still good.

Then, when night falls, so do they. Twenty-four hours is all they get, then they fall back to earth, dead and done. An empty husk with broken wings. Do you see what I mean? It's just the same. Me and the chavs, that's what we get: twenty-four hours when we're at our prime, swaggering down the street, tough and fashionable, all the girls wanting you, all the boys afraid and envious. And the fire in your eyes is burning brightly and your heart beats fast, because, for a short while, the world belongs to you.

You know what happens next, don't you? The fire dies down and becomes nothing but ashes. The girls move on. The boys go to university, then get jobs, and drive past you in the flashy car on the way to the flashy restaurant. And they're not frightened of you any more. And your life is over. You'll live for another fifty years or so, but your life is over, cos you've fallen back to earth, your wings all crushed and broken. And you know you'll never fly again.

And I don't want to accept it. I'm not going to accept it. I want a life, something to look forward to, some glamour that lasts beyond my twentieth birthday. And d'you know what? I'm going to find it. If it kills me, I'm going to find it.

I've learnt things, you see. Father O'Flynn said I was a quick learner. 'You have a mind like quicksilver, Danny,' he said. And right enough, I do. This last two weeks I've learnt enough for a lifetime. Take me mam, for instance. You see, I know I love me mam. I wish I didn't sometimes, cos she's a regular pain in the arse, mad as a fuckin badger, and an alchy to boot. Not to mention the fuck-awful boyfriend. But there you go. We don't choose our mothers, cos I certainly wouldn't have chosen her, but we don't have the option. Anyway, I love the silly cow and, surprisingly enough, she loves me. That's a new one, see. Didn't know that. I'm her son and she loves me, which means something, however crap and drunk she is. And – this is so heartwarming I can practically see the tears falling and the noses running, so, here we go, are you ready for it – and, knowing that the daft bat loves me makes me feel a tad better. God alone knows why, but it does. So there you are. One of life's profound mysteries.

Shall I tell you something? I know this is mad, but I believe it. In fact, I'm sure of it. I'm sure that Eleanor chose me. She picked me out, I know it, and she made a special effort for me. Just for me.

And that has to change things. Sometimes you open a door in your heart and find a whole new room that you never knew existed. It's hard to explain, hard to tell you. But something like that happened to me. When she spoke to me outside the abbey, well, it was the best moment of my entire life. It was like the stars had come to earth and started dancing. You know the Lord's Prayer, the pater-noster? 'For the kingdom, the power and the glory are yours, now and for ever.' That's what I saw. The power and the glory. The power and the glory, now and for ever. And how do you forget something like that?

So you see, things aren't the same.

And I'm not sure what I'll do, but I've got to do some-thing. Me and me chavs, we deserve better than what we've got coming. And in London you can't help but notice, cos it's all around you. Everywhere you look there's people living the lives you want but can't have. And I've got to find a way through to it.

I mean, there's got to be some way out, I'm sure of it. And I'll fuckin sort it, I know I will. I'm not going to give in. I'm not going to be satisfied with second best, with a crap, grey, daytime-telly, nothing of a fuckin life. I'm Danny MacIntyre, not some snivelling, run-of-the-mill tenapenny tosspot. I'm fuckin special, and I know it. And I've seen things you'll never even dream about.

Yeah, you just watch me. I'll crack the code, you see if I don't. I'm coming, ready or not. Claro? Ta bom.

THE END